THE EXPANSION BOOK 5
ALLIANCE

DEVON C. FORD

PRESS

First published by DHP Publishing in 2019
Published by Vulpine Press in the United Kingdom in 2020

Cover image by Jamie Glover at eruleanfuture.com
Cover by Claire Wood

ISBN: 978-1-83919-336-1

www.vulpine-press.com

"Equipped with his five senses, man explores the universe around him and calls the adventure science."
Edwin Powell Hubble

PROLOGUE

"Dropping from Fold space in three, two, one…" Rogers announced calmly to the bridge of the *Ichi*.

Perhaps calm wasn't the most accurate description. He sounded bored. Bored by repetitive routine. Bored by the recurring hype of excitement being marred by the monotonous undertone of constantly deflating hope.

"Scanners, tactical," Torres ordered from the captain's chair, though the ensign manning the station had literally nothing else to be doing.

"Working, sir," he responded flatly.

"Guns, anything?" Torres asked, leaning over the comm built into his chair.

"Negative pod one," came an almost robotic voice.

"Nothin' from pod two," Zero's voice came back, the only one of Torres's crew not to appear borderline depressed.

"G-class planet detected," came the news from the tactical station. Still, this exciting fact—the discovery of another planet capable of supporting life—did nothing to stir the crew into action above the bare minimum required to perform their roles. "It's less than one quarter light year away."

"Wide orbit, Mister Rogers," Torres instructed the pilot.

He would get the ship to their destination with the correct calculations and just the right amount of jump from their Fold drive.

Torres stifled a sigh of frustration. Maybe this star system would be the one to yield results after the dozens they had already located, orbited and scanned with no success.

That was, success for their primary mission goal and not just gathering information in the interest of science.

In terms of scientific research, their search had uncovered whole new worlds previously undiscovered even by ultra-long-distance telescope. This crew had done more for scientific discovery than any other explorer in history.

But that wasn't their aim.

They were on a ticking clock to find their enemy, wherever they were in the galaxy, and bring that information back to Earth for preparations.

So that the humans could launch a pre-emptive counterattack, many members of the crew guessed cynically.

"Entering high orbit," Rogers said, snapping more than just Torres from their daydreams.

"On screen," the captain instructed quietly, leaning back to regard the large viewscreen that acted like a bridge-wide wind- shield. His eyes sparkled, growing wider as he woke up to the utopia below them. "Well... would you look at that..."

"Readings indicate very similar conditions to Earth," the ensign reported. "Although almost ninety percent of the surface is covered by water."

"They have cold poles like ours," Sarvanto said as she leaned forward to look at the magnified image of the planet below.

"Not for long if I'm reading this right," Lieutenant Howard said over the open comm from the office he used as an astral navigation chart room.

"Meaning?" Torres asked.

"Meaning that I don't think the water level was supposed to be that high. I'm reading evidence of an advanced civilization down there; machinery, industry, widespread deforestation…" Howard explained. "The rising water level matches what we know about our own pollution back in the fossil fuel era. The atmosphere is significantly hotter than our own, which could account for the melting ice at the poles."

"Can corroborate, Captain," the officer at tactical said. "Equatorial temperatures are reading close to seventy degrees. Celsius."

"Remind me not to visit the equator down there," Torres said as an aside. "Any evidence of Va'alen or Kuldar technology?"

"Nothing on comm," the communications officer said. "Scanning wider frequencies."

"Okay, let's do another full sweep to be sure, drop a buoy and move on. What's the next location, Lieutenant Howard?"

"Next star system is a little over nine billio–"

"Contact!" shouted Rogers. He had seen the sensor reading before the tactical officer.

"Shields to full," Torres barked automatically. "What and where?"

"On the surface, energy spike from something matching an orbital rail gun."

"Half-second jump, Rogers," Torres ordered. "Shroud as soon as we enter normal space and loop back nice and slow. Tactical?"

"Sir?"

"You keep your eyes on those scanners and cry out *the second* you see anything you don't like, you got that?"

CHAPTER 1

Earth Orbit

"You have to do it," Petty Officer Payne said through the comm link. "The first one's hard, I'll grant you that, but just remember that if you mess this one up nobody will ask you to do it again."

"That doesn't help me much," Seaman Ikaika Kekoa said through gritted teeth. He leaned up tentatively to look out of the small observation port in the sealed lower rear section of their ship. "Wait, you mean if I fail the first attempt that's it? I'm cut?"

"No," Zero said as he joined them near the launch tubes. "She means that if you screw it up there won't be anything left of you to take a second attempt. You remember that poor bastard on Gaia?"

"Blackburn," Payne said. "He was called Blackburn. But he ended up more like blackberry jelly."

"Oooooh no," Kekoa breathed in a squeaky whisper, turning abruptly from the drop tubes. "No, no, noooo."

"You'll be fine, you big baby," Zero said in an almost fatherly tone. Kekoa was their youngest and newest team member and needed the reassurance, although his enormous size marked him as a freak of nature. "You finish these jumps and you're officially qualified. You can have your callsign and we can go do our job."

Kekoa turned reluctantly back to the drop tunes or, as he called them, the claustrophobic pipes of near-certain death.

4

There had been more than a few hurdles to overcome before the best posting in UN history ever could begin. One of those was the mandatory qualification of all troops assigned to Captain Torres's command on the *Bōken sha Ichi,* or just the *Ichi* as she was usually called, to CP or special operations standards.

For some that meant no work at all—seven out of their ten soldiers were already qualified.

For the other three, however, it meant updating their skill sets and undergoing additional training. Turner, being some- thing of a recreational atmospheric free-faller to the surprise of just about everybody, was already rated for orbital jumps. Payne seemed to enjoy it. But Kekoa felt unnatural jumping out of any vessel that could land safely.

As he squeezed himself into the tube—a tight fit for normal-sized troops in armor—he locked his boots into the disposable booster pack and recited the same circuitous litany they had been over more than once already.

"But why do we have to get out?" he asked. "Is the ship venting atmo? Have we run out of shuttles and life rafts? Couldn't we just land?"

"We have to get out, Kekoa," Zero recited from memory using his senior NCO voice, "because in this scenario we have troops in contact on the deck down there, and the thing, the *only* thing that will save their lives is an oversized, tattoed, ass-kickin' seven-foot-tall baby dropping from orbit. Now step to it."

"I really don't like thiiiiiiis," Kekoa whined as the tube sealed shut on him like a sarcophagus in space.

Zero, joining them on the drop just because, stepped in beside him as Payne sealed herself up on other side.

"Bridge from Zero," the sniper said into his comm. "Three in the pipes, ready for drop."

"Bridge acknowledged," Torres responded. "Geostationary orbit confirmed and holding steady. You are clear for drop on your mark."

"Roger that, bridge, commencing jump in twenty, nineteen, eightee–"

"Aw, *come on*, maaan! Just do a three-count and get it done!" Kekoa cried out in a voice much higher pitched than his usual rumbling baritone.

Zero smiled to himself, knowing that the added anticipation would torture the big guy.

"Mark!" he said, activating the drop for all three of them sooner than expected.

As one, the three tubes spun quickly on their vertical axes, pointing their heads at the Earth below as though they were human missiles. The tubes opened in an instant and vented them into open space. The rapid, explosive decompression served as their initial launch velocity and fired them at the planet below so that, even three hundred miles away, it blotted out their entire field of view.

If they turned their heads they could see the black of open space. If they looked behind them they would have seen the rapidly shrinking shape of the *Ichi*. Doing either, however, would result in screwing their trajectory so badly that they would land on Earth crispier than a turkey at the holiday meal they weren't allowed to mention under official UN rules in case it offended someone else's views and beliefs. Messing with the re-entry angle was a bad idea.

Most jumpers tell anyone who listens that it's all about the skill of the jumper and their nerves holding when the heat builds and the glow of the burn of the atmosphere makes their visors glow a cherry red.

Experienced jumpers, however, the ones who weren't angling for free drinks in return for recounting their accolades, would freely admit that nowadays the suit did all of the hard work for the atmospheric entry. The prototype armor their team possessed was a degree better still. The suit's software locked them up and refused to accept any movement overrides to the servos which held them in the right position.

In addition to that, these new suits used the onboard shields to make the process safer and more comfortable, only unlocking their movement abilities when the boost packs dropped away, and they slowed to the meagre speed of terminal velocity for the remainder of the journey.

Zero kept up a running commentary of their descent in the cool voice he would use for range practice on a summer's day. Kekoa, remaining stubbornly silent, hated him for that. Zero was making a point of sounding completely unphased by the whole process, despite what he knew about Kekoa's terror.

"Standby for booster separation," Payne said, trying to match Zero's tone, but achieving maybe eighty percent of his coolness. The devices stopped powering them toward the surface and their suits unlocked to allow free movement.

Kekoa stayed in exactly the same position, tucked up in a tight line and heading down like a spear. Beside him the other two started to spin and tumble, enjoying themselves as they flew around him. Payne was a natural, and Zero had chalked up almost twenty jumps in his service, although none of them combat drops. There were only thirteen surviving troops Brandt knew of in the whole UN who could boast that feat.

"Adjusting for drift," Zero said. "Kekoa, follow me." "Hrrrrrrrn-ghf," the big Hawaiian managed to grunt out. "Target site below,"

Payne piped up.

"Kekoa," Zero ordered, "call the ball."

"Standby... for repulser flare... in ten... seconds..."

"I was hoping for a three-count..." Zero mumbled to himself.

"Ready, ready, flare!" Kekoa said, his throat tight and constrained.

All three of them, already levelled out in a stable freefall position, felt the air driven from their lungs as their repulsers fired. The power grew intensified gradually instead of hitting full power straight away. This felt more like an old-fashioned parachute canopy than a burst of power that would injure them.

Their descent continued to slow, though the ground rushed toward them still at a sickeningly fast pace.

"Ghaaaaah!" Kekoa wailed as he activated the overrides. The repulsers hit full power when he was still twenty feet from the ground. He panicked, cut the power, and flailed in the air until gravity took hold of him and slammed him down.

Payne and Zero dropped in only fifteen feet apart and within a second of one another.

"*Oh!*" yelled an excited male voice. They turned toward where he was leaning on the nose of a sleek shuttle built like nothing else in the galaxy. "And the German judges award a solid seven point five to the sniper and the heavy gunner, but... but what's this? A surprise late entry by the Hawaiian team has been awarded a nine point two!"

"Screw you, Rogers," Kekoa said through rapid, desperate breathing.

"Now, now, Seaman." Rogers launched himself upright and walked toward the freight train that was Kekoa in his armor. "It's 'screw you, *Lieutenant* Rogers'," he chided him gently. "UN protocols should be adhered to at all times."

8

"Okay, cut it out," their commander, Leslie Brandt said. "You passed your first jump by virtue of still being alive. Good work."

"Yeah, but there was n–" Rogers tried to interrupt as the three jumpers removed their helmets.

"Ignore the lieutenant," Brandt said tiredly. "There are no bonus points for a superhero landing."

Rogers threw his arms—his left arm and his right prosthesis—up in silent exasperation.

"Load up," Brandt ordered. "We'll go back to the *Ichi* and get another jump in today before the final one in the morning."

Kekoa looked ashen; he had deactivated his helmet to gasp in real air. He filed up the rear ramp of their shuttle, the *Tanto II*, reluctantly.

"Hey, I've got an idea! Why don't we do the final combat simulation tonight in the dark?" he asked sarcastically.

Brandt stopped, looking at Kekoa wearing an expression he couldn't read before glancing at Zero.

"Good idea," Zero said, "I can make that happen. Nice idea!"

Kekoa said nothing, just traipsed up the ramp hanging his head like a scolded child.

CHAPTER 2

Orbital Shipyard 9, Earth Orbit

Orbital shipyard nine was officially a defunct station, which had been decommissioned close to forty years before. It was maintained by an automated AI system designed to keep it from colliding with any other floating object orbiting the planet, degrading over time or being destroyed by some other mishap to burn up in the atmosphere.

Unofficially, orbital shipyard nine was the blackest of black sites the UNID operated. It had recently been quietly upgraded with a shroud device to keep away prying eyes. That device had been tested and tweaked to encompass anything that docked with it.

The *Ichi* had left Earth to conduct void testing and systems checks before making a short jump to the Moon. They had returned a few hours later under shroud and had docked with the station where the real preparation work would commence, and where the newest members of the crew would be welcomed.

The team of ten troops had all been trained to CP standards and certified to use all of the cool prototype equipment and weapons they had along with them. Brandt insisted that they all must be to insane enough to follow her into the unknown.

The subject of their special operations qualifications brought with it the question of their callsigns. All but three of the squad had already been awarded such monikers, and an open meeting was called to discuss the remaining. The team gathered in the *Ichi*'s troop ready room which, finally, had had the heating issue resolved so they didn't slowly roast as they talked.

"As you know," Zero said as he stood. The small congregation hushed, and he was clearly enjoying himself, sounding every part the southern preacher his father had been. "The training staff usually award callsigns at the completion of the full course. Seeing as these three," he swept an open hand wide to present Turner, Payne and Kekoa, "merely qualified in the separate modules," he bowed his head slightly and placed a hand on his chest to convey the sheer emotion he felt at the duty laid at their feet, bringing smiles to the faces of those listening, "*I believe* this solemn duty falls on us. Commander?"

Brandt, mirroring Zero's over-the-top solemnity, stood and waved away the sarcastic whistles and sporadic applause.

"Settle down, kids," she said. "First up, we have our resident medic. Turner didn't do anything *too* embarrassing during qualification, to our bad luck, so I'll open the floor to suggestions."

"Doc!" shouted Marks. He was one of the three men brought by Beale. His callsign was Drop, on account of him screaming his head off when a koala bear—called 'drop bears' for their propensity to fall randomly from branches—landed on him out of a tree he was using for cover during his training in Australia.

"Doc?" Turner said. "Seriously? Imagination points deducted…"

"Quack?" Payne offered, earning a series of dirty looks from the rest of the squad. Her suggestion was ignored. She was not invited to make suggestions until she was inaugurated.

"Staples?" Zero offered, earning a chuckle from a few.

"Oh, I get it," Turner said with mock annoyance. "You pick on something I say too often and make it my name from here on, right?"

"Pretty much," Brandt told him. "You *do* tell people that a lot…"

"Because you apes are always getting yourself cut and hurt, resulting in me having to staple you back together? Can't I just stay as Turner?" he asked with a shrug.

"All in favor of calling Turner 'Turner' until he does something funny?" Brandt asked, raising a hand. The agreement was unanimous.

"Next up," Zero said as he took back the floor. "Y'all know her as the badass with the big gun, but the little-known fact about our Miss Payne here is that her first na—"

"I swear," Payne said in a cold fury, "if you say it, Master Petty Officer Conrad, I will shoot your balls off."

Zero, having been threatened by plenty of people in his life, merely smiled.

"She's called Daisy. All in favor of giving her the callsign Flower?" He paused as a metal coffee mug flew past his head, barely missing him as he leaned back. The mug hit the bulkhead behind him and spilled coffee onto the hardwearing rug, prompting a questioning look from the sniper.

"Chain?" Brandt offered. "As in daisy chain?"

Payne stopped reaching for the next nearest mug, the one cupped in one of Kekoa's massive paws.

Chain didn't actually sound that bad, at least not as bad as Kekoa's was sure to be. She sat back, feigning sullen boredom.

"All in favor?" Zero asked. All hands raised.

"Good. Now that brings me on to our newest member, not only to the UN and the team but also to the human race. Y'all know him," Zero said, "and damn if he ain't hard to miss anyway! Ladies and gentlemen, our boy, our own little monster, our baby Kekoa."

"Baby?" Kekoa rumbled, actually shaking the bench he was sitting on.

"Well," Brandt added, "you did cry like one during orbital drop training…"

"…and shit in your shorts," Turner added, shrugging an apology for chiming in.

"All in favor?" Zero cried. All hands went up and he turned to the huge man. "Hey, Baby," he said with a wink.

"Alright," Brandt said, calling her team to order after the laughter and camaraderie had aired long enough. "Med bay, let's go see Baby's girlfriend."

Kekoa argued against the description of Ensign Curtis, the doctor who was more R&D than MD most days. That said, he did turn into a six-foot-eight schoolgirl and blushed uncontrollably whenever she spoke to him. He'd been mesmerized by the pretty young woman ever since she had patched up his bullet holes. He had had the heroically dumb idea of laying the smackdown on a first gen mech with just his bare hands. Despite the aforementioned bullet holes, he'd won that encounter, terrifying people on both sides of the skirmish. With his armor on he was a whole new animal.

Their mandatory medical procedures involved undergoing a thorough medical prior to casting off, as well as introducing a new treatment to their bloodstream to be sure there weren't any hidden medical surprises that would affect their performance down the line.

The Nanomites—a secret tech developed in such shady settings that not even Curtis knew everything about their creation—would move through the body and assess, then attack anything that shouldn't be there. This included the removal of benign growths as well as other, more sinister, cell mutations. They also removed a degree of scar tissue, breaking it all down to purge it from the body via the kidneys.

Curtis privately thought that the technology could be adapted to extend individual human existence far beyond the natural one hundred years of current life expectancy. Or, to clarify, the current life expectancy for anyone who doesn't jump out of orbiting spacecraft, fight with huge aliens or go billions of miles beyond their home solar system into who knew what.

"Okey dokey. Seaman Kekoa, we meet again," Curtis said as she tapped at the datapad in front of her.

"Hh-hmf." Kekoa babbled involuntarily before coughing and gathering himself sufficiently to answer with actual words. "Doctor Curtis," he said quietly.

"Just a few standard questions before we start," she said. "Medical history. Are any of your immediate family suffering or have suffered from the following:

"Heart disease?"

"No."

"Liver or kidney failure?"

"No."

"Diabetes, either type one or type two?"

"No."

"Carpal tunnel syndrome?" Curtis frowned at the question but shook her head.

"No."

"Repetitive strain injuries to... to either hand?"

"No."

"Any problems experiencing erectile dysfunct–*goddammit!* Who has been messing with my datapad?" The waiting room erupted into laughter that had been building in pressure so long it could not be safely contained.

"Very funny," Curtis shouted through the medical bay so that their tormentors could hear her. "I'll be checking that box as a 'yes' on the permanent UN medical record of the next person who laughs!"

Silence, at least from the deeper voices, came at once.

The interviews were conducted with only minor giggling from a few and all ten of them were given a mild sedative and secured to a bed in the small ward as the Nanomites were administered.

They had expected it to feel weird, like having an army of ants running around under their skin fixing up all of their old injuries. Instead, the only effect they felt was the mild sedative. True to form, for fighting troops at least, almost all of them took the opportunity to sleep. Like food and shore leave, sleep was something they grabbed whenever and wherever they could.

They remained in the med bay overnight and had individual discharge interviews with Doctor Curtis the following morning.

After eating breakfast, they took the morning to get their heads squared away. Some were feeling a little subdued by the private news they had received.

"Briefing at thirteen hundred," Brandt said as she left. Most of them would hit the gym hard, then they would be at the briefing with their heads on right.

"Mission objective," Sarvanto said, smiling broadly at the assembled crew too large to fit into any single compartment onboard the *Ichi*, "is to systematically conduct a search of the galaxy in order to locate the Va'alen home world. The method is ours to freely develop, and we are provisioned for three months with double that time spent on emergency rations should we need them. We have a set rendezvous in the Centauri system in a little under ninety days. Captain?"

Torres nodded, thanking his flight officer for the introduction, and remained seated. The atmosphere among his crew was intentionally informal.

He gestured to the two aliens assigned to the crew of the *Ichi*. "Thanks to Asha, we have narrowed our search parameters from about a hundred billion stars to eighty-five billion, as the origin of the Kuldar world had be reliant on a red dwarf star."

He paused. A slightly nervous note hung in the air emanating from the two Kuldar indicated. "That said, a lot of regions of space we are discounting for a multitude of reasons, such as they are too close to the galactic core or they do not contain any red dwarf star capable of emitting the correct spectrum of light that the Kuldar evolved under." Torres stopped talking—the eyes of some crew members had glazed over at the mention of such, quite literally, astronomical numbers.

"Keeping it simple," he said loudly, "we're starting at the nearest stars and searching out from there. We're also not the only show in town. The construction of the new orbital plat- forms in the CS allows for manufacturing the deep space recon drones we talked about."

Those drones, each an unmanned ship the size of a small shuttle or a large ground transport, jumped in small bursts until they hit the right sector of space where they floated and drank in all of the sensor data they could. The drones also acted as sub-space signal boosters, a network that bounced comms all over the galaxy until human expansion had placed a station in every system worth colonizing.

"So, we're taking a drive without a map," Brandt said. "Only we know where and when we can resupply?"

"Pretty much," Torres said. This earned him a panicked look from the astral navigation lieutenant pressed into his crew. "As far as most of us need to know," he added quickly. "Lieu- tenant Howard will deal with the complicated stuff; we just fly the ship and take a look at what's there."

Lieutenant Howard, a painfully thin and peevish young man, stood up to speak. He always seemed to be in pain and didn't seem to get annoyed when his glasses fell down the bridge of his nose.

"We will move through the galaxy logically, jumping from system to system, and assess any G-class exoplanet we find."

The concept of the G-class planet—a planet in the 'goldilocks' zone where liquid water could exist and sustain life —wasn't a new one. The mission to set foot on as many as possible in three months with a view to locating the home of a terrifying race of alien warriors was more of a rarity.

Howard sat after waiting fruitlessly for any questions.

"When we depart each such planet, we will leave an encoded beacon in orbit to signal any subsequent search parties of our exploration."

"Everyone up to speed?" Torres asked. They nodded. "Good, Mister Harris, full engineering work-up including shield harmonics and Fold drive checks." The chief engineer nodded his assent. "Commander Brandt, your team are to have two on standby at all times if you could work out a rotation. I want those rostered gunners in the pods when we jump into any new system. Questions? No? We leave in four days. Dismissed."

CHAPTER 3

Orbital Shipyard 9, Mars

"You've got *what?*" Torres asked incredulously, leaning forward to get closer to the screen on his console.

"Seriously," Amare Eze said from millions of miles away. "There's a pizza joint, a burger place, a steakhouse, a bar—"

"Wait," Torres interrupted. "A bar? That a good idea?"

"Trust me," Eze chuckled. "The MP detachment are on that posting twenty-four-seven. In force."

"I bet, more for the civilians than ours I guess?"

"You guess right," Eze said. "They're worse than the troops but at least it leaves us free to do the really important work."

That important work, at least for the multiple units assigned to the surface of Gaia Néos, was patrolling the large sections of unsecured perimeter. This was not yet covered by the automated gun and re-pellant systems designed to ward off the unwelcome attentions of the local wildlife.

The engineers worked on their own schedule, however. They were to be fixing up those defenses atop the prefabricated sections of high walls, brought from the big resupply ships arriving almost daily from Earth. They started each day at eight in the morning, spent the first hour conducting a tasking meeting that mostly involved drink-ing coffee, then worked until around one in the afternoon. When they broke for lunch, they took another hour, followed by a recap of their daily tasking, before finishing up with a solid two hours of sedate work. Finally, their commander called a stop to the day's work in order to debrief his men and women.

Their slow work rate led to more than one clash between troop commanders and the senior members of the engineers.

Eze, left behind in interim charge of the Chief's unit, was given the temporary promotion to commander until Chief returned. He had remained by Dassiova's side to personally ensure his safety.

Whenever Eze challenged the engineer's slow rate of work, the topic of her brevet rank was raised to undermine the validity of her argument.

Many believed her rank would be approved on Earth when the bureaucratic machine turned, even though she had been promoted to lieutenant commander only months before. The formality of her promotion would take time, but the men and women under her command had no qualms as to her abilities or bravery.

Given the push for recruitment on Earth, with new volunteers lining up in the streets outside the UN recruitment offices, seasoned officers and NCOs would be in high demand. Entire new units would be raised to protect the large number of new territories. Each of those units would need a leader.

One of those newly raised units, rumors had it, would be given to Eze. She was indisputably one of the up and coming stars of the Va'alen conflict.

Those complaints, permanently refuted, served only to slow the work down even further until summarily abandoned. As a result, the troops from the units assigned to protect the unguarded sections of walls kept a frosty distance from the engineers. The engineers in turn made goading comments to the soldiers. This was where the five-hundred-strong contingent of military police troops came in.

"How long until the entire base perimeter is secure?" Torres asked her.

"Could be a month," she said. "Could be six. It would be faster if they invested in modifying the atmospheric shield emitters but I'm not in charge of R&D. No matter; my troops are rotating onto patrol escort duties after our mandatory stand down period."

"Safari?" Torres asked. "Isn't that what you call it?"

"We have standing orders *not* to kill the wildlife unless we are forced to," Eze told him. "Anyway when do you go?"

"You know I can't tell you that," Torres began chidingly. He interrupted Eze before she spoke again. "Four days. We're conducting final system checks and taking on all the supplies we can carry. We did a single jump past the end of our main planets."

"In one jump?" Eze asked, her eyes wide.

"Yeah, eight billion kilometers," he snapped his fingers, "done in minutes."

Eze had questions. She wanted to know what it was like out there, so far beyond the reaches of their own sun. She had been in the pitch black beyond the Oort cloud, as had everyone who had been to the CS, the Centauri System, but onboard massive fleet warships as part of a long sequence of shorter jumps wasn't the same. Somehow what Torres and his crew were doing was different, was *more*. She certainly felt it was more than what she was doing in keeping miners, engineers and scientists safe from vicious mammals that were only responding to the invasion of their world by aliens.

Aliens.

They were the aliens here, not the strange creatures which one minute appeared like dinosaurs and in another seemed like hideous monsters from the nightmares of imaginative children.

"When will you be back?" she asked, trying not to sound needy or lonely.

"The provisions should last us three months," Torres told her, "but we have rations to extend it for double that if we need to."

"Ouch," Eze answered. She tried to imagine three months spent living on the tasteless nutrition tablets. They were designed to give the body everything it needed but nothing it wanted. Her mind wandered to the long-term side effects of the pill's extended use, wondering if the psychological symptoms of starvation would manifest after long enough without taking any enjoyment from eating.

"Well, you know where I'll be when you get back," she said.

"Keep your chin up, beautiful," he told her, meaning every word. "Keep your troops in line, lead from the front, delegate well and ride the waves until you rotate out. They'll give you your own command, I'm sure of it."

She kissed two fingers of her right hand and held them out towards the screen, not wanting to say anything in case her cool exterior cracked. Torres did the same, returning the gesture until she cut the comm link. She stood to wipe at both eyes before returning to her duties.

Torres took a moment to gather himself. As much as he hated to even think it, and he would never admit it to anyone especially Amare herself, he found that their relationship often made things difficult.

Before, the concept of going somewhere for a twelve- or eighteen-month posting was fine. He was home wherever he was posted, and with only his mother left on Earth there was very little of value he was leaving behind.

He kept in touch with his mother, the admiral, but being a senior UN officer at a time like that meant that they had little to talk about other than the emerging situations on Earth, in the CS and now far beyond into the near-infinity of their own galaxy.

Now, leaving Eze behind for months at a time, he felt the twin pangs of both loss and jealousy. The latter emotion surprised him. He was a confident man, given his rapid rise in both rank and prime assignments, but the thought of other impressive young men looking at her while he was billions and billions of miles away left a sour feeling in his stomach.

Of course, sensibly, logically, he knew that she would be far too busy maintaining and honing both her skills and those of her unit to be sucked in by the attentions of others. Also, he knew her well enough—he suspected she would be pushing all of her troops to perform close to special operator standards. He wouldn't be surprised if there were a dozen or more applications to CP selection from her unit alone on their return to Earth after their deployment.

Still, good sense and logic never had a say when it came to the insecurities he didn't realize he had.

Torres shook off the feelings and stood, checking the time on the upgraded, smaller comm device on his left forearm. Ship's time was the rule of their lives now, running a standard Earth twenty-four-hour routine. It was important, physically and psychologically to maintain as much normality as possible when at sea for any length of time. The simple adaptation of day and night was the biggest step in achieving that.

The temperature controls and the ambient lighting onboard the *Ichi* were carefully set to mimic the passage of time on Earth in a temperate climate. Those who routinely rotated the night shift they found the slight chill in the air helped to keep them awake and alert.

By contrast, when they slept through the day, their quarters were also carefully climate-controlled to allow them enough sleep.

Their ship was fully provisioned, staffed by the best they had, and ready to push far beyond even the limits of human ability to see what stars existed.

CHAPTER 4

Barnard's Star, Six Light Years from Earth

"Reading a planet roughly... three times Earth's mass, sir," the ensign on the tactical station reported.

"I'm showing solid-state water over most of the planet, but the equator is showing elements of liquid water and dry land. Temperatures too low to support human or Kuldar life," Lieu- tenant Howard said.

"Life signs?" Torres asked eagerly.

"Some aquatic readings," tactical said.

"Comm, anything?" Torres asked.

"Nothing, sir, no readings."

"Okay," Torres said as he leaned back in the command chair and instructed their pilot. "Rogers, take us out again, tactical, standby for long-range sensor pulse."

The ship jumped again, pushing further away from Earth's sun to explore the exoplanets orbiting the Luhman and Wise stars in the Hydra constellation. They had spent four days doing that while their excitement was still running high, but as the mission clock ticked over into the second week with little more discovered than some alien wildlife the boredom began to creep in.

They spent a further two days in the Leo constellation, studying the exoplanets orbiting a star named Wolf 359. This was where they

25

encountered their first real element of risk—and resurgence of excitement.

"Sir," Howard said in a voice tinged with concern, "recommend breaking orbit and increasing distance from the star to—"

He was cut off as the ship shuddered under the shock of an impact to their shields.

"Report," Torres called out, righting himself in his chair.

"Shields are down," said the ensign at tactical, gripping the edges of his console as his feet rose. "So are the grav emitters..."

Torres bit back his retort as his ass lifted off the cushion. Everyone could feel that that grav emitters were out.

"Rogers, get us away from here," he said instead.

"Trying, sir," the pilot responded. His fingertips danced madly over the helm console. "I've lost maneuvering repulsers on the port side... unable to re-route power from here."

Torres wasted no time asking for confirmations or further explanations; if his pilot said it couldn't be done then he trusted the man's word. He hit the ship intercom on the console beside his chair and selected the engineering channel.

"Mister Harris, need a manual override to port maneuvering thrustors. Can you do it?"

"Standby one," came the shout over the comm.

The ship's display rotated slowly in a lateral roll, though they didn't feel it as they floated freely. It wasn't the true zero-G they had experienced before, but the grav emitters were running at about five percent.

"Re-routing auxiliary power from non-essential systems now. Manual reboot required, so hold on..."

Torres looked at Rogers who still tried to force some effect on their uncontrolled tumble through open space. The pilot nodded acknowledgement and frowned at Harris's next words over ship-wide comm.

"All hands from engineering... try not... err... try not to breathe too much for a while..."

As soon as he cut the comm, the gentle hum of air conditioning, the pumping of air circulating around the ship, faded to nothing.

Rogers's brow furrowed, and the majority of the crew's eyes shot wide as they realized what their chief engineer had just said. The bridge crew fought to strap themselves into chairs and hold onto their consoles. The door opened and the armored figure of Brandt walked in, her boots magnetically locking her to the deck of the bridge as the rest floated free where they weren't restrained.

She'd floated down the gangway to the armory and into her suit when they took a hit. After hearing Harris's announcement, she guessed that he had to manually reset some vital ship's system.

"What got us?" she asked.

"Solar flare," the floating ensign squeaked as Brandt hauled him back down by the waistband of his flight suit and wedged him under his console. "At least I think that's what it was. Took out our shield and fried a few systems."

As he spoke the ship began to shudder and some of the lighting flickered disconcertingly.

"I've got repulsers back online," Rogers announced. The tumbling view of the stars outside their bridge leveled out and settled into a featureless horizon.

"Engineering, report," Torres said over comm.

"Systems rebooting now, Captain," Harris answered after a pause. "All hands, standby for gravity."

He didn't give the crew long to prepare themselves. A second later everyone on the bridge thumped back down to where they should have been, with the exception of Brandt who remained firmly fixed to where she stood and deactivated the helmet of her armor.

"I need a full damage assessment," Torres ordered after a moment spent with his eyes closed, willing his stomach to adjust to gravity and stay where it was supposed to be.

"Primary shield emitter is fried, Captain," the tactical officer said. On most ships, or at least on ships not specifically designed for operations beyond their home system, that would represent a major obstacle in their ability to stay alive for the long term.

"Engineering to bridge," Harris called up.

"Torres here, go."

"Switching to secondary power grid," the engineer snapped. "We've got a cascade failure in primary battery banks. Expect some disruptions."

Disruptions, Torres considered, was a very mild way of his chief engineer saying that their source of power was suffering a chain reaction that would destroy the ship at an alarming speed. He swallowed, said nothing, and kept his nerve. If they were going down then the alarm would have sounded by now. He had to trust that his crew knew their jobs as well as, and often better than, he did his own.

"Fold drive still offline, Captain," Rogers announced help- fully from the helm. "It's mechanical, not a system fault."

Torres again forced his face to appear calm. He refused to show the cold, sinking sensation of utter and debilitating panic at finding out their only way of ever seeing home again was damaged to an as yet unknown degree. He took a breath, tried not to catch Brandt's eye, and gave his orders slowly and with calm purpose.

"Power secondary and tertiary shields through auxiliary power grid as soon as Harris has it re-routed," he said before turning to the tactical station. "Monitor that star, and don't wait if you see another ejection happening."

"Yes, sir," the ensign said, though unsure what he was looking for.

"Lieutenant Howard," Torres went on, "scan all the orbiting rocks of this fireball and find us somewhere we can sit safely sit for a while."

"Sir?" Howard asked.

"Our Fold drive emitter requires attention," he explained briefly, "and I don't relish the thought of going outside to take a look."

Howard, though pale, nodded and turned to his console. Torres, powerless to do himself, waited.

~

"You're sure this is the only place in the system?" Torres asked the astral navigation expert.

"No," Howard replied. "Of course not, but it's the only place we can reach without jump capabilities in the timeframe we have." His words sobered Torres, guessing that the next nearest place they could reach was almost half a year away at their maximum 'normal' space velocity.

"Okay, tell me about it."

"It's an exoplanet, a moon if you prefer, satelliting a gas giant. I estimate it to have a little over half of Earth's gravity, but it is solid ground," Howard explained.

"Atmosphere?"

"No way to be certain until we get there," Doctor Curtis said. "If we have to work EVA in suits then that's how it has to be."

Torres nodded, turning to his pilot—he preferred to involve everyone in a briefing if he could.

"How long to get us there?" he asked.

"Eighteen hours," Rogers shot back, "assuming nothing else breaks."

"Let's not rely on that assumption," their engineer said without the slightest hint of humor. Harris had almost had to be dragged away from the repairs he was undertaking to attend the critical briefing. He preferred to roll up his sleeves and be the first into the claustrophobic maintenance tunnels to fix a problem while his small team watched and learned.

"Commander," Torres addressed Brandt, "I want a full deployment when we land and protection laid out around the clock until we can fix her up and get underway again. Questions?"

"What if we can't?" Brandt asked.

"Can't what? Get home?" Torres asked. "We'll cross that bridge *if* we get to it. In the meantime let's make this work."

The others filed out, leaving only Brandt in the small briefing room with Torres.

"And the real answer?" she prompted him when they were alone.

"The real answer is I don't know," Torres said, rubbing his face with both hands. He tried to push away the stress of keeping his cool and collected mask visible for too long.

"We'll make it work."

Brandt smiled at him, a small and sad smile but a smile nonetheless. Bumping her younger captain affectionately on the shoulder as she exited, she left to brief her troops.

Eighteen hours came and went with only two more system failures to threaten their small existence in the great expanse of the galaxy. That stretch of time didn't bring their arrival to the small planet they expected, but it did bring them in clear enough sight of it to fire one of their many probes far ahead to start sending back data.

They arrived in orbit to find a thick ozone layer beneath them. The pilot identified a number of potential landing sites and chose the nearest and easiest to reach.

"It's going to be rough," Rogers said, "but so long as the repulsers don't die on me again we'll get down just fine."

His confidence was reassuring to the crew, who had had enough unknowns for now.

The breaching of the atmosphere was, just as their pilot had promised, rough. Two out of three of their remaining shield emitters were not running on full—one was damaged and the other didn't have the power. They could, Harris suggested, re-route the shield emitter directly to the singularity source but that would result in their immediate and catastrophic deaths should the shields overload and breach the reactor's containment.

Torres decided against that.

Brandt walked into the ready room where all of her team were crammed. Only two of them were already in armor, on duty to run the gun turrets.

"Beaver and Fangs on guns then," she said. She acknowledged young Lieutenant Beale by his callsign much to his annoyance. The other gunner was so named because he'd managed to get himself bitten by a snake during training. "Everyone else suit up and be in the hangar bay. Let's do this."

She led the way out of their ready room, the two armored troops hanging back to go their respective gun pods and provide heavy support to the remainder of the ground team. Brandt stepped into her armor, turning around as it opened up to receive her form and closing again to encase and empower her. She took her weapons and stepped into the drop tube, which would deposit her directly into the hangar below them. From there, she formed up her remaining troops by the side of their shuttle. One by one they dropped down with a metallic clank to join her.

"Brandt to bridge," she said over the comm. "Ready to deploy."

The *Ichi*, like so many sleek spacecrafts, seemed sluggish and heavy in atmosphere, like an ocean mammal ungainly and comedic on dry land.

The landing struts extended from the fuselage, unused for months since the ship had been stuck in a hangar on Earth. They sank into the first foot of dark, rust-colored dirt on the surface of the planet. As soon as the surface took their weight, the rear ramp, like that of a dropship only much larger, also sank into the dirt and spewed out eight armored shapes that deployed quickly to find the sparse cover and scan their environment.

The first thing Brandt noticed was that her suit's powered movement servos were working overtime in the heavier gravity. Had they been wearing the older generation of armor that would have been an issue. It would have murdered their battery power. Their new rigs, each with an individual onboard power supply, rendered that obstacle obsolete.

"Give me eyes, Zero," she said over the team channel.

"Bart up," the sniper responded. He sent the micro drone out of the pod up into the fierce wind that swept their exposed position.

The drone, used only once before to great effect, could identify and tag any organism or equipment, mark it as friendly or hostile, and transmit all of that data to the HUDs of the linked team on the ground below. It did all of that in seconds, so when it had been in the air for close to half a minute with no icons appearing on the inside of their visor displays, the team was confused.

"Nothing?" Brandt asked.

"Ain't nobody here but us chickens," Zero retorted.

"Push out a three-sixty," she ordered. "Eyeball everything. Specter?"

"Here," he said, the metallic twang in his voice courtesy of the major reconstructive surgery he'd undergone was as unmistakable as his accent had been before.

"Full circle recce of our position," she instructed.

He acknowledged her orders and set off. Brandt waved her hands in front of her body like she was doing a jerky form of Tai Chi. She was manipulating the topographical map provided by the drone they had nicknamed Bart.

"Zero, high ground four hundred meters east by northeast, you see it?"

A slight pause before her marksman responded.

"I see it," he said. "Moving."

"Roger that. Payne? Cover him."

"Aye, Commander," her heavy weapons operator answered.

The two of them broke cover and set off toward the nearby peak to give them a more commanding view of the ground.

"All units on ship perimeter," she instructed. "Push out fifty meters and hold." One by one they all acknowledged. "Beale, confirm gun pods have all friendlies painted green?"

Beale didn't answer immediately, which she took as a sign that he was double checking the facts before giving a response.

"Confirmed, Commander," he said. "Gun pod HUDs showing all eight friendly units in the green, over."

"Acknowledged. Brandt to bridge, LZ secure; send out damage assessment parties whenever you're ready."

CHAPTER 5

Carina Constellation, Twenty-Thousand Light Years from Earth

The crew of the *Weapon of God*, what was left of it, was forced to conduct over two hundred and ninety jumps, all of which were longer than their recommended safe operating limits.

The MEA, using stolen technology they hadn't developed, weren't looking for ways to improve and adapt to the longer periods spent in Fold space. As a result, the systems onboard the carrier began to fail one by one. Entire decks were cleared and sealed off, removing all power and life support in order to minimize their energy expenditure that was being sapped by the constant jumps.

No matter what problems were reported to General Chakour, he pushed them away, as though ignoring the protestations of his crew would render those problems irrelevant.

And then there was the crew members disappearing.

It started with a few non-essential personnel from the lower decks, but soon there were more. Each subsequent report of a missing engineer or a sanitation crewman who failed to report for their shift raised panic levels a little more.

Chakour chose to ignore them for the first few weeks, but even he couldn't deny the suspicious nature of the strange goings on.

At first, he had tried to limit the reach of the Va'alen to the single hangar deck they had originally occupied, but with so many warriors penned into a small space, there had been *incidents*. Even in translation, he had the distinct impression that the head Va'alen warrior was playing down the death of two of his own. With the last of the human-controlled security cameras in the bay, Chakour had seen footage of one warrior standing atop another as it slashed down with claws and ripped at the limbs of its victim. The footage cut out before they could see what happened to the corpse, if indeed there was one.

Attending the hangar bay doors with a contingent of armored guards carrying heavy rifles and energy-based shotguns, he identified himself and waited for the doors to slide open. The doors remained shut, so he tried again. Still they wouldn't budge.

The leader of his guard stepped forward and rapped the butt of his gun hard against the metal three times, in a temper. He stepped back and let the dull, metallic echo die away.

Chakour's temper was just about frayed to breaking point when the door finally slid open. Two hulking alien warriors barred their path, barking and crackling at them in the Va'alen tongue. The translation demanded angrily to know their purpose in disturbing them.

"I want to speak to Da'kath," Chakour said coldly, attempting to reassert some dominance. "Now."

The two alien warriors looked at one another briefly and stayed resolutely still. Chakour, incensed by the lack of respect they were showing him on his own ship, boiled inside and felt his face turning purple with frustration.

"Da'kath!" he yelled, embarrassing himself and under- mining his own authority even further. "I demand you—"

"You demand *what*?" Da'kath snapped from behind him, his words cutting Chakour off with a frightened yelp. He tried to straighten himself, to control his breathing, but failed at both.

"There are things I need to discuss with you," he told the supreme leader of the Va'alen.

"Come," Da'kath ordered him.

Chakour stepped forward, with his entire guard following automatically.

"No," Da'kath told him. "Bring one witness, otherwise my warriors might think you are an enemy."

The general swallowed, still fighting to control his nerves, and nodded to an unarmed aide.

"No, sir," said the troop leading the armed contingent. "I will go with you."

"It will be fine, Colonel," Chakour said in a failed attempt to sound reassuring.

The colonel, the man who had personally led the raid to recover the alien overlord, insisted that his general take a fighting crewmember. Chakour relented, stepping inside the hangar bay flanked by a single soldier as the doors slid shut behind them.

At once the soldier was seized and the rifle was stripped from his armored hand, as though the augmented strength the suit gave him was no more than that of a Va'alen child. The soldier was held firmly in claws the size of his helmet. His visor turned toward Chakour in a silent and expressionless plea for help.

"What do you want, coming to our place and making demands?" Da'kath asked Chakour conversationally.

The general cleared his throat, tried to ignore the risk the two humans were in, and spoke with as much authority as he could manage.

"There…" Chakour began, before clearing his throat and lowering his voice an entire octave. "There have been disappearances among our crew."

"What is this to me?" Da'kath asked, in the same bored, conversational tone.

The general faltered, unsure what accusation—for he was certain he wanted to throw out at least one—he intended to make to the massive aliens.

"What do your people eat, Da'kath?" he asked. "Did you bring enough supplies to last you this long?"

The supreme leader, the first warrior of the Va'alen, turned slowly to regard the small human who stood only to the middle of his chest. He leaned down to put hit chitinous head in front of Chakour's.

"You wish to know how we Va'alen survive? Here, we will show you."

He stood tall and crackled off a rattling noise, which translated through Chakour's comm as SKIN THE OTHER ONE.

Claws grasped Chakour. He flinched, but the claws held his head still to watch and pinned his body in place. The armored soldier he had brought was forced to the deck, held down by large claws and barbed feet. The general watched in horror as the armor was pierced, bent out of shape and torn open until the automated subsystems ejected the driver from the rig.

A thin young man emerged from the torn armor, an adolescent male complete with the whisper of a fluffy moustache, and was dragged to his feet. He shot a terrified look at his general. Chakour opened his mouth to scream a protest but Da'kath shot out a spiked claw to rest the tip at his throat. The message was clear. He fell silent as the soldier, suddenly so scrawny and weak in comparison to his captors, had the uniform torn from his body until he stood naked. He was lifted bodily toward a device about the size as a double bed. Noises filled the air as a machine started up. Chakour watched with dread as the screaming boy was lobbed effortlessly into the top of the machine.

The screaming stopped, only to be replaced instantly with a cut off yelp and a squelching, crunching, ripping noise as the boy's body was blended by whatever monstrous contraptions lay within the machine.

A chorus of excited clicking noises rippled through the hangar deck, like dozens of lobsters clacking their big claw tips together.

Da'kath held up all four clawed hands as he removed the threat of immediate death from the general's throat. This silenced the chorus at once. He stood beside the machine, quiet now after performing whatever barbaric function it was designed for.

"You wish to see how we sustain our bodies?" he asked Chakour, turning his near-featureless head and opening a gaping maw where a mouth should be. The machine had a spout, and from it issued a dollop of paste at his command which dropped into his open orifice.

Chakour stared in revulsion and terror, suddenly realizing where his missing crewmembers had gone. Somehow the truth was far worse than anything he could have possibly imagined.

"Can you pilot this vessel, General?" Da'kath asked as the other warriors lined up to take their shot of recycled human to sustain their bodies.

"I..." Chakour stammered, not wanting to give the full answer. He desperately tried to think ahead to what the aliens truly wanted. "I need maybe fifty people to make the ship work."

"Good," Da'kath told him. "We are almost at our home world, so you should send every one of the humans you do not need to us."

Chakour swallowed again, terror and disbelief fighting one another in his mind for primacy. He shot a glance at the square vessel where the Hive Lords resided.

"The Lords are sleeping," Da'kath explained, interpreting the glance, "entrusting us to bring them home."

"What... what will you do with me and the others who will help you?" Chakour asked with a defeated sigh.

Da'kath gave a rattle which the general interpreted as a laugh of triumph.

"You will live, as will anyone who helps us learn your technology to move between the stars."

CHAPTER 6

Gaia Πeós

The last day of rotation guarding the wall was as standard a day as any on the strange new planet.

Eze had to constantly remind herself that she was actually pioneering a new world, unsullied by humans except for a few outposts. She was leading her own unit on the new frontier, albeit with a temporary promotion in rank.

Their next duty of expeditionary escorts, or *safari* as the UN troops on the planet called it, wouldn't require the full strength of her men and women. As such, she rotated the active roster to put two-thirds of them through training and rest periods mixed with providing assistance to any personnel outside the walls of the compounds as needed.

That was what the units did best—hurry up and wait. Rush to get to a certain place for a certain time in full gear, only to be told to wait for orders. It was their bread and butter.

She was happy to delegate the command of the reactionary standby teams to her lieutenant commanders. One of those had been bumped up from lieutenant to cover her promotion to commander and so on down the line until a squad just had to make do without an ensign.

Anyone who ever served in a squad knew this was not a hardship. Now they no longer had to ensure their young officer wasn't losing

41

their equipment, getting themselves lost between the head and the mess hall, or feeling homesick.

Eze much preferred to take point on the safari missions, but she was also mindful that her duties as commander meant staying behind while other troops did the fun stuff at the sharp end. She sat back at camp updating company records and overseeing discipline drills run by the senior NCOs.

She rotated her personal command among all of the squads, hiding her pride at their enthusiasm to be following her personally into the unknown.

Twelve of her unit bore the small stenciled mark of a combat drop on their armor. Those were the survivors of the squad with whom she had performed an orbital drop from the hangar bay of a massive fleet carrier. These troops had accelerated their way to this very planet through the atmosphere to fight in a deadly stand-off until an orbital bombardment saved them all from annihilation.

That rare, vaunted badge marked those troops as elite and served to unite those who had earned it. Eze made a conscious effort not to show those troops any special treatment, but it was undeniably an experience they all shared. The troops dressed before her all wore the hopeful look of excitement that they too would find themselves in contact with their new commander and could boast of their exploits for free beer in some dive bar at the Lunar base one day.

"Squad!" barked the master petty officer as she approached. "'Teeeeeeen*HUH*!"

"At ease. Listen up," she said in a voice that was all business and no pomp. "Our task is to escort a team of scientists to a mountainous area. HUDs up." Her helmet activated to allow her to access the briefing package she had received and project it to them. Their helmets all activated for them to view the information.

"The ridge runs for approximately one hundred and ninety miles almost laterally around the planet on the largest continent halfway up the northern hemisphere. Flight time will be about forty minutes, which is also our ETA for support should we need it. Science team comprises of four, and their goal is to search for mineral deposits used in the research and development of weapons systems. We will be flying over the mountains at low speed with the ramp down scanning for these deposits before we search for an LZ to recover any we find."

The master petty officer, Ryers, cleared his throat.

"Ramp will be open, kids, which means you keep your asses in your seats unless me or the commander orders you otherwise. I see an ass off a seat, I promise you I'll be kicking it."

Eze smiled at the display. She and Ryers hadn't got off to the best start when she had been promoted to the unit, but her performance under combat conditions had softened his attitude toward her. More than that, he also bore the combat drop insignia and felt the bond as keenly as all of the others who had earned it.

"Any questions," Eze said, "save them. Load up."

Escorting scientists was a much better job than guarding a wall from big bugs and dinosaurs, but the prospect of rogue Va'alen elements remaining stranded on the planet could not be over- looked. Not if they wanted to stay alive.

Eze felt alive. She was riding in the back of a dropship in atmosphere with the ramp down as the weird and wonderful colors of an unfamiliar landscape zipped by below. She was doing what she was born to do.

The ride took the expected time as the bird swung its wings lazily back and forth, following the contours of the planet's surface.

"Approaching first site in thirty," the pilot announced over the channel, slowing the dropship to a hover as the sensor array under the chin of the cockpit scanned the rocky ground below.

Eze broke her own rules, ignoring the exasperated hand-waving of the loadmaster, and unfastened her restraints. She walked across the moving deck to where the scientists huddled over their ruggedized screens to assess the sensor feed.

"Anything?" she asked.

"Not sure," one of them said, identifying himself as the leader of the contingent or else just the loudmouth. Eze wasn't sure yet. "We have trace signals, but they're faint; either means there's not much there or it's buried deep."

"Pilot, ETA to the next site?" she asked over the channel. "Eight minutes, Commander."

"Recommend we try the nearest sites for a more definitive signal," she told the scientists.

"Agreed," said an older male scientist. "Let's do that; we can always come back to this site if the signals are stronger here than the others."

Eze nodded, having quickly ascertained the leader and the loudmouth distinction.

Eight minutes later they settled into another hover and immediately found far stronger signals from the surface.

"Sensor readings indicate a high concentration of the mineral at this site," the lead scientist said.

"Roger that," Eze replied. "Pilot, nearest LZ?"

"Standby one," the crooning voice came back. The dropship gained altitude as the power to the hover was increased, giving them a wider view of the area. The hover settled in again, the altimeter on Eze's display showing a thousand feet.

"Nearest place we can set down is… six miles out. We can get you to forty feet for a drop and exfil further out," the copilot told her.

She looked at the scientists, two of whom wore looks of abject terror, until their leader put a stop to the idea of jumping out into the cool mountain air.

"Our gear is sensitive, Commander," he explained. "Carrying it overland, as much as I'm unhappy with the walk, is our only real option."

Eze nodded, finding her own compromise and addressing the whole dropship.

"Listen up," she announced. "We're landing six miles out. Half the team stays with Boss Ryers and defends the LZ. The rest are on me with the science detail. I need demolitions to clear trees closer to the site for an extraction LZ."

The dropship, to the pilot's credit, fit into a gap in the massive trees that very few people would describe as a landing zone. The prickly needles of the long, low branches danced crazily in the updraft caused by the engines powering down. Eze stepped off the ramp to have her suit software automatically increase the ambient light to her vision; the tall trees obscured a lot of the natural light from the twin suns.

"Boss Ryers," Eze said over the comm.

"Behind you, Commander," Ryers answered as he filed down the ramp.

"Start work clearing this LZ wider," she ordered.

He nodded quickly. It was absolutely the right call. The spot was so tight to the dropship there was no way to see far enough into the dense forest to mount an acceptable defense.

"First platoon, on me," she ordered.

Eze detailed off certain troops to carry equipment and others to personally escort each of the four scientists who were wearing tough overalls instead of armor. The scientists weren't trained and rated to drive the suits. She identified her two troopers rated for demolitions and detailed them to fetch the equipment required for blowing trees out of the earth to clear an LZ closer to their target. The cutting tools they would need were already accounted for—the laser drills packed to dig the minerals out of the rock would perform the same task.

"Second platoon," Ryers said, "form up a defense."

He began firing off names and giving them orders to fell trees and provide the space and vision they needed, adding a few choice words where he felt them to be necessary. "And any of you dumbasses drop a two-hundred-foot tree on my drop- ship will be walking back to base, is that understood?"

Choruses of the affirmative echoed throughout the clearing as Eze set off toward their main objective.

CHAPTER 7

Exoplanet Orbiting Barnard's Star

"God *dammit*!" Harris exclaimed as he tried to drag the already heavy tool case down the ramp of the *Ichi*. "A little help here?"

He turned pointedly to the two junior engineers who seemed only slightly less fearful of Harris than they were of stepping foot outside the safety of the ship. They scurried forward, picking up a side each and relieving the chief engineer of his burden.

Harris stood and leaned back as though stretching a stiff lower back. "You just *had* to pick a repair spot with three times Earth's gravity, didn't you," he grumbled over the comm. Anyone listening wondered if he meant himself or was blaming someone else.

"You have my deepest, most heartfelt apologies and sympathies, Mister Harris," came Torres's sarcastic reply over the channel. "I'll let you pick the garage next time."

"Sorry, sir, I… I wasn't intentionally…" Harris muttered. He had forgotten that he still had an open comm.

"Just give me an ETA for repairs when you can," Torres told him more gently, but with a sternness that reminded the engineer of the chain of command and that they weren't exactly on vacation.

Brandt watched the two engineers lugging the case of tools toward the nose. They would spend at least half a day carefully removing the ablative polymer-resin armor plating from the nose of the ship to expose the mechanical workings of the spiked tip of their Fold

Drive. As she understood it, the protrusion was necessary—it extended beyond their ship and emitted the correct frequency of microwaves (and some other kind of science she didn't know) in order to shorten the distance between one part of space and another.

When they had first used the technology, before each subsequent jump was tested and recalibrated and rigorously assessed for ways to tweak it, she had assumed that the drives had given humanity the ability to travel great distances in an instant. It was only when the sheer, near-infinite scale of their own galaxy truly became apparent to her did she realize that such mind-numbingly incomprehensible distances still took time to travel.

What used to take hours now took seconds. What took a month before only took minutes now. Their current destination had taken them hours instead of a generation to reach if they had used the technology from only two years before.

The one feeling she was left with, when the scale of their world hit her, was of being so incredibly, unbelievably, infinitesimally small and unimportant to life in the galaxy.

She put their discovery of this faster-than-light travel technology right beside the ancient historical greats—fire, the wheel, electricity, harnessed singularity energy sources, and Nanomites. To the lives of every human being in existence, it made the kind of difference that there was no coming back from. This technology dragged all of them into a new era whether they wanted it or not.

She turned her attention back to her present and fired off some very commander-like orders to focus her mind.

"Zero, tell me what you see."

"Nothin' moving, Commander," the marksman said. He had both been fully alert to their comm channel and known the correct answer as though he refreshed the feed every two seconds.

Brandt checked her HUD to confirm with the suit software.

Technology was invaluable, but given the option she'd still prefer it to be backed up by the mark one eyeball of someone she trusted implicitly.

Payne sat beside the sniper atop the nearest spike of high ground in their immediate area of operations with her heavy gun on a detachable bipod ready to rock. She had come up with the ingenious solution to provide aerial support while they'd be stuck on the exoplanet, and had requisitioned one of the larger search drones from the *Ichi* to sit in a hover high over their ship. She had gotten Zero to sit his targeting drone on top of the larger piece of equipment first, which meant that his eyes-in-the-sky, which in turn fed all of their troops intelligence, could stay up there for hours without burning out its battery power to stay in the air.

When Brandt asked why they simply couldn't patch the smaller drone into the larger search one for targeting and telemetry, the snickering at her words was short lived. Payne had explained—a little too condescendingly Brandt felt—that the software for Bart was firewalled against everything but his armor. Brandt had given this information the shrug it deserved, caring more for the results than for the in-depth workings. Regardless, she was glad that her team had targeting information on their HUDs however it had been achieved.

She had tasked the search drones to run a perimeter beyond the scope of Zero's Bart, but the increased gravity put more strain on their small repulser engines and reduced their maximum flight time to about forty minutes. Staying still meant that the two search drones could recharge and take turns to hover with the little sniper recon drone sat on its back for close to three hours at a time.

She had done her commander duties and rotated the personnel out on the ground and inside the gun pods. She had stood down half of her team to rest in the ready room and allowed them to rotate and provide a reactionary force if they needed one. Such was the cycle of thoughts that ran through the mind of anyone commanding troops—everything was rostering and welfare and relief shifts. The last person she could give consideration to was herself, as though she had nine children to care for.

Children, she admitted to herself, who were likely baddest bunch of badasses in the UN.

"We're going to lose the light before you get that plate off, you know?" Harris's voice cut over the comm as he berated one of the other engineers for moving slower than he liked. "Make it pretty when it goes back on, not now, okay?"

Brandt smiled to herself, glad that it wasn't only her who was seen as a slave driver.

"Ah!" Harris exclaimed, still not realizing he'd left his mic open. "There you are, you little shit..."

Grunting and muttered curses punctuated the transmission, amusing everyone listening until they heard the next words.

"Okay..." Harris said. "That's not good... Bridge, you there?"

"Send it," Torres said.

"Yeah, Captain," Harris said with a resigned moan. "I've got about a week's worth of rewiring to get through here, and that's not counting the work inside to re-route the damaged battery cells. It ain't good, sir."

"You've got two days, Mister Harris. Bridge out." Torres said without hesitation, cutting the comm before his engineer could lodge a formal protest.

Brandt's HUD flashed an icon that indicated a priority incoming comm. She clicked the icon with her eyes, and enlarged it to see a secure channel from Torres's personal comm.

"Hey," she said. She knew this would be a private conversation.

"Hey," he answered, sounding more tired than he had over the open channel. She guessed he had excused himself and was now in his small but well-appointed private quarters. "So, the news inside is that we've lost roughly fifteen percent of our battery capacity and the Fold drive's wiring is fried. On top of that we've taken a ton of damage to the level one shields. How's it looking out there?"

Brandt spun a slow three-sixty as she thought. "Pretty damned bleak to be honest with you," she said as she took in the barren, rocky landscape. "Nothing moving as far as we can see, which is a good thing if you ask me."

"Well, there is that," Torres answered tiredly. "At least there are no aliens or dinosaurs down there."

"That we know of," corrected Brandt. "Or giant bug-crab bastards…"

"Yeah. Anyway, recommendations? Should we shut everything down for the night?"

"I'd say so," Brandt answered. "Shut it down tight but keep sensors on during darkness so we have a better idea of what's out there."

"What do you mean?" Torres shot back. "Are you seeing signs of life?"

"Nothing obvious," she said carefully, "but there is liquid water and vegetation and Bart has seen some holes that looked like tunnels about a mile out from our position. Between you and me, I'm not loving the idea of being outside without light."

"Agreed," Torres answered. "Start buttoning it up as soon as Harris calls it."

"Roger that, Captain. Brandt out." She waited for him to kill the private channel, then switched back to the team comm to give her next orders. She asked Harris for an ETA and instructed her team to

51

fall back to the ship one by one, leaving Zero in position until they had all returned. The engineering team, electing to leave the heavy toolbox where it was needed and not drag it back inside, stepped wearily up the ramp, looking forward to the artificial gravity inside and not feeling three times heavier than they were.

Brandt climbed up last after waiting for Zero to jog in carrying his long rifle. She hit the ramp controls to seal the ship from the alien landscape just as the last of the light faded.

"Rotate two-hour watches on the gun pods," she ordered over the team channel. "Specter and Turner take first watch."

She waited for the confirmations over comm and returned to the ready room via the decontamination walkthrough before stepping out of her armor. Despite the air conditioning inside the suits, she felt that blissful release of being free and allowing real air to brush over her skin. She never shook the sensation of wearing the old generation armor, and these prototype rigs were by far the best that ever been made, but that still didn't take away the claustrophobia she felt after any extended period inside the suit.

Catching up with Zero, she muttered to him in a low voice, "You get the feeling there's something out there?"

"You reading my mind again, Commander?" he muttered back. "Specter reckons the same. Them tunnels didn't dig themselves now, did they?"

"That's what I thought," she answered. "Stay ready."

"Picking up biological material on sensors," the ensign at tactical announced.

"Details?" Torres demanded.

"Unknown, sir, readings on three sides and…"

"And what, Ensign?"

"And they're… they're gone, Captain."

"Gone where?"

"Just… gone."

"Give me a visual," Torres ordered. The viewscreen lit up, showing an ambient-light-enhanced review of the alien landscape, empty and still.

"Commander Brandt to the bridge," he ordered.

He pointed a finger at the comm officer, who then turned away to relay the instructions. Almost a minute of tense silence went by, the bridge crew staring at the viewscreen, until Brandt walked in and asked for a report.

"Bio readings all around, now they've just disappeared," Torres told her.

She didn't respond, but tapped at her comm device.

"Gunners, Commander Brandt," she said, then waited for the twin acknowledgements. "Anything on visual?"

"Negative," Kekoa responded from the pod he was crammed uncomfortably into.

"Same," Beale answered from the other side of the ship. "Switching to lowlight resolution. Standby."

Brandt waited a few moments.

"Still nothing, Commander. What exactly are we looking for?"

Brandt decided not to tell them the worryingly ambiguous news that biological material had been detected and had now disappeared. Instead, she reminded them to keep their eyes peeled.

"This could be a long night," she whispered to herself before turning away to ready her weapons and armor.

CHAPTER 8

Gaia Neós Mountains

"Commander Eze?" came the call over the comm.

The rushing wind accompanying the transmission made it immediately obvious that the hail didn't originate with any of her troops.

"Here," she responded. "Go ahead."

"How much... how much further is it to the objective..." came the breathless response.

She stopped and turned to look at the scientists, each shadowed by one of her armored troops. One of them held a hand to his side and wore a pained expression. The pace she had set was one that any of her troops could sustain all day, even without powered armor. But the science team they escorted was clearly lacking in even the basic fitness she would have expected from the non-fighting branches of the UN.

"Platoon, halt," Eze announced. "All-around defense."

No acknowledgments came as her troops fanned out to adopt positions in cover and her marksman made straight for the nearest appropriate high ground with the spotter. The other half of that specialist sub-unit matched the pace and direction. She allowed herself a small moment of satisfaction that her people were well-drilled. She walked back to the scientists who had all collapsed onto smooth rocks. She disengaged her helmet as she smiled and approached.

"Science division not much for PT?" she asked a little goadingly.

"Last time someone made us do a morning run," the female scientist said, before pausing to drink water from her canteen, "there was damn near a mutiny."

"What do you say, Petty Officer Bowers?" Eze asked, glancing into the now exposed face of the junior NCO escorting the female scientist. "Reckon there'd be a mutiny if I drilled you sorry bunch harder?"

Bowers, his own helmet removed, smiled like a masochist. "I'd say not, Commander," he replied.

Eze returned his smile, pleased with the loyalty and love from her unit, and stood to address the whole expedition via comm.

"We rest for eight minutes," she said.

"Why eight?" the lead scientist asked, still holding his side as though direct pressure would remove the muscle cramp.

"Not a biology major, then?" she asked. "Last reports out of the UN medical research center say that inactivity after a forced march causes a build-up of lactic acid in the muscles if you stay still for more than eight minutes. Makes it harder to get moving again and increases the risk of muscle cramps. Are you not rated to use armor?"

The lead scientist exchanged a look with the female but neither explained.

"Let me guess," Eze said. "It goes beyond the scope of your departmental budget for the training, maintenance and use of suits for science purposes?"

"Something like that," the leader said.

"Well, if we have to come back out and there's the chance of any kind of distance to cover, I'll see about getting a few of you trained up to use our spare rigs." Eze saw the look of excitement and surprise in their eyes, so added quickly, "Strictly off the books, you understand?"

Rushed murmurs of agreement to keep such arrangements on the downlow met her question. She nodded and strolled away to tour the position they would occupy for the next seven minutes.

When they moved out again, setting an intentionally slower pace, Eze sent two troops to scout farther ahead of their main force. She was never one to miss an opportunity to drill her troops in the field.

Keeping an open ear and a muted mic on the main channel, she checked in on the LZ.

"Ryers, Commander Eze," she said on a private channel. She had left the master petty officer in charge, despite the nominal leadership of the young lieutenant.

"Ryers, send it, Commander, over," his gruff voice shot back.

"Sitrep?"

"Making good progress, ma'am," he said. The sounds of creaking and cracking loud in the background indicated the fall of a tree larger than their barracks. "We're on schedule. How about you? Over."

Eze stifled the small huff of amusement as the NCO insisted on using the sign-off tags for every single transmission. She couldn't help but feel he had the makings of a seriously badass command chief when the next available slot came up for his seniority. She entertained the thought of asking him to come with her on promotion if she ever got the chance to take a new unit under her wing.

Mentally shaking the tumbling thoughts away, she responded. "Terrain is making progress difficult for the civilians. Estimate forty minutes to the target area. Any sign of hostiles?"

The pause on the other end made her think he was politely waiting for her to say 'over,' but he came back anyway.

"Negative hostiles. Guessing the dropship coming in would scare off just about most nasties, over."

"Roger that, Ryers," she said. "Stay sharp. Eze out."

She cut the private comm and reactivated the mic to her team channel.

"Siviter, Kembery, sound off," she ordered, hailing the two she had sent ahead on reconnaissance.

"Siviter here, Commander," came a whispered response. This was strange since inside their helmets sound didn't carry, but habits of human nature were hard to override. "Standby."

Eze stopped, bringing up the menu inside her visor and expanding the roughly mapped terrain with her gauntleted hands as a virtual control. She found the two green icons about a mile ahead of them near the objective.

"Some sort of... of *nest* here, Commander," Siviter's voice came back. "In a clearing... there's bones and..."

"Left flank!" barked Kembery's higher pitched voice over her male partner's report.

A burst of gunfire, abruptly cut off, sounded in stereo from the team channel and via the external feeds to their suits. The platoon froze, dropping into cover instinctively as the troops nearest the science team pushed them down to cover them. A scream over the channel pushed Eze into action. She ordered half of her team to stay with the principals and secure them before detailing five others to follow her.

This was the reason she pushed them hard, the reason she didn't want the monotony of guarding a wall and allowing complacency to creep in, eroding their sense of danger at their alien surroundings. The troops she ordered to her side fell in with her fast pace, working in pairs; being an additional gun in a unit designed to work in multiples of two was a quick way to get shot by friendly fire.

"Siviter!" she snapped into the channel. "Kembery! Report!"

Neither answered as she ran, her HUD showing a rapidly decreasing distance to the two stationary green icons that morphed into outlines of armored humans when she neared them.

Only one other outline flared on her HUD. Massive and shining in red, it reared upward onto huge hind legs and issued a bellowing roar at the approaching shapes.

Eze, time slowing to a fraction of the speed of her thoughts, registered a few important facts.

One green outline was slumped at the base of a gargantuan tree that had to be at least fifteen feet across at the base. The other outline flickered as Kembery's vital signs blinked out and flatlined. The beast, for there was no other word she could use to describe the thing, dropped back down onto all fours to fill the space beneath the tree cover with a shrieking, screeching noise like a blade scraping over glass.

The long, talon-like claws on its front paws raked at the chest armor under the crushed helmet leaking what used to be Kembery's brain matter. The claws were dragged like knives over the polymer resin armor, as the creature scratched to find a way inside the hard shell of the new thing that had wandered into its world.

"Open fire," Eze ordered, ducking behind the tree where Siviter lay still. She mag-locked her rifle onto her back over her right shoulder and reached around the base of the tree to grab the ankle of her injured trooper and drag him out of sight of the thing.

Siviter's armor had gone rigid, preserving whatever injured muscle and tissue and bone was left inside until surgical intervention could be sought. No doubt the safety mechanisms of the suit's software had also pumped him full of pain meds to stop the screaming.

The animal was close to the size of a ground transport and covered in the thickest, shaggiest coat of fur Eze had ever seen. It bellowed in rage and pain as the bullets hit the thick, wet fur and pierced into the flesh underneath. She drew her rifle from her back and pulled the butt tight into her shoulder as she rounded the tree and knelt, drawing a bead on it and squeezing the trigger.

The thing, which looked similar to a grizzly bear crossed with a rhinoceros, turned to face her, locking its eyes onto her visor in a moment of bowel-loosening terror. The suns, shining through the trees like a downward slash of orbital fire support, glinted off the long claws like they were diamonds. Instead of running or charging like any large animal would, the bear-thing snatched up the ruined body of Kembery in what remained of her armor and spun to release it like the projectile of some ancient siege weapon.

Eze barely had time to react, throwing herself aside just in time for the boot of the thrown body to impact her right arm where she flinched to protect her head. That arm crashed back into the chest of her armor and her rifle disintegrated under the force.

Dropping the fragments of her destroyed gun, she got back to her feet. The force of the blow had knocked her down like a bowling pin. Once standing, however, Eze found the animal had gone from her sight. Her brain also registered the lack of weapons fire.

"Where is it?" she demanded.

"No idea, Commander," responded one of her troops. She got on the channel and informed the main part of her platoon to be on the lookout for something that was like a double-sized grizzly bear about the same mass of a small elephant, when a long, oozing dribble of thick liquid strung down just ahead of her from the trees above.

She didn't have time to think, only react.

She didn't look, no matter how much her body screamed at her to do it. Instead she threw herself forward into a combat roll to get back to her feet and turned in time to see—to *feel*—the thing dropping from the thick branches above where she had just been. It held up one front paw, bigger than Eze's leg, and readied to charge her.

"Commander! Get out of the way!" came a shout.

She imagined someone lining up a rifle and seeing their commanding officer far too close to the target to be able to pull the trigger.

Eze didn't answer. She rocked back on the balls of her armored feet and began to sprint toward the thing at an enhanced velocity. It charged her, lumbering but accelerating faster than any mammal with that kind of bulk had a right to. As it stretched out the glinting talons on its one good front leg to slash her, she leapt higher, sailing over the outstretched claws, as the armor on her right greave responded to the command she gave on her HUD.

The wide-bladed short sword, an addition designed and hastily retrofitted for close-in work against the Va'alen, shot from the armored sheath as she timed her strike to perfection.

Knowledge, she knew, was often more important in a fight than any level of skill. For example, fighting against a man without armor meant that, without fail, she would take the first presented opportunity to deliver a punch or a kick to the groin. The knowledge of that sweet spot was worth more than the ability to overpower her opponent.

The beast she faced, the one that reached out to tear through her armor, was a vertebrate. Which meant it had a spine, a central nervous system running from a control center —the brain. Unlike the

Va'alen there was no way she could believe this thing was an exoskeleton.

As she leapt, timing her downward motion with the exposed blade, she stabbed down at exactly the point she would expect the spinal column to be exposed between the shoulder blades of the huge, terrifying thing.

The blade bit deep, the added weight of the armored person wielding it pushing it deeper than could have been achieved without the augmentation. With strangled cry the creature went limp. The momentum of the savage charge dragged Eze along with it, for them both to tumble and skid along the forest floor. Once they came to a stop, she withdrew the blade and rolled away from it, drawing the pistol from her thigh as she regained her feet. Without a thought, she emptied the entire magazine into the head of the monster to make sure it didn't rear up after they all thought it was dead.

She was sure she'd seen that movie.

CHAPTER 9

United Nations Medical Research Facility, NYC

"Cut the crap, Doctor," Dassiova complained, "and just tell me when I'll be cleared for duty."

The doctor, nominally senior at the medical facility attached to the UN headquarters in New York, sighed. He had just about suffered enough bile from the admiral. His entire staff had, which was why he found himself dealing with the man personally.

"Admiral," he explained tiredly for the third time that day as he reviewed the latest test results, "there's nothing *physically* wrong with you so far as we can tell—"

"So, sign your damn form and clear me for duty," Dassiova interrupted.

"—but as I've explained before, countless times, the untested medical procedure that saved your life requires long-term research to ensure you won't relapse. What if the injuries you suffered that the Nanomites fixed simply unraveled? Believe me, Admiral, you'd want to be inside of a sterile medical facility with some of the territory's best surgeons if *that* happens."

"Before you did your five-day online course to become a doctor," Dassiova said without regard for the consequences, "did you happen to sell insurance?"

"Admiral Dassiova!" the doctor erupted, having suffered enough with that last insult in a long line of similar abuse. "If you want to be released then that's fine. On your own head be it. But neither I nor any of my staff will clear you for active duty until we are satisfied that the repairs conducted by the Nanomites will hold permanently. Understand? This technology wasn't *designed* to repair catastrophic soft tissue trauma. It was designed to combat hidden infections in the body and repair minor damage like degraded cartilage and negate the need for orthopedic surgery. *Minor* damage, Admiral. Minor."

Dassiova boiled inside but let out only the smallest hiss of vented pressure before he spoke. With a gentle sigh of resignation, one not mirrored in his eyes, he relented with a wave of his hand a lay back on the bed. The doctor took that as permission to carry on unabused as Elias Dassiova closed his eyes and tried not to recall the moment that a cockroach three feet taller than him swung a razor-sharp claw to slice open his entire gut.

He tried not to re-live the sickening slow-motion replay of the savage blow arcing toward his midriff as he sucked in his gut.

Tried not to think of the searing, white-hit pain of the claw slashing a rent through uniform and skin and muscle alike.

"Have you experienced any dizziness, nausea or headaches?" the doctor asked him, snatching him back from the brink of his memory spiral.

"No," he said. "Fully intend to when you release me and I can get good and drunk though."

The doctor ignored the poor attempt at levity.

"Tell me if there have been any sensations that you would consider to be different or unnatural," he asked, scrolling his finger down the datapad he held.

"The only thing that's *unnatural*," Dassiova grumbled, "is that I've been sitting on my ass waiting for you to sign me off while my fleet is out there fighting a war."

The doctor sighed heavily again, lowering the datapad and lifting a hand to rub his eyes with forefinger and thumb before pinching the bridge of his nose.

"For the last time, Admiral," he said in a voice that hinted he was dangerously close to the edge, "the war is over. The aliens are gone from the Centauri system. The Middle Eastern Alliance has been crushed and UN troops control every part of the territories they subverted. There *is* no war!"

"Maybe not right now," Dassiova said sulkily.

The doctor blew up and damn near threw the datapad across the room.

"Fine," he said, all semblance of professionalism gone. "You want out? You got it. Just let me do one more round of tests and, assuming they are all okay, you're out. Believe me, we don't want you here more than you don't *want* to be here! You're... you're *demanding*, and every single one of my staff has complained to me about your behavior. If *I* could complain to someone about your behavior, then I would!"

He stopped, seeing the cold and unamused look on Dassiova's face.

"That how you usually speak to a fleet admiral, Doctor?" he asked in a worryingly controlled voice.

"I... my apologies, sir," he stammered.

"Ah forget it," Dassiova said. "So long as I'm out by the morning we're all good." He sat back, compliant and calm. "Now, I need a secure comm link to... well, you don't need to know where to. And get someone in here to fetch me some coffee, would ya?"

The doctor opened his mouth to protest, but shut it because he realized, in defeat, that there was no way he could ever win an argument with this man.

"Admiral," Director Chase Ettington said as he sat at the console and smoothed down his tie, "how can I help?"

"You can help by sorting out my orders ready for tomorrow morning when I'm cleared for active service."

"I don't have direct authority over UN postings and orders," he began. He faltered as Dassiova pulled the datapad closer to his face, achieving the same effect as leaning across the table at the man if he were there in person. One of the reasons he was so influential, had risen so far and so fast in the shady world of inter-territory back-channeling, was his ability to read a room and know his audience.

The director's senses told him in that instant that bullshit wouldn't wash with the admiral, and the admiral knew where the real power came from, otherwise he would have contacted some friendly senior admiral at UN headquarters.

"I won't bother with the party line," he said. "You'll get your ship back, but you won't be heading straight for the CS."

"Oh?"

"United Nations Earth Command," he said grandly before rolling his eyes. "That's what the combined security council is calling itself this week. They've decided to maintain two fully-equipped fleets until manufacturing and recruitment can fulfill the requirements to garrison the habitable worlds and provide sufficient transport and protection—that's no real secret. But the decision to maintain a battle-ready armada near to Earth is a safety measure everyone agrees on until the eventual construction of orbital defense platforms around here, the Moon and Mars is scheduled and completed."

"So I get my fleet back and we sit in space waiting to be attacked? Why aren't we taking the offensive to the enemy?"

"That's..." Ettington hesitated. "That's in hand. Don't ask for any more details because you won't get them."

"Fine. Can I assume that Vernay's Tenth will have to rotate back home to take up the defense and my Ninth will go back out?" Dassiova asked hopefully.

"That's a fair assumption, Admiral," Ettington said. "I'll make sure you have a transport ready for when you're discharged from the medical research center."

Dassiova nodded once, his version of a thank you, and cut the comm.

"Admiral on deck!" yapped the ensign as he stepped down from the rear ramp of the dropship.

"Can it, Romano," Dassiova said, although without the venom he usually reserved for the young officer who manned his main tactical station.

The admiral walked over to him, returned the salute briefly with a hint of a smile and reached out to brush an imaginary speck of dust from the second vertical star on Romano's right breast. He had to get it out of the way soon before the young man, the *boy* if truth be told, burst with excitement at showing his recent promotion to his commanding officer. Romano beamed, trying and failing to hide his immense pride at promoting almost a year ahead of expected.

Dassiova scanned the hangar deck, seeing far more people than had good purpose to be there. He was about to ask his troop commander, his trusted Chief, to order them all back to their duty

66

stations when he realized they were probably off-duty staff who just wanted to see him return to the *Indomitable*. That realization threatened to overwhelm him. To save having to accept personal gratitude and well-wishes from all of them he tapped at his comm device to connect to the bridge to speak to the officer in command of the massive ship still docked to the orbital shipyard.

"Commander Childs here," the comm chirped.

Dassiova was happy with that. The man had been a competent captain on smaller ships, and from what Dassiova knew of him, held no arrogance. He was happy to have him along as a sub-commander for the carrier.

"Commander Childs, this is Admiral Dassiova," he said.

"Honor to have you back aboard, sir," Childs answered.

"Honor to be here. Get me a ship-wide channel from here, if you please?"

There was a short pause until Childs reported, "Ship-wide channel open, standby for transmission from fleet Admiral Dassiova."

Dassiova grimaced a little, feeling on the spot in front of the thousands of crew just on this carrier alone, not counting the members of all the other ships in his fleet he'd have to address soon enough.

"Crew of the *Indomitable*," he said, speaking into the mic of his comm device but making eye contact with the people arrayed in the hangar bay for his arrival. "It's my honor to be back, but we don't have the luxury of time to congratulate ourselves on our last mission; we have work to do. Trust in each other, trust in your supervisors and officers, and trust in me. Let's get it done. Dassiova out."

Cheers rang out in the hangar bay, making him flush with color—he wasn't one for attention. He walked out of the docking level and toward the bridge, taking his bag of personal kit from the crewman who had expected to carry it all the way to his quarters for him.

"I may be an admiral, son," he said, "but that doesn't mean I'm too important to hump my own gear."

He dumped the bag on the sofa in his quarters after taking a brief report from the bridge and waving Childs back down to the chair he offered to vacate. Setting up the coffee machine, which he saw with a smile had been filled, cleaned and repaired ready for use, he made himself a pot. Once he poured a cup, he sat down to enter his credentials with the bio implant in his left arm.

"Computer, current posting for Captain Torres," he said.

"Captain Torres is not on the UN deployment roster," the computerized voice replied.

"Computer, locate Commander Kyle Torres."

"Unable to comply; Commander Kyle Torres is not on the UN deployment roster."

"Computer," Dassiova tried again. "Current posting details for Commander Leslie Brandt."

"Commander Brandt is not on the UN deployment roster."

Dassiova sat back, confused and suspicious, muttering, "… the hell did they get to…?"

CHAPTER 10

Exoplanet Orbiting Barnard's Star

"Shields to full," Sarvanto snapped. He pointed at the ensign at the tactical station who jumped to comply. The tall flight officer calmly took the young officer's station to cut down on the time it would take for orders and information to be relayed through another person.

"Can you give me anything more than 'biological readings,' Mister Sarvanto?" Torres asked.

"Reviewing sensor feeds now, Captain," Sarvanto responded, only slightly distracted by the data streaming over his console. "Aha. I've adjusted the filters to electromagnetic and infrared and it looks like..."

Torres shot an exasperated look at Brandt before turning back to his flight officer.

"Looks like what?"

"It looks like a few individual readings combined to overload the sensor array; like picking out one person in a crowd of twenty..."

"Be clear," Torres demanded. "Are you saying there are twenty bio-signs combining as one?"

"Yes," came the terse reply. "Only... I apologize, Captain, please allow me a moment to interpret the data."

"Fine, but I need a line on whether whatever is out there is hostile or not and I need it now."

The answer came from Rogers who had taken his seat at the helm to monitor sensors and do something since he couldn't fly. A slight hum vibrated the *Ichi* and caused him to call out to the bridge.

"Contact, port shields," he announced. As soon as the vibration had begun, it stopped.

"Somebody give me something to work with here," Torres prompted, a hint of annoyed frustration creeping into his voice.

"External visual coming online, sir," Rogers said. "Enhancing for low light using infrare—"

"What the hell is that?" Torres asked, seeing what looked like a leech the size of a fully grown adult human rear up and attach itself to the shields, making their landed ship vibrate again.

"Unknown," Sarvanto answered, "but sensors indicate there are now six of them attached to our outer shields."

The hum of vibration increased noticeably after he reported that. Torres glanced at Brandt who nodded in return and opened a comm channel once more.

"Gunners, open fire."

The response was nigh on instantaneous. She guessed that both her second-in-command and her newest recruit had their thumbs on the fire controls ready to tear up the alien worms the second they were cleared hot.

Rumbling, chattering vibrations rippled through the ship as the two gun pods articulated to fire and clear away all of the alien worms attacking them until both fell silent.

"Clear," Kekoa reported.

"Clear," Beale echoed. Brandt turned to Torres and nodded, who in turn looked up at his flight officer and asked for a report.

"Outer shields reduced by nine percent, sir," he said.

"They appear to have drained the main power somehow without being repelled by the... standby..."

"Multiple incoming biological signs," Rogers barked.

"Gunners, fire at will," Brandt ordered. The dull rattling of their surroundings began again. What nobody would say out loud was that with their damaged and depleted battery stacks, they had no hope of maintaining a constant fire to clear away whatever the things were. Until a better option presented itself, however, Brandt would keep the main guns firing. She tapped at the console behind her and hailed the ship's main engineer.

"Harris, I need you to deploy as many of your engineers as you can to the armory."

Heinrich, the man responsible for maintaining the weapons and armor, was a former UN troop from Germany with injuries that had left him with prosthetics and unable to fight on the front line. He had found himself at a loss for many years until the posting aboard the *Ichi* landed in his lap. He sounded out of breath as he answered.

"I am already making my way to the armory," he answered without waiting for a question. "What is it that you need?"

"I've got engineers en route to the armory," Brandt said with as much efficiency as possible. "I need every pulse rifle and heavy gun we have calibrated to the same shield harmonics as the ship like our main guns are."

"Understood, Commander," Heinrich answered. He accepted his task without question and knowing that he would find out the why long after he had achieved the what part of the equation.

Brandt killed the channel and glanced at Torres. His eyebrows rose as he guessed what she was going to do. She nodded once as she stood, so much conveyed silently through the gesture between friends, and hit the pre-programmed button on her comm to open a channel to her entire team.

"Full gear and weapons for immediate deployment," she said simply. If she knew her team, most of them would already be on their way to join whatever fight was happening.

The team's rifles were strewn over every available surface where the armorer threw each weapon after the engineers programmed the shield resonance harmonics into them as fast as they could. This re-programming allowed the pulses of lethal energy to pass through the shields unchecked. Each rifle was then snatched up and loaded with a fresh battery pack by the team member who ran to jump into their armor.

Zero arrived wearing nothing but his skivvies and walked into the room as though nothing was wrong. He stood before his armor and wait for it to open up to accept his almost entirely naked form.

Turner, arriving with at least a PT shirt in addition to regulation underwear, did the same as he padded barefoot toward his rig.

As Brandt's armor closed around her and the helmet activated to bring up her HUD, she opened up the team channel and addressed the two men in the gun turret control pods.

"Beale, Kekoa, talk to me."

"There's a lot more of them now," Beale said. By not addressing her by rank, he betrayed his concentration and elevated stress levels.

"Roger that," she said.

She picked up a rifle and began attaching as many spare battery packs to her armor as she could possibly fit before her form was totally disfigured. Many more and she wouldn't fit in the drop tube, but she hoped her example was being followed by the rest of her team. The decision to take as much ammunition as possible wasn't difficult to make, given that the ship's guns were firing almost constantly.

"Listen up," she said just as the ground beneath her feet opened up and she dropped to the deck of the shuttle bay with a metallic clang. "We're going outside via the main shuttle bay doors. Hold firm under the main fuselage inside the first shield layer." She ignored the fact that the first of their four shield layers was gone, damaged and depleted by the impact of the solar ejection. "Spread out. You're all cleared weapons free as soon as we deploy."

The sounds of other metal clangs echoed around her as, one by one, the other eight members of her team landed in the shuttle bay with her.

"Standby for shuttle bay decompression," she announced to the bridge via comm, waiting for the hissing noise to fade to nothing as the bay became equalized with the outside atmosphere.

They ran down the ramp, HUDs flashing with squirming red outlines as they fired and spread out to combat the wall of flesh pulsating against the outer shields.

"Report, Commander," Torres said earnestly into the comm.

"Multiple contacts," she replied. "All around. They appear to be attacking the shields."

"I can confirm this," Sarvanto's voice cut into the transmission. "Outer shields are down thirty percent. Whatever these things are doing, it is draining our power reserves rapidly."

"Take 'em out, Commander," Torres growled vehemently.

"Aye aye," Brandt answered, depressing the trigger on her rifle and letting fly with an entire battery pack of pulse shots on rapid fire. She cycled the weapon twice like that, cutting down beast after beast as her shots passed through the layers of shielding and taking them down like she was harvesting crops. All around her the shields glowed faintly as though being hit by enemy fire, and the noise of six other rifles thrumming away resounded inside her helmet under the constant thudding pulses of the ship's turret guns.

The only other noise, apart from a low frequency shriek she couldn't identify, was the heavier sound of Payne's heavy pulse blaster which she swung in wide, sweeping arcs from left to right and clearing an entire section of shields over a hundred meters wide. The gun, affixed to the support bracket that popped out of the front of her armor, didn't need reloading like their pulse rifles. It fed directly from an oversized battery pack built into her armor and, as such, she was worth half a platoon of firepower.

Brandt fired and reloaded, fired and reloaded until the ground at her feet was littered with depleted energy packs for the weapon. Taking stock of their situation without relenting in her fire, she realized that no matter how many of the creatures they killed the attack never seemed to abate. There was some- thing ominously terrifying about the enemy numbers.

CHAPTER 11

near the Crab nebula, Perseus Arm of the milky Way

The Va'alen home worlds, Chakour learned, were quite unique in that there were four habitable planets all inside the same star system. The star, a red giant putting out a strong amount of low light, heated four worlds, each slightly larger or smaller than Earth.

Da'kath told him of the legends of their ancestors, explaining how they had been four different clans who spent generations viewing one another with powerful devices and had eventually learned to communicate between the planets.

By the time their ancestors had evolved sufficiently to cross the divide of space between worlds, one of the clans tried to dominate the others. Years of war erupted without any one clan able to exert enough control over the others to win a decisive battle.

"And that," Da'kath told him as he sipped from a bowl of recycled biological paste that turned Chakour's stomach, "is when the Hive Lords came to our ancestors to unite us. Our people believed them to be gods at first, coming from the heavens to speak directly to our minds, but they dispelled these myths. They were like us, they said, only much, *much* older.

They knew things about the universe that my people could not even dream of, and in a way that did make them gods.

75

"They showed us how to grow the armor that marks us as true warriors, how to construct new ways to generate power so that we did not have to rely on the burning of our natural resources and scorch our planets just to travel to new ones and do the same all over again."

He sipped again, apparently enjoying the vintage much the Chakour's horror and Da'kath's amusement.

"They helped us evolve," he went on. "They showed us new ways to explore the galaxy by making our ships faster and constructing the gateways between other worlds."

"And your clans united to become the Va'alen?" Chakour asked. He had forgotten for a moment that he was entertaining a monstrous alien close to twice his size, as it sipped on the recycled biological matter of one of his non-essential crewmembers.

"No," Da'kath said darkly. "One of the clans, the weakest one that did not take to living adorned with the honor of the armor," he bashed a fiercely proud claw into his rock-hard breastplate, "escaped. My ancestors flew to their world to crush them and enslave them, but some of them fled in a ship that was capable of harnessing the power of the gateways, just as this ship and the other ships of the humans can. They fled like cowards leaving their own people behind."

Chakour said nothing, looking away as Da'kath's grotesque maw opened and a thick tongue protruded to lick the contents of the dish.

"We colonized every world in our reach, recycling every race we encountered, and when we were searching for minerals during our expedition, we found evidence of the traitors."

"The Kuldar?" Chakour asked. The mere mention of their name could be enough to send Da'kath into a furious rage. He hoped he would kill him. At least that way, the torture of watching his ship taken over and stripped of everything useful while his imprisoned crew were led away one by one to be 'recycled' would end.

Da'kath growled, which came out as a basso clicking like heavy ball bearings being rolled down a granite staircase.

"Yes," he said icily. "And humans intervened on their behalf. By the laws of my people, humans have become the sworn enemy of the Va'alen. They are traitors much the same as the despised *Kuldar* and will all be treated with the same hatred they deserve."

"Including me," Chakour said, earning not even an acknowledgement from Da'kath.

The door to Chakour's private quarters opened. This no longer surprised him, since he had been ordered to remove all locking protocols from every part of the ship and allow the alien hitchhikers full access to wherever they pleased. The only exception was the storage bays used to imprison what was left of the non-essential crew like some kind of fresh meat farm.

"Supreme Leader," a warrior said, bowing and shooting an unreadable gaze at Chakour, "we are within communication range of our home worlds."

"Excellent," Da'kath said as he stood and dropped the dish, complete with the smeared remains of the contents in front of the ship's former captain. "Send word back that we have returned in possession of the technology to travel between all stars as we please. I will inform the Hive Lor—"

"Forgive me, Supreme Commander," the warrior said, not sounding at all sorry for his interruption, "but we are receiving a message. It is... it is a distress call."

CHAPTER 12

Exoplanet Orbiting Barnard's Star

"Captain," Rogers said quietly, "this isn't going to work."

"You got a suggestion there, Lieutenant?" Torres answered. "Or are you just flapping your lips?"

"Permission to recall the team and take off?"

"Achieving what, exactly?" Torres answered.

"Be ready to take off but only as an emergency measure on my say so."

"Captain," Sarvanto said, "I have a suggestion."

"Well, let's hear it," Torres snapped, allowing too much frustration to creep in.

"Cease fire and drop all shields," he said, earning a stare of incredulous silence from Torres. The captain seemed about to say something unkind, to dismiss the suggestion as suicidal foolishness, when his intelligence kicked him, and he tapped at the console beside him to see the information that had prompted the suggestion.

He knew Sarvanto was no fool. The man was a highly skilled engineer. He had been a part of the team responsible for the development of the *Ichi*, which was still, as far as they knew, the most advanced spacecraft ever built humanity.

"I'm listening," he said. Sarvanto bent back to the console and continued tapping his fingertips against the icons in an impressive display of skill. "Outer shields have fallen below forty percent. We have roughly ten minutes before they are through and we have no idea what they will do then."

Torres stared at him, willing the explanation to come quicker.

"My theory is that these creatures aren't attacking, they're *feeding.*"

"From our energy shields?" Rogers asked.

"From our energy in general," Sarvanto said. "If we remove the food source, we remove their reason for what seems like an attack."

"How do we test the theory?" Torres demanded.

"We have to power down everything and see if they lose interest."

"And if they don't," Rogers argued, "then they're inside our shields and we're dead."

"Not necessarily, Lieutenant," Sarvanto said before turning back to Torres.

"Permission to launch a singularity warhead at a target one kilometer away from our position."

Torres considered it. The warheads, their *nukes*, were an irreplaceable commodity until they resupplied in the Centauri system in two and a half months' time. Weighing up the loss of a warhead against the loss of the entire ship and crew, it was an easy decision to make.

"Fire when ready."

The audible *crump* noise of the launch was strange to all of them—they had never fired a warhead inside atmosphere before and had never heard what one sounded like. The tense wait seemed far longer than the eight seconds the projectile took to arc through the air a short distance and detonate just above the surface a kilometer away from their position. The delay in finding out if it worked was even longer.

"Confirmation that some of the readings have broken off to head for the impact site," Sarvanto said, almost panting as he breathed out in relief.

Torres hesitated, torn between a pull to make a rapid decision and jump on the first possible solution to present itself. He glanced at the shields, knowing that they would hold long enough for him to get a second opinion.

"Asha, come in," he said into the comm.

"I am here, Captain Torres," Asha responded.

"Time isn't a luxury we have," Torres said a little melodramatically. "The ship seems to be under attack, and I need to know if you're sensing anything from the attackers. Intent. Anything that could help."

A tense couple of seconds passed by before Asha spoke.

"I will try to make my answer brief," he said. "I—*we*—sense nothing from outside the ship, which means one of three things. Whatever is out there is capable of masking their brain patterns, they are too complex and evolved for us to sense or that they simply have no thoughts and are acting on what you would call *instinct*."

"Good enough for me," Torres answered. Given that what they had seen on external sensors seemed to be an enormous but largely unevolved creature, he put the most stock in the theory that their behavior was instinct-driven and that they were trying to feed on their energy shields.

"Bridge to Commander Brandt," Torres said. "Standby to withdraw all personnel and deactivate all energy shields."

A slight pause on the other end of the comm was ended with, "*What?*"

Thundering weapons fire dominated the next few seconds of transmission until her voice came back.

"Say again, bridge," she said. "Confirm you want us to surrender?"

"These things feed on energy," Torres said. "Withdraw all personnel back inside and power down."

Brandt, still firing and trusting the volume of her fire to hit something, considered her orders for another few seconds. She trusted Torres. She trusted the entire crew aboard the *Ichi* but this... this felt very unnatural.

"Cease fire," she ordered her team. "Including gunners. Cease fire, cease fire."

She waited until the unfathomable orders had been received and she recalled all of her ground troops back to the shuttle bay ramp.

"Inside, power down, deactivate shields," she instructed them then added further orders over the comm. "Gunners, power down but stay in position; I want to be able to go hot if this doesn't work."

Two acknowledgements, as unhappy as the rest of the team had sounded, came from the heavy gun pods.

"Brandt to bridge," she said. "Clear."

The shields were dropped simultaneously, and the wall of slimy, black flesh stopped writhing and pulsating in the same instant. They dropped back to the ground, almost confused, and began to slither around in search of something to draw power from.

"Inside," Brandt ordered. "Now."

Another *crump* of a launching warhead pounded the air as the things, like flat worms now that they weren't so agitated, raised what she guessed were their heads. They followed the trail of the missile as it looped back down to the ground in the distance. As the team ran back up the ramp, the majority of the worms turned and headed for the oddly muted explosion where the warhead had landed.

Pausing halfway up the small ramp to the shuttle bay, Brandt turned to make sure she was the last inside. Half a dozen of the worm-creatures pulsated along the dust toward the running troops. Brandt glanced at the last two on her HUD, seeing Payne and Marks—one of Beale's men they called Drop—running toward her from near the nose of the ship.

Realizing that they weren't going to make it, Brandt raised her rifle and began stitching the wriggling creatures with fire. Running recklessly close to her shots, Payne made it up the ramp and past her commanding officer just before Drop did, and as his fear triggered the armor to respond and activate his shield.

The response from the two surviving creatures was instantaneous and violently sudden.

Rearing up and striking like venomous snakes, they lunged for the trooper, flying through the air while Brandt fired in vain to intercept them. Shots from over her shoulder punched steaming holes into the lead creature, its momentum still carrying it on its intercept course and knocking Marks to the deck. He rolled to try and break free, shouting in rage and fear, as the second, undamaged creature, hit his armor with a wet slap.

Both Brandt and Specter, who had been firing as he ran back down the ramp to support her, dropped their weapons for fear of punching holes through their own man's armor. He screamed, the sound shutting off instantaneously as the readings from his suit vanished from Brandt's HUD.

"More coming back," Specter warned as he reached the stricken soldier first.

He lifted him by the arm and slashed a wide blade across the body of the creature. It fell away from Marks, leaving a sticky residue, to flop onto the rising ramp and remain still. Brandt joined him and they dragged the limp suit of armor back up the ramp with no idea as to the state of the man inside.

"Pressurize the shuttle bay," she called over the comm, "and get a medical team to my location."

"Report," snapped Torres. "Have you got casualties?"

"Unknown yet," she replied. They dropped their burden to the deck and waited for the atmosphere to equalize before getting his suit open. "What are they doing out there now?"

"Not sure yet, concentrate on your team," Torres replied, cutting the comm. Someone yelled that the shuttle bay was safe; the doors opened and Doctor Curtis ran in with a trauma kit.

"Outta the way," she called with authority. "What happened to him?"

"One of the... *things* landed on him and his suit went dark," Brandt said, already working on a theory she couldn't quite put into words yet.

"Get this thing open," Curtis demanded, tapping impatiently at the armor that was nothing more than a fitted sarcophagus.

"It's dead," Brandt answered, seeing no power signature at all from the still form. "I think that thing drained it somehow."

"Stand back," Specter called out in warning as he pushed a maintenance cart toward them, repulsers humming as the weight was held off the deck. He stopped beside the unmoving trooper and dropped to his armored knees, clanging the deck heavily when he flipped the man easily and lifted a secure access port to attach cables.

On Brandt's HUD, the suit flickered back into existence again and a second later the helmet retracted with the sound of a loud gasp for air from Marks.

"Brandt to bridge, no casualties," she reported. "Repeat, no casualties. What's happening outside?"

"Nothing good. We're working on something. Standby."

"I'm okay," Marks said as he fought for breath. He had been running out of air for a full minute in a sealed suit with no power. "I'm alright, just... just get me out of this thing."

"Not enough power to trigger the emergency release yet," Specter said. "Just hold on."

Brandt stood, turning to catch Zero's concerned look and outstretched hands as he silently asked what the hell they were supposed to do now.

~

"Mister Harris," Torres asked, "how is the plan coming along?"

"It's coming, sir," Harris replied via comm. "But for the record I think you're insane." He left off his nagging doubt that the plan might get them all killed or worse—stranded about a million years from home to starve to death.

"Duly noted," Torres answered, before finding Rogers's gaze on the bridge. "If you would, Lieutenant?"

"Yes, sir," the pilot answered. "My pleasure."

~

"Make a hole, people," Harris barked, scattering the soldiers milling on the deck of the shuttle bay.

Ahead of him on another repulser cart, he and two other engineers pushed a small cylinder wrapped in a dark metal. It hummed gently, and Brandt recognized it as their one and only replacement singularity power source. She said nothing as it was pushed past her. It was followed by an excited Nathan Rogers who was zipping up a jacket and pacing confidently toward their shuttle, which Harris was busy loading with the power source.

"Explanation, anyone?" Brandt said loudly.

"Captain thinks these things are feeding on power," Rogers said. "Wants to use the spare drive to keep them off us."

Brandt found she had nothing to say to that, in spite of the million thoughts she had bouncing around her head.

"Shotgun," she said, stepping forward to climb onboard the replacement for the ship both she and their pilot had crashed in.

"Negative, Commander," Zero said, forgetting for a moment that he was no longer the official second-in-command of the ground troops.

"Come again, Master Petty Officer?" she said in a measured tone.

"He's right," Specter told her. "We'll go; you need to stay here in case it doesn't work."

Facing a minor mutiny designed to keep her mission effective for as long as possible, she had to accept their offer and vacate the shuttle bay as the *Tanto II* took off like the pied-piper equivalent for alien worms.

CHAPTER 13

Gaia Neós

Acting Commander Eze, reminded of her brevet rank, waited on the uncomfortable seats outside the base commander's office. Ryers had accompanied her, even though she had assured him she could manage an ass-chewing all by herself. In return, her NCO assured her that it wasn't fitting for a commander to walk around a base full of— as he put it—civilians and assholes, without someone to shout at them for her.

She accepted the loyalty, knowing it was nothing to do with chivalry and more to do with making amends for giving her a hard time when she was first assigned as the unit's second in command under the Chief.

"Enter," bawled a lazy voice from inside the office.

She stood, ignoring her crumpled uniform as she refused to apologize for being an operational soldier. She shot a crooked smile at Ryers to convince herself she wasn't worried. She stepped inside, saluted a little slower than regulations dictated, and tried to stop her face from falling.

If Commander Franks didn't recognize her, she sure as shit recognized him.

The overweight, piggy-eyed cruel man had been dumped in a backwater posting the last time she had seen him, but somehow he had managed to get himself shipped out to the sharp end where, she highly suspected, he was seriously underqualified to be.

"Lieutenant Commander... *Eeez*?" he said.

"*Ay-zay*," she responded, the word 'sir' not making its way to her head let alone out of her mouth. "And it's commander."

Franks fixed her with a malevolent look, did not invite her to sit, and reminded her of her place.

"At the very best it's *acting* Commander until such time as the UN refuses to ratify a promotion clearly given with undue haste," he said, his drawling accent oozing arrogant privilege that she wasn't sure was aimed at her gender, rank, the friends she kept or the color of her skin. Could be any or all.

"Now," he said, leaning back in his chair to expose more of the gut straining the material of his uniform, "I have here a report from the science detachment that you put them in danger on some kinda recreational hike instead of getting the mission done as ordered."

Eze knew full well that the report from the science team said nothing of the sort, nor would their superiors twist the facts so elaborately. No, this was purely Commander Franks electing to interpret the reports in the way that best served his interests. Knowing that he had likely already put his seal on the damning report about her performance as being a young woman in charge of a fighting unit—something he had never been awarded as he was completely useless—she decided to play her own cards.

"I doubt that's what the report says, *sir*," she said with as much respect as the accusation that he was a liar could hold.

Franks went red, then parts of his face turned a darker shade of purple. She wondered briefly if she had actually killed him simply by making him angry, but instead of suffering a stroke or catastrophic heart failure he released his held breath and turned on her.

"You," he snarled, levelling a finger at her, "don't know your place. You don't even have the authority to access this report, let alone decide whether to level accusations at me—"

"You don't remember me, Commander?" Eze asked, using his rank as the most respectful way to address him without being sick in her own mouth.

Franks hesitated, looking down at the datapad as though it would magically access his memory.

"Remind me," he said.

"You'll recall a while ago," she said, "Commander Torres and I arrived to relieve you of one of your officers on the Lunar penal facility?"

The triumphant smile of power melted away from his face as he recalled the fear any sensible person felt when two UNID operators arrived unannounced.

"Brandt?" Franks said, dragging the insignificant name from his memory. "Yeah, what happened to that washout?"

"Commander Brandt was heading up the security detail with UNID for negotiations with the Va'alen in the Centauri system," she said flatly. "In fact, she and I fought off the enemy counterattack on a flat hilltop about thirty miles from here."

Franks's face fell; his jowly cheeks sagged. He was defeated. He'd gone after someone who was more connected than he was and hadn't thought to check his facts first. To make things worse the upstart who, in his opinion was both too young and delicate in appearance to be attached to ground troops let alone lead them, helped herself to a seat opposite his desk.

"How did you get off the Moon and out here anyway, *sir*?" she asked confidently.

"I... err, management of the facility was contracted out to a private corporation," he mumbled dismissively.

"Hyper subsidiary I'm guessing," Eze said confidently. "That left you at a loose end?"

Franks nodded silently, cheeks wobbling again.

"I'd have taken retirement instead," she said as she stretched. "It can get dangerous this far from home." He said nothing, his expression revealing that retirement hadn't been offered, neither had a safe posting training the flood of new recruits.

"Well," she said as she rose, "if there's nothing else, I'll be off. I'm the on-call QR-Team Commander." Leaving the room without a salute and knowing that she couldn't have done more to intimidate the man, Eze made a note to cover her bases and check with the science team what exactly their report entailed.

Crystal Mining Site

Their two dropships arrived the following morning, relieving the other half of their unit who would rotate back to base and take over as the quick reaction team should she need backup on a larger scale.

Her troops had cleared a forward site in a hurry to evacuate their one dead and one injured soldier. It had been widened and levelled to allow enough two craft to land side by side.

"Dust off," she said to the pilot of her dropship after she had been the last to dismount. "Bring that engineering team straight back."

"Aye aye, Commander," the pilot said.

He whined the engines back up to lift the ship off the deck and whip the ground with debris, before taking off to return with the people she had requested to make the site more accessible.

Twenty-seven hours—the daily rotation of the planet they were on—after the emergency evacuation and discovery of the rich vein of crystals, the site had been cleared and leveled enough to land a dropship. Another twenty-seven hours and the engineers had brought out enough equipment to establish shelters and storage for the science team who were working ahead of the mining operation.

Actually digging the crystal out of the rock was a relatively simple task, other than the fact that the precious material was volatile and could easily trigger a chain reaction that split the entire mountainside apart if they used laser cutters of demolitions too close to it. That meant that they had to do it by hand, old school. That meant being exposed to the elements and the wildlife in the mountains for an extended period.

They needed to create a safe environment to work and establish secured supply routes, which led to a forward operating base with a cleared perimeter and a killing ground of empty space extending forty meters beyond the heavy fencing.

Guard towers had been erected using scaffolding-type poles that came in kits even a ground-pounder could put together with the instruction manual uploaded to their HUD.

Eze, fighting off the rushed reports of her junior officers, toured the site where half of her unit was busy constructing defenses and guarding their perimeter while the other half was at a forward operating base fifteen minutes out from their mountain. That location was being similarly constructed, but using prefabricated materials instead of the harder work required to make their position safe.

Eze kept going, breaking away from the reports, giving orders that she considered simple common sense, and agreeing to suggestions that her people had already come up with but just needed reassurance. She made her way to where the science team was set up near the exposed part of the crystal vein.

"Commander," the female scientist who had been part of their original expedition said in warm greeting, "come to see what the eggheads are doing?"

Eze smiled back, a little embarrassed but also amused that the science team had caught on to what her ground-pounders called them.

"As a matter of fact, I was," she said with a small smile of apology.

"Well, here it is," she said, holding up a small tube of clear resin bearing a large shard of azure blue glass flecked with dark veins of purple. "We're calling it thuridium."

"It's pretty," Eze said dreamily, momentarily forgetting she was a senior commander of ground troops with a history of special operations deployments. "What's it for?"

The scientist opened her mouth to explain, but another voice cut over them.

"I'm sorry, Commander," the senior scientist said. He cast an angry look at the person who was evidently about to share facts outside of her authority. "We're not permitted to discuss our work."

Eze pulled a face, taken aback by not his words but his tone.

"In fact," he said, "we are being sent a security detail today in case you don't already know, and I'll need your people to be kept out of this immediate area." He stared at her pointedly until she got the hint and backed off.

Eze returned to the work her unit was undertaking, catching the eye of her dogged senior NCO.

"The hell was all that about?" Ryers asked. Eze responded with a question of her own.

"You hear about a separate security detail ordered to this location?"

"Negative," Ryers said with a frown. "Want me to check it out?" The sound of a dropship coming in low answered for her.

The smoother design based on the standard craft combined with the darker color already sowed the seed of the answer in her mind.

"That's not ours," Ryers said.

"And ten to one it isn't our engineers with another ride," Eze answered as the ship flared in to land.

Both she and Ryers activated their helmets before dust and twigs peppered their unprotected faces. Eze tried to break into the comm channel of the ship and demand the pilot's orders but found her command authority didn't cut it.

Ryers figured something was wrong as the armored troops exiting the tail ramp didn't show up on his HUD as outlines—either green or red. The black armor gave it away visually, as Eze recognized a private military contractor unit heading straight past them toward the scientists without even an acknowledgement.

CHAPTER 14

Exoplanet Orbiting Barnard's Star

Repairs to the *Ichi* went slowly once the sun rose. The *Tanto* had flown slowly over the landscape away from the damaged ship with the power source suspended beneath it and, as they had hoped, drew the flood of writhing creatures away with it.

"From what I can ascertain," Howard explained as his glasses slipped down his face once more, "the surface of the exoplanet conducts some kind of electromagnetic energy—"

"So, the whole ground outside is a live wire?" Torres clarified.

"Not exactly," Howard said peevishly. "This current as such needs a conductive element to be absorbed, which is what the secretion from the creatures appears to be."

"So they ooze on anything with power and literally suck the power out of it?" Brandt questioned.

"Essentially, yes."

"And why are they nocturnal?" Torres queried, earning a shrug from the scientist.

"It's rather beyond my specific skill set," Howard admitted.

The events of the previous night were pretty raw and Rogers had held the *Tanto* in a hover for nine hours far enough away from the *Ichi* that the creatures were more attracted to that than they were the ship. With the alien creatures drawn away, the *Ichi* had powered down as much as possible to avoid looking tasty, and the captain wanted repairs conducted immediately.

Torres had asked if the repairs were possible in space through EVA procedures and, as much as Harris hated to admit it, they were actually possible under those circumstances.

"Possible, sir," he said, "but highly advised against."

"Noted," Torres said. "Can you get the drive operational today?"

"Operational? I hope so. Good as new? Unlikely."

"Estimating the amount of stress on the Fold drive to get us back to the CS, will we make it with a patch-up?"

Harris rubbed his forehead with a frustration bordering on insubordination. "The longer I stand around answering..." he hesitated, "...questions, the longer the whole thing will take. You want us back in space before nightfall? Let me work. Sir."

"Get to it, Mister Harris," Torres said. "Anyone and anything you need is yours."

Harris left without another word, scurrying off to continue the vital work outside the ship now that the writhing mass of six-foot leeches had disappeared underground. He had a detail guarding him, but most people seemed unconcerned that the creatures could reappear during the daylight.

"I'm more concerned with what they hide from during the day," Brandt said to Torres, raising a valid but unwelcome point.

She left the briefing, feeling overdue for some sleep. She intended to get out of her armor in the ready room and curl up on a couch there so she could be good-to-go if called upon. Being the commander, however, she had more than enough things to do before she could sleep.

She checked in with Beale, reassured that he had the gun rotations in hand. She checked who was on watch out on the ground with the engineers, then checked that she had a whole eight hours before she took a turn and went to their ready room. There she found Zero sitting still as a statue in the corner of the room with his arms folded and his chin resting on his chest.

He lifted his head when she walked in, prompting her to apologize for waking him.

"Don't worry about it," he said as he stretched his neck from side to side. He'd been awake throughout the night standing watch in the open side door of their shuttle in case the creatures got organized and formed a leech pyramid or something to reach them. They hadn't; they'd just milled around in a slippery pile underneath the ship until just before dawn when they slid away to get back underground. "Quicker we're off this rock, though, the better."

"Amen to that, brother," Brandt agreed. She sat, groaning slightly as she lifted first one boot and then the other to put her feet up on a chair opposite her. "Just going to close my eyes for ten." Her eyelids drooped instantly, not hearing an answer as she was already out.

"Wake up, let's go." Zero's voice cut through to her, waking her in an instant.

She leapt up for her armor but relaxed as Zero began to call whoa like she was a runaway pony.

"Relax your pants there, Commander," he said soothingly. "Just lettin' you know we're about to take off."

"We are?" Brandt asked, checking her comm device to see how long she had slept. "How…?"

"Harris thought 'screw this,' apparently, and just bypassed the whole Fold drive through the shroud array like it was made for that. Reckons it'll hold but we're without a shroud and have half shields with precious little backup power."

"So, a few weeks in and we're already looking like hammered shit?" she asked.

"Pretty much, but at least we're flyin'."

Brandt rubbed her face, shuddered to think what she looked like, and grabbed a cup of coffee on her way to the bridge.

She walked in, slurping the drink as she walked and sketched a ghost of a sarcastic salute at Torres who looked as red-eyed and dog-tired as she felt. She took a seat beside him, with Sarvanto was at the helm controls in place of Rogers. Brandt cast a concerned look at Torres.

"Curtis made Rogers sleep," he muttered as he leaned toward her. "He was adamant he could fly all night and all day. I sent him to get a stimulant shot and she made it a sedative."

"Isn't that against her oath?" Brandt murmured back at him.

He shrugged, guessing that she was doing no harm in ensuring one of the crew rested when they needed it.

"We are good to go, Captain," Sarvanto reported from the helm.

"Good," Torres said as he straightened himself in the chair. "Take us up, engage shields when we hit ten thousand feet."

"Aye aye, sir," came the response from tactical.

"Let's see if Harris is as good as his word," the captain added to himself.

It took them twelve jumps, each one requiring a long pause in between as the power supply was running very slowly. A manual recalibration check was needed on each trip through the nothing between different points in space. Other than dropping a warning buoy near to the exoplanet they had landed on—one set to shout far and loud that it wasn't the vacation destination it appeared to be—they had ignored their mission for the priority of reaching the Centauri system where the *Anvil* would be waiting for them. There they could put the *Ichi* up on the ramp and fix her up.

The added bonus, Torres thought privately, was that there might be an opportunity to visit the surface and see Eze.

He kept those thoughts private, though, not wanting to confide in anyone but Brandt. She knew just as well as he did the pressures of hiding a relationship from the prying eyes of the UN and, more specifically, the UNID.

The ship dropped out of Fold space on the far edge of the twin suns. They were unable to call ahead due to their damaged subspace communications array, so they hailed the nearest ship and received a surprise.

"*Ichi*, this is *Indomitable* actual," Dassiova said with intrigued amusement. "We weren't expecting you for another month and a half. Everything okay?"

"Good to see you here, Admiral," Torres said with genuine warmth and relief. "We got a little beat up and need to hit the shop."

CHAPTER 15

Gaia Neós Orbit

The *Ichi* was cleared straight away for priority docking with the *Anvil* where Harris took charge of the engineers sent to help. He called it 'taking charge,' but others might have called it something less kind, like slavery.

Torres, along with Brandt and Asha, requisitioned a drop- ship to head straight for the *Indomitable* and their old commanding officer. The last time the two humans had seen him, he was still undergoing revolutionary and highly classified medical treatment to save his life from injuries he had sustained and should never have survived.

The rest of their crew had been ordered to remain onboard their ship until directed to do otherwise. Beale was left with the responsibility of having the non-crew engineers from the *Anvil* escorted everywhere they went. The easiest way of achieving that was to assign each one of them a member of the team—everyone felt sorry for the young guy who had Kekoa standing uncomfortably close to him, breathing loudly.

The detachment of three landed in the now familiar hangar bays built purposely for the many dropships that came and went from the fleet flagship. Torres politely refused the escort to the bridge.

"You sure, sir?" the crewman asked as he cast a sideways look at the first alien he had seen up close. "Can get a little confusing is all."

He tried to ignore the insistent elbowing of another crewmember who eventually got his attention.

"You know who that is, dumbass?" he asked, smiling at Torres apologetically. The crewman shrugged.

"I've got this, Seaman," Torres reassured him. He turned to leave the hangar deck to the sounds of the man being berated by the rest of the deck crew.

"You go away for a few months," Brandt sighed wistfully, "come back and all the crew have changed. I bet nobody remembers you were captain of this tub for, what was it? An hour?"

"Six days," Torres responded equably, not rising to her goading remarks. "And if you recall it was my orders that saved you from going down in flaming, heroic glory on the surface…"

Both of them felt an uncomfortable sense tickle their minds. They turned to glance at Asha who seemed torn and uncertain what he wanted to say.

"Spit it out, Asha," Torres prompted.

"He means that you should ask the question you want to ask," Brandt clarified. The Kuldar struggled badly with human language metaphors.

"I do not understand this conversation," he said. "It is clear to me from the conversations we have had, Commander Leslie Brandt, that you respect Captain Kyle Torres deeply. You have confided in me your gratitude for the orbital bombardment that rescued you and your team as you feared your imminent death, and yet you say these things that are… derogatory?"

Torres caught Brandt's eye with a smirk but stayed silent.

"Couple of points there, Asha," Brandt said. "One, when someone *confides* in you, you aren't supposed to mention it again and two, I'm busting his balls. It's what we do to our friends."

A sharp stab of embarrassment was quickly overtaken by more confusion.

"So this busting of balls is what you intentionally do to cover your true feelings?"

"It's how we ro—" Torres interrupted himself and reworded the sentence. "Like the commander said, it's what we do. You've never heard troops insulting each other when you know they're friends?"

Asha made a hmm noise but said nothing. When they reached the access door to the bridge, they scanned their authority to gain entry and waited for the doors to slide open.

A commander Torres recognized but didn't know well stood as they entered. They had been expected. His nametag read Childs. He offered a hand to Torres as the two men exchanged surnames and a nod. Childs, who hadn't been onboard the *Indomitable* the last time Brandt had been in the system, turned to her.

"Pleasure to meet you, Commander," he said with a winning smile. He faltered as he experienced a sensation of mild revulsion laced with hilarity and embarrassment. He stammered, unable to understand what was happening, until Asha cleared his throat and stepped forward.

He wasn't exactly clearing his throat, but he approximated the noise a human made clearing their throat to act as a social cue he had observed. It was his way of stepping in, of saying 'excuse me,' and he liked to use it almost as much as he enjoyed the ritual of the handshake.

"I am Asha," he said, "mate to our queen." He was still unsure how to explain his rank and standing among his people to humans. "I believe that with Commander Leslie Brandt you may be what you humans call, 'trying too hard'?"

Childs stammered again, blood rushing to his face as the alien pumped his hand.

"We're still working on his social graces," Torres explained apologetically. "The admiral in his quarters?"

Childs nodded, finally receiving his hand back from the alien who had just publicly embarrassed him on the flagship's bridge.

⁓

"Come on in," Dassiova said, sounding almost happy. "You get docked to the *Anvil* okay? No problems?"

"It's all good, Admiral," Torres said. He accepted the offered hand as an excited Asha pressed close for his turn. "Appreciate the sealed bay and the security detail though."

"Gotta keep you spy types out of sight, right?" Dassiova asked as he shot a smile at Brandt. Asha reached out to shake his hand and Dassiova accepted it happily.

"Asha," he said.

"It is good to see you, Admiral Elias Dassiova," Asha said as his lips curled up in a smile of anticipation. The others got the impression that something funny was about to happen from his barely suppressed humor. "I did not think I would see you alive again after the Va'alen almost cut you in half because you should be dead from such an injury."

The room went silent, with a stunned Dassiova staring into the face of the Kuldar who still shook his hand and issued a hissing laugh.

"Relax, Admiral," Asha said. "I am trying to bust on your balls."

Torres and Brandt erupted with uncontrollable laughter, and the mouthful of coffee Brandt had just taken left her face in an atomized spray.

"Asha," Dassiova said quietly, as he shot a disapproving glance at the two senior officers falling about like children, "you be sure to leave my balls alone in future."

The *Ichi* was damaged worse than Harris wanted to let on. He couldn't let their captain know the odds of them spontaneously detonating, or that every time they re-emerged from the nowhere of using the Fold drive he suspected there was a good chance they'd simply cease to exist.

The list of things that could go wrong with a malfunctioning Fold drive was long, extensive and bordered on the supernatural with the wild theories thrown about. Harris didn't want to consider the possibility of re-appearing in normal space back in the seventeenth century or an alternative reality.

None of that had happened, he was almost certain, but his relief at getting back to the CS was greater than anyone onboard.

"All of these," he told the three engineers. He spread his arms wide with exaggerated movements over the primary and secondary battery banks. "All of these out."

"You sure you don't just want the scorched ones out?" one asked. He pointed at the blackened marks extending half-way up the primary and on just one corner of the secondary banks.

Harris fixed him with a stare. "That's like getting gangrene in your foot and just cutting off the toes. You got X-ray vision?" The engineer shrugged at him. "So you can't tell which ones are damaged. That means you take them all out, just like I said, and replace them with *all* new ones. I don't want even the slightest chance of a cascade failure."

The engineers did as he asked them, figuring the difference between replacing some and replacing all was nothing to them. They'd be on to the next job as soon as this one was finished. Harris left, poking his head back around the doorway to check they were starting to work and shooting a quick nod at Payne who leaned against a bulkhead wearing a gun on her thigh and bored expression on her face.

Harris occasionally trusted others to do some work on his ship, but ever since he had first been vetted and cleared almost four years before to even see the schematics for the *Ichi*, he had still been there for the vital parts that had brought her to life. He'd personally oversee the complete wiring for both new battery banks—mainly because he didn't want to have to vent the whole section into space to kill the electrical fire cascading from cell to cell in the battery banks like he had to before. He'd also been working on the way to prevent energy feedback and the same damage happening all over again.

Harris headed down the open shuttle bay ramp to turn back on himself and head for the nose of the ship. A familiar voice yelled from up on a mobile inspection platform.

"Something about what I just said you didn't understand?" barked a voice that spoke of humor hidden behind the intolerance in his voice. "Remove the emitter array *without dropping it*! Ass!"

"Hey Paterson," Harris called up to the man who had helped him bring the ship to life so long ago on the Moon.

"Harris." Paterson raised a hand to wave. "If this was a rental," he yelled down with a smirk, "you'd be better off torching it and saying it was stolen."

"Yeah," Harris grumbled to himself. "I know."

CHAPTER 16

Gaia Neós Orbit

The *Ichi* was in more of a mess than Torres had been led to believe. When he had been given the official estimate of when they would be back at sea, his eyebrows rose so far they became part of his hair line.

"Come again?" the captain asked his chief engineer. He could not accept that he was facing almost another week in delays.

"I'm sorry, sir," Harris said, looking as tired as he felt. "The damage is bad. Like, *really* bad. Like, there's no way we should've actually made it back bad, but the alternative was sitting in empty space with no sub-space comms and no way to repair her."

Torres seemed to bubble up like a kettle coming to the boil, but he took a breath and settled back down.

"Two things," he told his engineer. "One, don't ever leave me in the dark about that kind of stuff again." Harris nodded his agreement through half-open eyes. "Two, go get some sleep. That's an order."

Harris perked up, his lips starting to flap with protests, but Torres held up his forefinger in gentle warning.

"Yes, sir," he said, relenting.

"Doctor Paterson can oversee the repairs," the captain told him firmly, "while you are on a mandatory twenty-four-hour stand down. I'd suggest you spend at least half of that asleep, and you should see Doctor Curtis if that's going to be an issue for you."

Harris's drooping eyelids and slack face reassured him that it probably wouldn't be.

"I'm standing down all of our crew for the same time, so this isn't special treatment. Every bit of repair work is being conducted by Paterson's people and the admiral has deployed his troops to keep our hangar secure from prying eyes."

"Yes, sir," Harris said again. "I'll just check in with Paterson before I—"

"He knows what needs to be done, Harris," Torres said. "I guarantee we won't set off until you've inspected every bit of work they do. But for now, get your ass to your quarters or I'll have you escorted to the med bay where you can catch a tranq. Your call."

Harris knew when he was defeated and shuffled off to reacquaint his exhausted self with his rack.

Torres had caught up with the full facts that they'd missed since they had been so far off the grid they weren't able to keep up with current affairs. Dassiova, after less than three weeks patrolling their home system, had been ordered to jump to Mars and begin swapping over his assets with those of the Tenth Fleet in the Centauri system.

The last ships to switch had been the two carriers; Admiral Vernay had formally handed control of the defense of the Centauri system over to Dassiova, just as he did the same for Earth and the surrounding space.

It didn't surprise them to learn that all of the long-distance mining operations had been shut down. Those efforts had been diverted to gathering the resources in their new territory. The fact that the operations weren't government led, however, was a twist.

"Makes more financial sense to work in partnership," Dassiova told him, "at least that's what the official line is. The rumor mill is churning out other things, like the fact that with the military efforts and the cost of producing the new ships and all that the UN is down on the bank balance. They can either borrow from the private corporations or they can strike up deals and give away all that new land." Torres pulled a face that showed how uneasy he felt with the that.

"Yeah," Dassiova agreed. "I'm not a short-term gains kinda guy either but whatever."

"What does that mean out here?" Torres asked.

"It means that certain operations on the surface are now in the hands of the private companies and we just provide the main bases to work from. Hell, on that moon of yours they've already got a working mine and are melting down ore to stock- pile it by the hundreds of tons to ship back. Every vessel sent out here has to take stuff back with them; never move an empty cargo hold and all that."

"Hmm," Torres answered. He sipped his coffee and said nothing more on the matter.

"You planning on getting down to the surface?" Dassiova asked pointedly, knowing who was down there important to the captain.

"If there's time," Torres admitted. "She doesn't know we're in the system yet; we're not due here for almost six weeks. I'd have to take a look at her roster."

"You mean this one?" Dassiova asked innocently, sliding a datapad across the table to him.

Torres looked at it—her unit was stood down for the next thirty hours until they were deployed as protection detail on another science expedition. Try as he might, Torres couldn't hide his excitement.

"Good," the admiral said with a smile. "You can bring her back up for me when you go see her."

Torres swallowed, keeping his face neutral as he interpreted the meaning of the orders to take Eze away from her command.

"Remind me why we're here again?" Brandt asked Torres as Rogers threw the new *Tanto* around in the atmosphere. Torres glanced at her and Specter, then frowned as he was jostled in his seat too much to be normal turbulence.

"You mind keeping both hands on the wheel there, Lieutenant?" he asked loudly to toward the cockpit.

"Sorry, Captain," Rogers replied. "Just getting a feel for her in atmo."

"Try not to crash like last time," Brandt added in a low voice.

"If you recall, Commander," Rogers said, sounding a little annoyed, "there was an issue of a major electrical storm and an orbital railgun slug taking one of her wings off that led to the demise of this girl's predecessor."

Brandt ignored the remark and reiterated her question to Torres with a raise of her eyebrows.

"Because," he explained, "bored troops on shitty postings like to see heroes of the UN from time to time. It gives them something to aim for."

"Aim for as in target practice?" Specter answered—more Jake Santana than cybernetic super soldier right then.

Torres ignored the remark just as Brandt had done with Rogers.

"And because you don't want to be on your own when you tell Eze that she's losing temporary command of the unit assigned to the *Indomitable* now she's back in the CS?"

The shuttle flared in to land, Rogers's showmanship making him honor-bound to make it look good—he came in a little fast and turned on a dime to rest the small craft on its landing struts perfectly.

"*BOO*-yah," he crowed to himself, since nobody else congratulated him.

Torres smiled with a small shake of his head, not enjoying the way the uprated grav emitter dialed up the power in response to the higher G-forces of the pilot's maneuvers.

The tail ramp lowered and the passengers exited, walking past their armor secured to the deck of the craft. Instead, they walked onto the surface of the planet wearing just fatigues with sidearms strapped to their thighs. What they carried made Brandt feel a little naked; they were under orders not to parade prototype equipment and weaponry before the masses of troops. Carrying the singularity-accelerated sidearm made Brandt glance at Specter's oversized pistols on each leg. But since nearly every part of him—the parts that weren't human anyway—was prototype, he seemed to be exempt.

"Check in with the base commander first?" Torres suggested, leading the way toward the building likely to be headquarters. Prefabricated bases like this had a standard feel to them, and he'd probably be able to pick out the landmarks at any UN base on any planet.

Chow hall, barracks, stores, administration block... it was as much part of their uniform as the rank insignia.

The base commander, informed of their unannounced visit, intentionally kept them waiting. Franks had been rattled by his brush with Eze, and he had tried to check for information on her other postings. In doing so, he had worryingly found big gaps of which his clearance didn't show him details. The sudden arrival of other officers, also promoted since he had last met them and shrouded by the veil of classified missions, had sent his nerves nosediving off a cliff.

"I'm sorry, Commander," the young female lieutenant adjutant lied smoothly. "The base commander is on a conference call and can't be disturbed at this time." The winning smile was just as false as her words. They had all heard Franks's outburst and refusal to see them. Her smile was as much her armor as their suits and shields were.

"Not a problem," Torres said as he stood and returned the smile with a more believable air. "We won't be in the way of anyone, just here to see a few people. If you could pass these orders on for me?" He handed her a data slate, like a smaller version of the datapads they used for hard data that wouldn't normally be transmitted. "Compliments of the Fleet Admiral," he added loudly, adding insult to the man who had refused to see him but was undoubtedly listening from behind the door.

They left the office, heading for the barracks area as Torres tapped at his comm device. "Better get hold of Amare before those orders hit."

She answered his call, sounding shocked but happy that he was there, until the suspicion kicked in.

"Where are you?" he asked. "I've, er, I've got orders for you…"

"So my promotion isn't going to be ratified?" she asked glumly. "Listen," Torres said comfortingly. Brandt and Specter had melted away on hearing the news, giving them privacy.

"I don't know that's what it is for certain. All the orders say are that you have to report back to the *Indomitable*."

"No," she corrected him sternly, "they say I have to report back to the *Indomitable* and the unit stays here."

"Look at the recall list," he said, trying to find some light at the end of the tunnel for her. "It's you, two officers and three NCOs."

"Two of those are owed shore leave," Eze said. "One is coming up for end of service in four months." She stood, cuffed at her face in shame that she was showing how upset she was. "It is what it is," she declared. "You mind giving us a lift or should I go schedule a dropship?"

They arrived a few hours later, after Torres and the others had been given a quick tour of the newly constructed walls with their automated defenses. The group stepped up the tail ramp carrying large duffle bags in their armored gauntlets.

The orders said that their replacements would be sent before the end of their stand down period, and the unit was left in the hands of the senior lieutenant commander until their new CO hit dirtside.

CHAPTER 17

Gaia Neós Orbit

"*Tanto* from *Indomitable*," the comm officer onboard the carrier responded to their request to dock. "Request from actual that you transport personnel cargo to the forest moon directly to save our dropship scheduling, over."

Rogers acknowledged the polite request for what it was: a direct order from a fleet admiral to take the six troops directly to the disturbingly memorable habitable planetoid.

"Change of plan," he said over the shuttle's intercom. "Request from the admiral to take you good people direct to your next post."

"Wait," Eze said. "What next post?"

"Orders say forest moon orbiting the main planet, Commander," Rogers responded. "Our ETA is about eight minutes." He went on in a low voice as though he had forgotten to mute his mic, "and unlike last time I think I'll land gently instead of whistling-in like a rock…"

Nervous glances were exchanged in the back of the shuttle, the interior a little cramped by so many people and their equipment, not to mention the next-gen mech folded for transport.

"He's joking," Brandt said. "Last time he crash-landed here it wasn't his fault."

The nervous looks didn't fade.

The environmental controls in the cockpit responded to the pilot's increased body heat and sweating by lowering the temperature of the filtered air it directed at him. He gave the usual commentary to his passengers, but something in the terse way he spoke made Brandt glance at Torres. He nudged his chin toward the cockpit, his implication making her frown, eyebrows meeting in the middle and her lips pursed. He shrugged, like always not understanding what he had done to annoy a woman, until it hit him that Brandt had been beside Rogers when they had crashed here before. His expression showed a simultaneous realization and apology for forgetting. He unstrapped to make his way to the co-pilot's seat.

"You doing okay, Lieutenant?" he asked, after killing the internal comm. He sat and strapped in again. Torres went with 'lieutenant' and not his surname or first name as he wanted Rogers focused, professional, and with his head firmly on the task.

"I'm good, sir," he replied. His face was flushed and his breathing faster than usual.

"Well alright then," Torres said softly. He leaned back and projected the aura of a man relaxing for a journey he knew was totally safe. "Take us in."

The landing was perfect. It wasn't showy, wasn't flashy and had no trace of the pilot's personality. It was completely by the book. Rogers said he had some checks to run on the *Tanto* and that he'd be there if anyone needed him, which gave him some time to reflect.

He flexed his right arm, working the hand and the forearm muscles—or the cybernetic equivalent—to try to alleviate the stiffness he felt. He knew the aching was phantom, just like the stabbing pains of white-hot electricity he felt during his night- mares three times a week watching the limb be physically torn off again and again.

The former Va'alen base on the moon was as Brandt recalled it. With the addition of temporary human structures and technological in- stallations, it now took on a kind of hybrid-Frankenstein air, which she found less than appealing. She was glad that Rogers had elected to keep himself with their little ship instead of heading back into the base. It was there he had been imprisoned and tortured before the dismemberment which had luckily been his last memory of the place.

The perimeter was guarded but with a relaxed feel, as though they weren't expecting any real danger or imminent assault. Nothing was anticipated, either rogue Va'alen warriors left stranded from their brief war or the myriad wildlife intent on attacking the new species that had entered their food chain.

Salutes were thrown at them as they headed for the central col- lection of buildings. This they assumed to be the headquarters, based on the setup of a typical base, and they passed a unit on parade in PT gear. Given the red faces and heaving chests, the session had probably just ended but there was some- thing curious about the unit.

"Ateeeeeeeen...*HUH!*"

One of the master petty officers stood at the head of the unit beside a single lieutenant commander and bawled, before turning crisply to stamp to attention himself and hold a salute to the passing party. They returned the honor, slightly perplexed by the display since there were senior officers travel- ling this way and that all over the base.

"Probably going to go home and tell everyone how they fought beside the great Commander Brandt and Captain Torres," Eze muttered darkly, only half in jest.

"We would all be so lucky as to claim that," Specter said in a serious tone. Brandt shot him a look, in case one of his implants had gone awry. The sideways smirk he tried to hide told her that he wasn't malfunctioning—he was just being a sarcastic ass.

"And you are?" the lieutenant at the adjutant's desk demanded. He took in the non-standard armor of Brandt and Specter too late. He started to stammer, realizing that the front rank of newcomers to his overworked and understaffed station were all commanders.

Eze said nothing, just handed over a data slate with the personnel details of her and her troops.

"Oh!" the lieutenant said. "We weren't expecting you until tomorrow."

"What?" Eze said. "Here? As in I'm posted here?"

"Only for final stage familiarization training, obviously," the lieutenant said, his smile wavering as he read the confusion on her face. "You... you are aware of your orders, Commander?"

"Assume I'm not," Eze said carefully, leaving the invitation open for the man to explain.

He tapped at his console feverishly, locating the orders before reciting them.

"Orders sent... almost two days ago. *Indomitable* returned to the system and all troop personnel assigned to her are recalled from Gaia when replacement unit has successfully completed final stage familiarization training."

"That's all well and good, Lieutenant," Eze said, "but I had no such orders. I received some today directly from the admiral recalling me and four others before we were redirected here. Care to explain?"

"Yes, Ma'am," he said. "Your unit's been waiting for you. For all of you..."

Brandt huffed in exasperation and annoyance, stepping around the desk to lean over and peer at the screen.

"Huh," she said with a lopsided smile. "Well, would you look at that..."

"Look at what?" Eze barked. "For God's sake will someone tell me what the hell is going on?"

"Be easier if I just showed you the unit personnel roster," Brandt said. She gestured, inviting her to look and force the adjutant lieutenant to lean back even further to avoid another armored woman invading his workspace.

There on the screen, plain as day, was the unit roster. Suddenly it made sense; the unit outside who had thrown up formal parade salutes even though they'd just finished their PT weren't saluting just anyone, they were greeting their new CO.

Eze's name was right there, at the top of the chart spilling out and down via the name of her unit's senior NCO.

"Huh," Eze said, glancing up at the frowning Ryers. "You know anything about this... *Chief?*"

His eyes went wide, and his mouth split to reveal white teeth in a grin very unbecoming of a newly promoted command chief petty officer.

"I'll take that as a no," Eze said as he fought to get his face under control and for the senior NCO scowl to reassert itself.

The other three had also been awarded early promotions to bolster the experience and leadership of the unit of mostly fresh recruits.

This had been the way the UN could rapidly grow their troop numbers to meet the growing need—by seasoning a group of recruits with some spicy veterans to lead and train them.

"These orders sent two days ago," Eze said. "Show me."

The lieutenant, allowed to lean back in and reclaim his workspace, brought up the orders stating congratulations from some admiral back on Earth Eze'd never heard of, and confirming her temporary promotion to commander. It went on to list the other four personnel promoted to her new command, informing her to report to the forest moon which they'd given some nonsensical numerical designation to, in order to complete the last phases of build-up and familiarization training before being deployed back to Gaia Néos after four weeks.

She waved her hand over the console screen, gesturing for it to scroll up until the details of the sender and recipient were exposed at the beginning of the comm.

"That son of a bitch," she muttered. "Franks received these redeployment orders and didn't pass them on."

"Well, it doesn't matter now," Torres said, though he sounded like he was trying to head off a revenge plot before it had the chance to blossom. "Why don't you go and introduce yourself to your unit?"

CHAPTER 18

Near the Crab Nebula, Perseus Arm of the Milky Way

"What do you mean, *distress call?*" Da'kath demanded, stomping over to the small console on the bridge of the *Weapon of God* and shoving the smaller warrior bodily out of the way.

"It is from the far colony," the warrior said, "but the words make no sense."

Da'kath played the message back, the 'glyphs rolling across the screen of the console from bottom to top for him to read and replay twice over. He turned to Chakour and pointed a vicious claw at him.

"Make the ship travel to new coordinates," he ordered. "Now."

Chakour stayed stock still, hands clasped behind his back and pointed with his chin to one of his surviving crewmembers. He stepped forward nervously to the navigation array. The jump was plotted and the man at the helm permitted to work the controls to send the carrier disappearing into the nothing between two places in space and time. It wasn't that the Va'alen, for their violent and brutish appearance, weren't highly intelligent and couldn't operate the ship themselves, but the controls were too difficult for them to manipulate. It was easier to keep a small crew of humans alive to do what they needed. Each human was watched at all times by at least one Va'alen, and every task they undertook was monitored and memorized.

117

The eight gunships that docked to appear as part of the super-structure of the carrier were gone, jettisoned in deep space far beyond the reach of any planets. Chakour had at first been fearful that their crews would die a long, slow death until he learned that the minimal crews had been brought into the main carrier before the craft were cut loose.

No sense in wasting good meat.

The man at the helm, his straggly facial hair greasy and unkempt since his personal hygiene had been abandoned, did as he was told without question. Some of the crew still held a shred of rebellion in their eyes, as Chakour did, but he knew that a person could only be tested for so long, could only be pushed so far before they broke.

He'd seen it happen. One of the bridge crew had lasted over a week after the majority of the crew had been locked away. He had finally cracked like an egg over the smallest thing and launched into a futile and furious rage, beating his fists impotently against the near-est alien. It had seemed confused at the pointless assault, shocked even, until a glance at the senior warrior had been returned with a shrug of permission. The memory of the crunching noise the spiked claw made as it punched through the man's chest cavity still echoed in Chakour's ears.

"Jump complete," muttered the man at the helm lifelessly. His dead eyes focused on nothing ahead of him. He had thought of jumping them into the nearest star and kill them all, but as each jump was plotted under the watchful gaze of a hostile alien, he had little chance of doing so undetected. Those thoughts had been long since forgotten, and a numb acceptance of their eventual death be-came something to look forward to.

Da'kath, lounging as best he could in the once-resplendent com-mand chair too small for his huge form, rattled off a series of hisses and clicks at one of the others who began tapping at the communication console. The translation devices had all been deactivated specifically so the humans could be kept ignorant of what their captors were saying. That many of them understood and spoke English was an oddity that confused them before more important matters pushed it aside. Chakour guessed that they were just naturally gifted at under- standing languages, putting him to shame as he couldn't decipher a single click of the Va'alen tongue. The conversation carried on back and forth, and not even their tone could be interpreted like a fellow human speaking another language could be.

An excited conversation began when a signal was received in return, prompting Da'kath to stand and pace the bridge as he seemed to dictate his message for transmission. He stopped twice, firing nervous glances at the man who tried to retain a shred of dignity in spite of the predicament he and his remaining crew were in, until he finally snapped.

"What do you know of this?" he demanded, rounding on the much smaller human and leveling a sharp claw tip at his face.

"Know of what?" Chakour stammered, unable to keep the fear from his words.

"I will find the truth in him, Supreme Commander," hissed another Va'alen voice from behind him.

Chakour spun, the claw tip brushing the back of his head and making him yelp. He found himself staring into the blank gaze of the smaller warrior who went everywhere with Da'kath, the one who must be the supreme commander's mate.

"I swear," Chakour pleaded, "I don't know what... what's happening?"

Da'kath issued a hissing grunt of impotent anger, pushing Chakour in the back. This pitched him forward into the chest armor of his mate who rattled off a snarl of aggression until he righted himself. He resisted the urge to wipe his hands on his crumpled uniform after touching the beast.

"My people have been attacked while the expedition was out of our system," Da'kath growled.

"Not by us," Chakour declared vehemently. He hoped that it was true, and that humanity hadn't found their way there ahead of them with an armada.

More orders were rattled off in the Va'alen tongue and the ship was directed to the nearest planet.

"Ch'akal," Da'kath said formally, "this ship is yours until I return. You have my permission to dismember any human who defies you."

Ch'akal, a warrior of impressive size with deep gouges and scorch marks in his chest armor, bowed reverently and accepted the honor of being left in charge. Da'kath stomped from the bridge, turning only to glance back at his mate and fire off an order.

"Bring that one," he said as he pointed at Chakour. "If he lies, I will tear him into many pieces myself."

Protesting weakly, Chakour was powerless to stop himself from being unceremoniously dragged from the bridge of his ship. The toes of his boots scuffed along the deck until he could right himself and walk. He was thrust ahead of the female warrior and forced to keep up with the angry pace of the alien leader, as every Va'alen they passed stopped and bowed their heads to the procession. He recalled sourly how he had once been the one to command that fear—which he mistook for respect—when his own crew had stopped to salute him everywhere he went.

His fears grew as they approached the large hangar bay where he had foolishly believed he could contain the aliens. He had had plans of transporting them like cargo to demand a high price in technology in return for the schematics of a working Fold drive. His breathing began to speed up as he feared that he wouldn't be kept alive to test the truth of his words but instead would be fed into the recycling machine and consumed by the Va'alen as a biological paste.

"Supreme Commander," a Va'alen hissed at Da'kath when they entered, bowing as he spoke the words. "Am I to—"

He was cut off by Da'kath speaking Va'alen.

"My mistake, Supreme Commander," he said in their tongue, shooting a hungry look at the frightened human. "Shall wake the Hive Lords for you?"

"Yes," Da'kath told him. "They will decide what they want to do. If they ask, tell them I have gone to the surface to see the destruction for myself."

The warrior bowed again as he retreated and Da'kath led the way into the cockpit of the bulbous spacecraft as Chakour was bundled up behind him. He was thrown into the rear section and stayed curled up on the deck where he felt it was safest to remain still. As Da'kath's mate climbed inside, however, she dragged him to his feet, forced him into a chair that was too large and stayed silent as she placed a diagonal strap across his body. It was too large to constrain him properly, but he doubted voicing any such concerns would be treated with sympathy.

The ship powered up, a spinning, thrumming noise of increasing intensity roared from behind and below where he sat as the craft lifted off from the surface. It moved slowly along the deck to the airlock exit, instead of what Chakour expected through the forcefield with a matching shield harmonic. The Va'alen hadn't uncovered all of their secrets yet, he realized. This gave him some small hope of surviving the ordeal he was going through.

The sound disappeared as the airlock went into vacuum, save for the gentle hum inside the ship. Immediately Chakour floated up out of his seat until the strap caught him hovering a hand's width from where he should be. The ride didn't take long—about as long as dropship transfer between fleet ships—and he saw the large, orange arc of a planet grow until it obscured the entire view ahead of the ship. Rumbling through the atmosphere with the heat inside the ship growing uncomfortably higher made him sweat. He slammed back down to the seat painfully when gravity re-established itself with un-ceremonious speed. He made a mental note of another piece of tech-nology he could trade just to try and make it home alive, refusing to be honest with himself about the true likelihood of doing so.

The landing was hard. Back on Earth it would be called a tactical landing, excusing the lack of comfort in order to put a ship on the deck as fast as possible without killing the occupants. As the engine shut down, Chakour was dragged from his seat and tossed down to the light brown dust that covered the flat landscape.

Hisses and jeers answered his arrival along with angry demands to know what he was. He rose to his knees, trying to appear as small as possible—not difficult given that even the smallest Va'alen were a head taller than most humans. He watched as a warrior close to Da'kath's size pushed his way to the front of the gathering crowd holding a curved sword glinting with the color of polished bronze and a fat rifle in another of his four claws. He stood before Da'kath. Chakour feared that he was witnessing some kind of showdown.

"Who are you?" the warrior demanded of Da'kath. "Why have you come to this place? All of our reinforcements left after the enemy moved on."

"I am Da'kath, Do-Ch'aal of the great expedition."

"I am Gru'thunn," the warrior responded, claiming his own status as equal to Da'kath's, "and I am in command of this sector."

"How many warriors do you command?" Da'kath asked.

"I have the honor of leading twenty pairs of warriors sent here after the attacks," Gru'thunn replied.

Da'kath, if he could mimic the human gesture, would have smiled.

"I led one thousand warriors to the nearest stars and fought a great war with a new enemy," he bragged. He deliberately left out the salient facts that he now commanded fewer than fifty warriors in total and had lost that war, putting him at a roughly equal standing to the one before him. The bravado worked; Gru'thunn bowed his head to him.

"Supreme Commander," he said quickly as a formality.

"What enemy?" Da'kath demanded as he turned and pointed a claw at Chakour. "Are they pathetic bags of meat like this thing?"

"No," the other warrior replied, staring loathingly at Chakour. "They fly in the skies in small craft like blades and fire on our settlements. We shot one down. It is this way, if you will follow me."

CHAPTER 19

Gaia Neós Orbit

As happy as Torres was for his partner Eze, there was a sadness at having to leave her behind. He tried not to show it, though. He had been proud and excited for her as she had almost skipped away with barely a goodbye. She was now the commander of a unit of troops; once she remembered that, she adjusted her gait accordingly.

He had gone a different way and gained command of a ship. It was a famous, one-of-a-kind ship with one of the most important missions in human history, but that didn't stop the stab of jealousy from hitting him.

He had commanded teams before. Had led platoons and squads and half-units. He had been the second-in-command of a special operations CP team. But he had never commanded a full unit, and that stung his pride.

"Relax," Brandt said. "She'll be there when we get back."

"I know," he answered as he smiled at her, "and we have a job to do."

They did. The *Ichi* had been painstakingly restored and improved with round-the-clock engineering teams working on the ruined power conduits and ravaged battery stacks until every component was replaced and rigorously tested. When she was repaired to her former status, Harris then personally oversaw the second stage and fitted additional redundancies to prevent a power overload from ever happening again.

"Energy has to have somewhere to go, you see?" he explained to Torres. Paterson stood behind him nodding like a demented dog. "Like lightning?"

"Yeah, I get you, so you've fitted an earth rod?" the captain asked. His lack of understanding made the doctor and the engineer scoff in amused sympathy.

"If our shields get struck, like with weapons fire, it dissipates and reduces the integrity of the barrier until that gets restored. It wears it down," he explained gently, as though Torres's brain might struggle to comprehend the concept if he went too fast. "But with a massive spike like the solar flare we encountered, the amount of energy was too much for the shields to cope. Like a blunt-force attack."

"So, what are you saying?" Torres asked.

"Any power sufficient to overload the shield capacitors instead of just wearing them down now gets re-routed through a heat sync, essentially converting it to something like an exhaust gas."

Torres took in a long breath and held it. His thought was still not fully formed when his mouth was ready to start responding.

"Two questions," he said. "One, you've fitted the *Ichi* with a lightning rod that converts solar flares into farts?" He had to raise his voice and speak quickly to stop Harris turning purple with anger at how his engineering genius had been described. "And two, why can't we do that for any kind of energy hitting out shields?"

"Because it doesn't work that way, sir," the engineer replied sulkily. "It works for an energy overload."

"But you've made it work for this, so why can't you change it? You've just told me you've converted the energy of a solar flare into harmless exhaust heat, right?"

"Yeah," Harris said, drawing the word out hesitatingly, as though he was going to be asked to come up with a second and third miracle to accompany his first.

"So, why can't that energy be used to, say, charge a weapon or feed back into something useful?"

"Because it's unrestrained," Paterson said, chiming in to try and help the beleaguered engineer. "It has to discharge at once and not be contained anywhere, otherwise we just end up with the same feedback problem we had the first time."

"Hmm," Torres said. "But you can convert an energy hitting our shields into a by-product without degrading the shield integrity?"

Harris and Paterson glanced at one another, neither wanting to admit that they had been so consumed with achieving one goal that they had failed to recognize a combat application for the process.

"In theory," Harris said carefully. "We could test it…"

"Outstanding," Torres said with a wide smile. "Let me know what you come up with. Jumping off in twelve hours unless something goes wrong with the testing."

"What testing?" Harris asked. He thought he was aware of any scheduled maintenance checks.

"The testing where I get someone to fire on our shields to see if your new," he waved his hand at the wires and conduit pipes behind them, "thing works."

"Aaaand *this* is where I get my ass back to my lab," Paterson said, taking an exaggerated step toward the door. He was forbidden from stepping foot off the ship, from leaving the safety of the fleet, or going to any planet that could be deemed hostile.

His wife wasn't part of the UN, but he wholly believed she'd know if he broke those rules.

Eight hours later, after what Harris felt were some suspiciously easy calculations and some rather annoyingly minor adjustments, the *Ichi* sat in space far beyond the orbits of the suns or the planets.

"Open a channel to our escort," Torres said to the comm officer.

He tapped at icons on his console, then turned to give the captain a nod.

"*Ichi* to *Hammer*," he said.

"*Hammer* actual," Captain Hayes responded. "Changed your mind yet, Captain?"

"Negative," Torres replied. "Coming to an all-stop for you to take a firing solution."

"Understood," Hayes said. "Keeping the channel open."

Beside Torres his chair console emitted a dull beep prompting him to open the text only comm from the other captain.

…SO I CAN HEAR YOUR SCREAMS.

The text comm was Hayes's idea of a joke. Torres smiled and tapped out a message back.

ONLY IF IT DOESN'T WORK. SAY SOMETHING NICE AT THE CEREMONY.

"All stop, shields to full," he said loudly to his bridge. He waited for confirmations before opening a comm to his engineering section. "Ready to conduct initial tests, Mister Harris?"

"Ready as we'll ever be, Captain. Recommend the *Hammer* starts small and builds up. Energy weapons only."

"I'm not of a mind to order a frigate to fire warheads at us," Torres replied.

"Torres to Hayes," he said over the live channel to the other ship. "Fire when ready."

The *Hammer*, a ship as over-powered as it could be without tearing itself apart, lined up at a safe distance should the recon ship go up like a supernova. In case this didn't work, Hayes had taken the pre-arranged position so that the forward guns of his ship could fire at angle over the *Ichi's* bow, and hit their shields without ever lining up a firing solution that hit their hull.

Their energy weapons were harmonized to their own shields' frequency so that the bolts of energy passed through without causing damage. However, as every ship ran a slightly different configuration, it was almost impossible to find the exact frequency to allow those shots to pass straight through the protection of whatever they fired on.

At least it was at the moment, but the captain was sure someone somewhere was working on a way to render shields obsolete.

"Ready forward gun batteries," he ordered. "Half-second burst on my mark."

He paused a few seconds to allow the exact solution to be programmed before giving the order.

"Fire."

Orange pulses flared out from the twin Gatling-style guns on the forward hull of the frigate, lancing across the twenty kilometers between the warship and the smaller reconnaissance vessel. Watching on screen with his breath held, Hayes saw the shields of the *Ichi* pulse and flare bright blue as the fire struck them. He waited a second before his nerve broke and he spoke over the open communication link.

"Torres, you still there?" he asked, unable to hide the concern in his voice. He knew the power of the weapons fire wasn't anywhere near sufficient to cause them any serious damage, but since they were trying to re-route that power there were any number of things that could go wrong.

"Still here, Hayes," Torres said. "Shield integrity down… only two percent. Heat syncs holding. Fire again, and ramp it up."

The testing had gone on for close to an hour before the risks of the experiment were too much. With the heat syncs disabled, a three-second barrage from the frigate's forward guns lowered their outer shield integrity by close to forty percent. With Harris's new system up and running, that loss was reduced to a little under ten percent.

The discovery of their extended shield abilities had far-reaching consequences for any future clash with the Va'alen. The aliens had yet to fire on them with anything but directed energy pulses. Harris opened a comm link to Paterson in his lab on the *Anvil*, confirming their research and passing on the final specifications.

The fleet's frigates, their working warhorses, would be retrofitted as a priority.

"Don't be taking the credit for all of it," Harris warned Paterson, mostly in jest.

"Relax," Paterson told him. "I'll give you props for assisting me."

"Asshole," Harris said, laughing.

"Seriously though," Paterson told him. "This is real cutting-edge invention. It'll save lives. Catch up with me when you get back to civilization and I'll show you the paper we'll have written together."

CHAPTER 20

Va'alen Planet, Edge of the Crab Nebula

Da'kath, incensed with rage that his people had been attacked, sought any avenue to vent those emotions. He kicked the downed enemy craft—the only one brought down to redress the balance of so many dead—until his warriors were forced to hold him back.

What made it worse was that the mates of those warriors killed had no way to exact revenge on their enemy through the Path of Ending. Driven insane through the loss of their telepathic link, the surviving Va'alen had scored themselves across the chest of their armor and sought anything they could kill.

Some had to be put down by their own people to save them from ripping the limbs off any innocent survivor. Others, the pain of loss and the impotent rage coursing through them like a poison, had taken their own lives, plunging their blades deep into their bodies to end their suffering.

Da'kath had heard of this happening only once in his long life. Now, however, him he saw before him evidence of a dozen more dead at their own hands. It sickened him to his core. The anger burned out eventually, leaving behind a cold fury that cleared his mind as he appraised the alien craft.

"Break this thing open," he ordered in English, turning to Chakour with a claw levelled at his face. "If there is a human inside, I promise you a slow and agonizing death."

Chakour swallowed, hoping that whatever was in there wasn't human.

He'd never seen a ship like it before. It was small—only large enough for a solitary humanoid, like a single-seat fighter plane from Earth's history. The need for small fighters had fallen away after the world peace accords and the forming of the UN territories, but he had seen enough historic footage to know the devastation and havoc just a single fighter could wreak on an undefended village.

He'd never seen this composition of metal before either. He couldn't be sure of the true color, since no matter where he turned it caught the dull red light of the sun, like a sunset under the red glow on his own planet. It shimmered anywhere between a bright silver to a deep purple like that of a polished gun barrel. He made a few observations, however. There was no spike protruding from the front of the ship, not even the evidence of broken-off remnants. That meant that these ships probably belonged to a larger vessel capable of faster-than-light travel, much like the gunships that had been part of his carrier.

He realized he was making assumptions, considering that whatever had attacked the Va'alen towns might not possess that level of technology. But given the destruction they caused, he highly doubted they weren't an advanced race.

The Va'alen warriors tried brute force, not unsurprisingly, but the metal alloy was oddly resistant to their blades and claws. One of them bellowed for the others to stand back and he braced himself with a wide stance, aiming his pulse rifle from the hip. The shot, wound up to full power, was designed to burst open the bulge that everyone expected to be the cockpit.

The bright pulse of energy ricocheted off the ship with a noise that vibrated the air, forcing Chakour to flinch. His movement brought attention, especially from the Va'alen native to the planet who hadn't seen a human before. Laughs of derision hissed and crackled over his head.

"Pfft," he hissed half under his breath. "At least I'm not the cockroach trying to crack a nut with my head."

"What did it say?" rattled the warrior who had been thrown back into the dust by the pointless discharge of his weapon.

Chakour watched the interaction between the warrior and Da'kath, who had suddenly transformed from his captor and tormentor to his only chance of survival. He understood not one word of the response, but he understood the body language of the warrior Da'kath evidently insulted.

"He said you are a mindless lump of gristle," Da'kath growled at the warrior, "and *bo'reth* shit has more intellect than you."

The warrior launched himself at Da'kath before he had finished speaking, in a reckless, ruthless onslaught with no thought to the consequences or any logical plan of attack.

Da'kath's warrior escorts stood close but stayed suspiciously calm and still. They knew what Chakour did not: the words and the attack were a challenge for seniority and authority and should be respected. It was between these two warriors until one died or yielded.

Da'kath let the warrior fly at him, stepping back and aside as he launched a brutal kick into the air where he had just been standing. He tripped him, then felt the ground shudder under the big warrior landing hard. He flailed wildly, swinging claws at Da'kath who leaned his body into the attacks, robbing them of their momentum. He forced the reckless warrior to the ground to stand over him, pinning the arms on both sides with his knees and dropping on top of him.

Slowly drawing the blade from his lower back, Da'kath placed the tip of it in a ridge between the thick plates of scarred chest armor.

The warrior at his mercy froze, intoning a low, rumbling clicking noise that prompted the watching Va'alen to join. Without a word, Da'kath rose, sheathing the blade and offering a claw to his vanquished challenger.

To Chakour's surprise he accepted the offer The warrior was pulled back to his feet as though he hadn't just been a moment from losing his life. The conversation went on, the flow of it lost as the non-verbal cues of the aliens were near impossible to follow, until Da'kath turned and spoke to Chakour in English.

"He says that if you know better, you should open this thing yourself."

Challenge accepted, Chakour gave a small bow of acknowledgement and asked for a closer look.

He ignored the clicks and hisses of the Va'alen watching him. He was the subject of their humor and derision, but he continued to methodically search each part of the small ship for a way inside.

The whole thing seemed to be made from a single piece of alloy. He could detect no welds or seams anywhere on the fuselage; in fact, he could locate no straight edge or flat panel at all. This worried him—only nature made things without straight lines.

He reached the back of the ship, remembering his electrical mechanic university training, and peered into what seemed like a large, single exhaust. He recognized elements of what looked their human repulser technology, but on a much larger condensed scale. Still he found no discernable way inside.

"It must be underneath," he said, as much to himself as to the few Va'alen who understood his language.

Da'kath heard, ordering warriors into action in their tongue. This forced Chakour to step back hurriedly as three large warriors gripped the sharp edge of the craft and flipped it over. There, directly underneath, on what he had assumed to be the belly of the ship but what he now realized was the top, was the clue he had been looking for. He saw a long, bulbous stretch of the same alloy, with a thin line tracing around it where it met the flat part of the fuselage.

"There," he said almost triumphantly, before seeing that the Va'alen were about to smash open the cockpit. He cried out to stop them. "Wait! Just wait!"

The warriors hesitated, looking to Da'kath as though for permission to ignore his pet and carry on. He waved them away.

"What do you see, General?" Da'kath said, sounding almost respectful in the way he spoke to his prisoner.

"I see…" he said, hesitating. "I think I see an access panel. Give me something to pry it open with," he ordered, forgetting for a moment to whom he spoke.

Just as he recognized that, he heard the long, singing scrape of a blade being drawn from a scabbard. Chakour looked up to see Da'kath standing over him, huge sword held close to his neck. Abruptly, Da'kath flipped the blade so that the hilt swung in a low arc toward the human, as he deftly caught the wide blade near the point.

"This *casha'al*," he said, "this blade, belonged to my sire's sire and he forged it himself on this very planet."

Chakour reached out nervously for the hilt, expecting it to weigh much more than it did. Da'kath didn't release the full weight into his hands until he had finished speaking.

"If you break it, human," he warned, "I will use the pieces of it to cut you into a thousand, thousand slices."

Chakour, not trusting himself to speak, nodded and took the weapon. He carefully placed the point into the seam of a small, oval-shaped panel on the flat surface of one wing and worked it into the gap. Next, he used his weight to lever down on the end. For a sickening moment the blade flexed, threatening to lose the battle of physics, but the panel sprung open with a twanging noise to expose wiring. He handed the blade back to Da'kath with relief and asked for anything that could supply power to the panel. He wanted to overload it. A device was brought under the Va'alen's orders and Chakour performed the simple trick of pumping an unknown circuit with more power than the conduits were designed for.

It worked, as much to Chakour's surprise as the aliens', but the cacophony of their response made him throw himself down with his hands clamped over his ears.

CHAPTER 21

Deep Space

"I don't understand, Captain," Howard said in apology. "The coordinates were good, and Lieutenant Rogers has put us precisely where we wanted to be—"

"Obviously," Rogers muttered.

"—there's just no star here."

The astral navigator shrugged as though there was no other explanation for it, and Torres was sure at any other time that the riddle would have intrigued him. Right then, however, it was just another pain in his ass.

"Tac," he said, "long-range sensor sweep and tell me if there's anything interesting here. Guns, stay sharp until the sensor sweep is complete. Everyone else, prepare for another jump if it comes back negative."

Ripples of affirmative acknowledgements came in person and via the open comm system as they waited while the sensors ran a basic check of their surroundings. That minute would have been tense at one time, back a few months ago when they were constantly on high alert. Now, though, they were used to finding that there was nothing out in space apart from their little ship, and the odd planetoid where leeches grew to five feet and lived off pure energy.

So many wonders out there, so much space and so many places to discover as the first humans. None of it held any excitement for them.

"Negative on sensors, sir," reported the ensign at tactical.

"Next coordinates if you will, Mister Howard. All hands prepare for jump."

"Dropping from Fold space in three, two, one…" Rogers announced calmly to the bridge of the *Ichi*.

"Scanners, tactical," Torres ordered from the captain's chair.

"Working, sir," the ensign responded flatly.

"Guns, anything?" Torres asked.

"Negative pod one."

"Nothin' from pod two," Zero reported.

"G-class planet detected, it's less than one quarter light year away."

"Wide orbit, Mister Rogers," Torres instructed.

"Entering high orbit," Rogers said a short while later.

"On screen," the captain instructed. "Well… would you look at that…"

"Readings indicate very similar conditions to Earth," the ensign at tactical said, "although almost ninety percent of the surface is covered by water."

"They have cold poles like ours," Sarvanto said.

"Not for long if I'm reading this right," Lieutenant Howard said over the comm.

"Meaning?" Torres asked.

"Meaning that I don't think the water level was supposed to be that high. I'm reading evidence of an advanced civilization down there; machinery, industry, widespread deforestation..." Howard explained. "The rising water level matches what we know about our own pollution back in the fossil fuel era. The atmosphere is significantly hotter than our own, which could account for the melting ice at the poles."

"Can corroborate, Captain," this from tactical. "Equatorial temperatures are reading close to seventy degrees. Celsius."

"Remind me not to visit the equator down there," Torres said. "Any evidence of Va'alen or Kuldar technology?"

"Nothing on comm," the communications officer reported. "Scanning wider frequencies."

"Okay, let's do another full sweep to be sure, drop a buoy and move on. What's the next location, Lieutenant Howard?"

"Next star system is a little over nine billio—"

"Contact!" shouted Rogers.

"Shields to full," Torres barked. "What and where?"

"On the surface, energy spike from something matching an orbital rail gun."

"Half-second jump, Rogers," Torres ordered. "Shroud as soon as we re-enter normal space and loop back nice and slow. Tactical?"

"Sir?"

"You keep your eyes on those scanners and cry out *the second* you see anything you don't like, you got that?"

"Brandt from Torres," chirped the commander's comm.

"Here, go ahead."

"Evidence of orbital railgun technology on the planet," Torres told her simply. "No current danger, but I'd be obliged if you prepared a team to investigate. Current planetary observations are available to you… now." He transferred everything they knew directly to her comm.

Brandt was already stepping into her armor, so didn't open the data packet on her device but let the suit fire up so she could access it on her HUD. Using a combination of eye-clicks and hand gestures, she selected a team of six and elected to leave the other four onboard under the command on Beale.

"Report to the shuttle bay," she told them before opening the channel to the bridge again.

"Six including pilot or do you want Specter to drive?" she asked.

"I'll keep Rogers at the wheel up here," Torres told her. "I might need him if another orbital gun pops up."

"Understood," she said. She selected weapons and spare battery packs for her rifle and pistol.

Specter, Zero, Payne, Kekoa and Fangs—one of Beale's original men who was cross-trained as a medic but not up to Turner's standards—assembled at the rear ramp of the *Tanto* as she briefed them.

"Listen up," she started, keeping her briefing short and to the point. "Orbital rail gun battery on the planet unveiled as we entered orbit. We've jumped out of line of sight and will be entering atmo away from it, where we'll come in low and fast. There's no indication of other defenses, but that doesn't mean there aren't any. We will investigate and report back. Questions?"

"Any signs of life down there, Commander?" Kekoa asked. He wanted to know if this was a research deployment or a combat one.

Before she could answer a klaxon sounded and the red emergency lighting flickered.

"Standby for emergency jump," the speakers announced ship-wide as a tremor ran through the deck beneath their feet.

"Bridge to ground team," Torres hailed. "Second and third gun batteries unveiled."

"Do we have an insertion window?" Brandt asked.

"Negative at present. Considering options to destroy one of the guns from orbit."

"Understood. Consider combat drop if that's an option; no sense in hostile action if we can quietly disable one from the surface."

A pause filled the channel for a moment before Torres acknowledged her suggestion. Behind her she heard a groan, quickly stifled, and shot Kekoa a glance. Zero nudged him with an elbow as he checked the action on his marksman rifle, prompting a dull clang of metal as their armor touched.

"Don't you want that combat drop badge?" he asked.

"Not desperately," Kekoa answered. "I mean, if I have to then, sure…"

"Bridge to Commander Brandt," chirped the comm in their ears.

"Go ahead, Captain," she answered.

"Stand by for drop. Recommend EW and demolitions equipment."

Brandt acknowledged the order, and turned back to her team to see Payne opening a weapons locker. She strapped a belt of compact demolition charges down the length of her right leg and secured them with the mag-locks. Specter took a small case, fixing that to his lower back and nodded at her before they made their way to the drop tubes. She called ready over the channel.

"Commander Brandt, helm," replied *Ichi's* chief pilot. "Target window is available. I'll have to jump in and jump out, but you'll have maybe forty seconds to get clear. Disable the gun on your target package and it'll give us plenty of room to bring the *Tanto* in afterward."

"Aye aye," she chimed. The knot of apprehension in her stomach churned as the thought of what they were about to do hit home. Adrenaline pulsed through her.

Her suit registered the increase in pulse and breathing rate, just as her display highlighted the other team members experiencing the same physiological responses. The only absence was, predictably, Specter.

They filed into the tight tubes, fixed their armored feet into the booster packs, called ready. Then, they waited for the order to go as the tubes rotated to tip them upside down.

"Ready to execute," Rogers said to Torres. He turned slightly in his seat to look at the captain's face as he gave the order. Torres gave him a confident nod.

Brandt steadied her breathing, feeling the rush of blood to her head as the artificial gravity caused it to run down—or up. She waited for the word. She had to do nothing but prepare herself.

"You'll be out of comm range until we jump back in," Torres said in her ear. She glanced at the communications icons and noticed that he had opened a private channel to her. "Disable that gun and send up a beacon. God speed. Torres out."

"Standby, standby... *jump*."

The rapid depressurization of the tubes fired them into space as the bright blue of the planet below filled her view. As soon as they were clear of the ship, she imagined the *Ichi's* shields re-engage while the rocket pack on her feet fired up to accelerate her to ludicrous speeds.

Her armor was locked out rigid. All she had to do was watch the HUD and cross her fingers, figuratively speaking.

Rogers had done well, putting the ship on the very edge of the atmosphere before blinking away again. She knew the ship had gone when the signals from their home vanished from her HUD.

They entered the atmosphere after only seconds in powered flight, their spacings equal and their descent synchronized. Zero kept a running commentary to the team, some- thing only she knew was his coping mechanism for drops.

Everyone else thought he was cool with it. He was cool about everything else, after all. Brandt knew he hated it, but his stone-cold persona wouldn't allow fear to show as a weakness. Like her, he'd overcome the fear as he did the thing that had to be done.

Travelling through the atmosphere was fast, and soon the noises changed as they were burning through the air heading straight down until their flight attitude varied.

"Adjusting course to compensate for—*Whoa!*" Zero exclaimed as a bolt of bright blue the size of Kekoa shot past them at unimaginable speeds. In truth it had passed close to a kilometer away, but close was a relative term in space.

"You ever seen an orbital gun acquire a target and fire that fast?" Payne cried out.

"Focus," Brandt snapped.

They hurtled through the upper atmosphere of the planet covered almost entirely in bright blue water, heading for the spit of high ground where the rail gun sat.

CHAPTER 22

Unnamed Planet

"Approaching target in thirty kilometers, prepare for break- away," Zero reported.

As soon as he had said the words, Brandt's booster pack stopped firing and detached from her feet. This then unlocked the movement of her armor, though she remained locked in a nosedive.

They held their nerve, keeping a tense silence as they descended at the lower speed of terminal velocity.

"Arrest descent in forty seconds," Brandt announced. Nobody acknowledged but she saw green lights across the board for the other five members of her team.

Their retro-repulsers flared, ramping up in intensity to slow them down before firing hard a hundred feet above the surface. Their target was a rocky plateau, surrounded by the azure blue of what looked like deep, tropical waters. Six thuds, all in rapid succession, marked their arrival on the planet. Guns were drawn from where they were mag-locked to armor. A hasty perimeter was established as they pushed out in a rough circle to each announce 'clear' in turn.

"No hostiles," Brandt confirmed.

She was the last to speak, as she checked the distance and bearing to their objective. They'd landed less than half a kilo- meter from the slightly raised summit that from higher up had appeared to be natu- ral. On the ground now, using the zoom optics of their suits, they

144

could tell it was a structure built atop the high ground. Bizarrely, there appeared to be no gun, nor was there any sign of one as they dropped.

"Where the hell is it?" Payne asked.

"Move out," Brandt ordered. "Three and three, cover and move. Go!"

They bounded toward the structure. Three of them provided cover from either standing or kneeling positions, as the others moved a hundred meters at a time before adopting similar stances. As Zero stopped at the head of their fast-moving team three hundred meters short of the objective, he launched the small drone built into a pod on the back of one shoulder.

"Bart's up," he announced.

In a moment, they could expect a god's eye view of the battlefield, complete with target recognition icons. Nothing showed on Brandt's HUD, only the five green arrows pointing to the precise location of her team members. Stopping one hundred meters from the raised rock structure, she called a halt, sending Specter and Kekoa ahead as recon. The rest of the team waited as the two soldiers bounded ahead, covering the distance in one sprint while the other four were offering covering fire, until Specter called to them.

The closer they got, the more they recognized the structure to be purpose-built. There were even chunks of roughly carved rock piled up like a wall with the outer faces left intentionally uncut to give the appearance of natural rock for all but close inspections.

"Energy signatures from inside," Specter said.

"Three sixty," Brandt ordered. She pointed at two of the team, indicating they head forward and to the left of the structure, while she advanced to lead the others around the right side. There was no discernable way inside, so she ordered the most physically capable of them to climb.

Specter mag-locked his rifle to his back and crouched to leap, sailing almost ten feet in the air. He landed on the rock face halfway up and began to climb. The wall wasn't a sheer cliff, but the gradient of the slope meant that traversing it without armor or ropes would be hazardous. He disappeared over the top before calling out over the comm to the others.

"Access panel," he said. "Better get up here."

They climbed, satisfied that their backs were covered by the little drone hovering high above them scanning the area. Reaching the top, Brandt saw the panel and gave Specter a nod to open it. She didn't need to tell him to watch for for improvised explosives on the hatch; of all of them he was prob- ably most aware of the risks of explosions. No markings gave any indication of the species who had built it, but the level of technology was on a par with their own. Given that the planet seemed to have been abandoned many years before, that put them in the realm of dealing with a more advanced alien race.

The panel came up after some persuasion. As it was forced open on seized hinges, the heavy metal creaked a tortured scream.

"Guess that's the doorbell," Kekoa muttered.

He turned his attention back to the outward defense over the sights of his rifle. Specter, kneeling by the gaping aperture, poked his head and shoulders down inside as the lights on his armor lit up to a command.

"Clear," he announced.

"Specter, Fangs," Brandt said as she stowed her own rifle on her back and drew the pistol from her thigh, "on me. The rest of you stay sharp."

She dropped feet first into the hole after Specter, landing with a loud, echoing *clang* as her armored boots hit the solid metal of the deck ten feet below. They were in a narrow, sweeping corridor. It seemed to form a circle around the summit, which would make sense if a large orbital rail gun was designed to pop up out of the middle section. From that position it could acquire a targeting solution on something so far away it was invisible and launch a supercharged slug at thousands of miles per hour. Ahead of them, illuminated by the harsh flashlight beams on her shoulders and forearms, a doorway came into focus.

Specter checked it again and opened it, turning the central handle like a wheel. The door protested more than the hatch above, and Brandt had to lend her augmented strength to it to force it wide. Steps went down into the darkness. As Specter stepped inside a hum filled the air and dull, red strip lighting flickered into life to light up the stairwell below them.

"I guess we go down," he said. She nodded.

"Topside," she said over the comm, "we might lose signal. We're going down. Fangs, hold this position as comm relay. Ten minutes without confirmation before you come after us."

Zero acknowledged the order up top, lining up a ten-minute countdown on his HUD before he had to go down into whatever was there to bring his commander back out.

Eight tense minutes later, the comm came to life.

"Zero, get a beacon up," Brandt announced breathlessly.

"Confirm the gun is down, Commander," he asked.

"Confirmed," she told him. "When they get back to orbit tell them we need a science and engineering team down here. Make sure they bring Asha. Out."

"Beacon up," the comm officer announced to the bridge of the *Ichi*, which was a safe distance from orbit of the planet.

"Jump us back, Rogers," Torres ordered.

He felt slight vibrations under his feet in answer. Seconds later the image on the large viewscreen changed to a much closer version of the planet they had been watching for a tense three quarters of an hour.

"Comm link established, opening channel."

"Ground team this is the captain, report." Torres called out.

"Zero here, sir," the sniper responded. "Request from the commander that you send down a science and engineering detail. She stipulated it should include Asha, over."

Torres hated this part of command. He'd have been the first to volunteer for the detail. He wanted the chance to get off his ass and put boots on the ground of an alien world, but his place was in the big chair, running the whole show.

Asha had been overjoyed at the chance to don the armor custom made for him back on Earth, but seeing as he hadn't completed anything but basic human combat training, he wasn't permitted to join the troop team. His inexperience would be a hazard. Harris delegated seniority to one of his more trusted engineers so he could go down and play with alien machinery.

Lieutenant Howard nominated himself, despite giving off the vibe that he was a comfy seat kind of guy. When Torres raised his eyebrows at the request, he shocked his captain with a quiet, rare moment of bragging.

"I'm fully combat rated, Captain," he said. "Didn't you know that before I came aboard?"

Torres accepted the admonishment.

Even Rogers's boyishly hopeful request for permission to fly the shuttle made the captain feel like he was being abandoned. Nevertheless, he gave his permission and sat on the bridge to watch them fly away toward the orbital cannon that had sparked so much interest.

CHAPTER 23

Rail Gun Bunker, Unnamed Planet

"Is Asha there?" Brandt called up through the hatch. "We need him down here."

A surge of nervous excitement washed over her—their alien friend had heard her words and could barely contain himself before dropping down into the outer layer of the bunker.

"Down here," she called.

She turned and led the way toward the stairwell. He wasn't armed, but the armor combined with his natural height made him look more formidable than she had previously seen him. Brandt stopped on the stairs, feeling hesitation and unease. Realizing the projected emotions came from the Kuldar, she spun around to look at his mirrored visor reflecting the dull, red glow.

"This feels..." he began, unsure of himself, "somehow familiar."

"Wait until you see this then," Brandt said. "Prepare to have your mind blown."

She explained further when she felt his wave of shocked panic at her words.

"It's a human saying," she said to calm him. "It means that you won't believe what you're about to see."

He relaxed, chuckling nervously in a deliberate imitation of humans, and followed her down.

The stairwell carried on, but she led the way off at the first sub-level around a central plinth to a control room. Power conduits ran around the room which had been bypassed to cut power to the main gun. Asha stopped directly in front of the plinth, holding up both hands while Brandt and Specter watched him intently.

With a flourish, the display flickered to life, bathing the room in a soft, green glow of the gun schematics.

"Have you seen this kind of technology before?" Brandt asked.

"This?" Asha asked, distracted by the display. "No. But whoever built it uses a variation of our language and coding. It is... it is more new than our own."

"Newer?" Brandt asked, unintentionally correcting his grammar. "But this place has to have been abandoned a few hundred years ago."

Asha gasped, stopping his navigation through the display and forcing a spike of shock over Brandt's consciousness.

"What is it?" she asked, her voice full of concern as she felt his emotions more than her own.

"It is... *Kuldar*. My people created this thing."

"It's *what?*" Torres said over the comm, leaning forward in his chair. "I thought you said it was more advanced than our own tech, so how could it be Kuldar if they've bee—" He stopped, connecting the dots on his own.

"You're certain?" he asked. "One hundred percent?"

"Without a doubt, sir," Brandt said. "Asha has confirmed that the language is the same as their own, only *different*."

"Different as in it might be older?" Torres asked, still searching for the easier conclusion.

"Negative, Captain," Lieutenant Howard said over the open channel. "The similarities in older and younger versions of the same languages are easy to spot if you know what you're looking for. This indicates that Asha's written form is the older version. That would tie in with the tech level, too, as it's way more advanced than anything the Kuldar had when we first encountered them."

"Talk to me about that," Torres said. He was annoyed that he hadn't yet seen the inside of the bunker. Since it was shielded, it wouldn't allow a signal to be transmitted into or out of it unless they hacked into the hardwired net connecting the handful of working sites still active on the surface of the planet.

"The railgun isn't that dissimilar to our own," Brandt said. "Although that isn't surprising given that our high-level tech is taken from Kuldar designs."

"But the targeting acquisition was faster than our own," Torres offered.

"That's true, sir," Howard interjected. "In terms of the hardware it isn't *that* far advanced, but the operating systems are much faster than our own."

"Okay," Torres told them. "I need detailed analysis, samples, and if possible, download the data core of that gun's operating system so we can study it. Let me know if you need anything else from up here."

"Will do, Captain," Brandt answered. "Surface out."

She turned to the assembled crew members of the ground team who had congregated to hear the conversation they weren't all plugged in to. Brandt gave orders, deploying people to specific jobs whether they were necessary or not just to have the area clear of tourists. She asked Asha to help Howard access the operating system to get the download Torres wanted, but they found that was difficult without the gun's systems operational. If the gun was fully operational, however, their ride could get blown out of orbit and they'd be stuck travelling millions of miles home in a small shuttle.

"Okay," Howard said to Brandt. "We think we've isolated just the data recording section of the operating system, if you're ready for us to bring that online?"

"Do it," she said. She then opened a channel to everyone on the ground. "All hands, standby. We're bringing the core online. Sing out of you see something you don't like."

Silence reigned as Brandt, unsure what to expect, held her breath for something bad to happen. Nothing did. She was about to open the channel to Howard and Asha again when her suit translated a slight rumble in the ground through her feet and up into her brain. The radio barked to life inside her helmet.

"Contact," Zero said.

The dull twang of his weapon forced the speakers in her suit to deaden the noise of the report. Two more voices added their own reports to the maelstrom as shot rang out on all sides.

"Someone tell me what the hell is going on," Brandt demanded, as she climbed out of the gun control bunker to the surface.

They had inexplicably come under attack.

"Bart up," Zero responded. Brandt's HUD showed twenty red arrows moving to point the direction to the attacking force. She wanted to ask what they were and where they came from, but all that would do was slow down someone desperately cycling their weapon.

"Aarghuuuh," came a transmission.

The commander glanced at her team display to see that it was Fangs transmitting. She also saw that his personal shielding was down whereas everyone else's was up. She got topside and drew her pulse rifle off her back. One of the red arrows grew larger on her display and moved quickly as it pointed directly behind her. She didn't spin around, but dropped and rolled aside to get back up to one knee and fire her rifle from the hip.

The heavy pulses rocked the silver armor of the humanoid thing attacking her, bouncing back as big scorch marks appeared on the metal-covered abdomen. The build-up of energy proved too much for the attacker and it came apart in two halves.

She stood upright, still seeing the red arrow in her HUD pointing at the thing by her feet. Glancing down she realized that the upper body section was crawling toward her. The right hand raised up to point at her.

Only it wasn't a hand—it was a pulse blaster built into the arm where the hand should be.

She fired again from the hip, drilling shots of energy through the outstretched limb and into the head until the red marker disappeared.

"Headshots," she called out to her team. "They still fight unless you take the head!"

"What the hell are these things?" Kekoa roared.

He dropped his rifle and ducked the wild swing of one of them running at him from behind. He couldn't have concisely described what had just happened, but the neural interface to his suit combined with the drone's view of the battle space allowed him to see the attack without seeing it. He clenched his now empty gauntlets, feeling the long spikes protrude ready for a close-quarters brawl. He pivoted on one foot to bring his right fist up into the head of the thing that had tried to decapitate him. It came away from the body, the head still stuck on the spikes, as Kekoa was pitched forward by three heavy shots hitting his back. He lost half the power his shields possessed with those shots. The percentage marker began to rise again slowly as the onboard power source started to regenerate the shields. He didn't have the confidence that he could take many more close, direct hits.

Kekoa pitched the decapitated head of his last victim at the attacker that had shot him in the back. He then snatched its head back so it couldn't see him deliver the brutal stomp to its knee, snapping the joint backward. The gun hand began to fire and he grabbed it, bending the arm down so that the shots pumped into its own head at point blank range.

Snatching up his gun again, he fired on two more heading for where Payne was saturating the three attacking with her heavy support weapon.

"Thanks," she said briefly, aware of the surroundings like he had been courtesy of Bart.

"Count five left," Zero called out. His gun twanged again twice in rapid succession and he changed his assessment. "Count four."

They fought, desperately and with all the fury of a tight-knit group who had seen hell together. When the last of their ambushers was punched apart by a collection of energy pulses, Brandt called out for a check on their people.

"Sound off," she snapped.

Voices come back in answer, luckily including Fangs who had been dazed and had gone offline while his suit had to reboot.

"Howard," she called, "sound off".

Nothing.

Shooting a glance at Zero, Brandt started running for the hatch to get back to the bunker. The sniper tossed his rifle to Payne who caught it easily and mag-locked it to her back.

They ran recklessly down the stairs underground, all the time calling for Howard to respond hoping that it was just a glitch in their comm channel or that he couldn't hear them so far underground.

They were wrong.

Bursting into the control bunker, Brandt whipped up her weapon to cover another one of the things that attacked them. It was slumped against the far wall like a drunk and tired human. She saw scorch marks and holes punched through the chest plate, with a dark puddle of what looked like oil in the poor light. Rounding the edge of a bank of monitors she saw it wasn't oil but blood—Lieutenant Howard's blood.

It looked like he'd been in an explosion. The light armor of his protection suit had been blown away, severing his right arm at the shoulder. Brandt dropped to her knees to see if she could access the suit and stem the blood flow, but when she flipped him over, she saw that some of his neck and half of his head had been taken by the blast. Resting him back down, she looked up at Asha who still held the blaster pistol and stared at the thing he had killed.

"Asha," Zero snapped, wary of the gun in his hand. "*Asha!*"

The Kuldar snapped back to reality, lowering the pistol and looking at the sniper.

"I'm sorry, Master Petty Officer Zero," he said, "I did not..." A flashing red light, pulsing with urgency, filled the bunker with an eerie light.

"We must leave," Asha said hurriedly. "Now!"

They ran up the stairs, dragging Howard's body without the care he deserved. As soon as they got topside, Brandt called a retreat to the *Tanto*, shouting at Rogers to get ready for dust off.

"Ready, Commander," he replied, sounding out of breath.

They sprinted the distance to the ship which was already ramping up the whining sound of the repulser engines.

"Commander," Payne said. "The water. Look!"

Brandt looked—the lapping waves of blue water near their small spit of high ground vibrated like an earthquake was coming. She stopped at the rear ramp, counting everyone onboard. There was a shriek from one of the engineers as they saw the broken form of the attacker that had come for Rogers while the rest were assaulting the gun position. The pilot had dispatched it and had the forethought to bring it onboard for study as the rest were running for their position.

"This is very bad, Commander Leslie Brandt," Asha said. "Very bad."

"I'm getting that vibe," she said as the ramp rose and the ship took off hard. Before it had fully sealed, she felt the shockwave of the huge detonation on the surface as the bunker self-destructed.

CHAPTER 24

Orbit of Unnamed Water Planet

"Okay," Torres said, sitting heavily in the chair at the head of the table in the mess hall. The briefing room wasn't large enough to comfortably hold all the crew members he had wanted assembled. They were gathered to brainstorm the meaning of what had just happened. "Talk to me. Current sitrep?"

Rogers cleared his throat. "Our orbital pattern is safe. There were six active railgun bunkers on the surface from what we now know, as all of them went supernova at the same time. Seems like our hack of the system triggered some kind of planet-wide cleansing protocol. The explosions were big—equivalent of a forty megaton nuclear blast. Five of those sites were above the waterline with the sixth estimated to be partially covered by tidal swells. There isn't a visible piece of land on the planet's surface now. Total water coverage."

Brandt spoke next, giving a brief rundown of what had taken place on the surface below.

"Asha has confirmed that the tech on the planet was Kuldar, or at least so close to Kuldar that it can't be a coincidence." She paused as they felt a small swell of pride quickly stifled by the alien who must have enjoyed being described as a key member of the crew. "The issue is—and this was confirmed by Lieutenant Howard before he was killed—the tech and the language are more evolved, more advanced, than what we know current Kuldar tech to be."

Torres looked at Asha, expecting to read his facial expression as he would a human member of his crew but getting nothing. Surprising him, Asha spoke.

"We cannot ignore the chances that my people were not the only Kuldar to survive the purge of the Va'alen," he said, leaking small slithers of nervous tension which made a few people shift position uneasily.

"If more of my ancestors survived and created this place, we must assume that they continued to advance given the materials and resources available to them. My own people had small numbers and were left with very little." He shrugged unnaturally, as though he was merely copying the human gesture.

"Understood," Torres said. He put the prospect of another version of the aliens aside for now and hoped that if they were still out there they wouldn't be a war-like clan of massive bugs like the Va'alen. "And the robot things? Tell me about them."

Brandt responded. "Humanoid, tall, made from some kind of shiny alloy that was partially resistant to our weapons—my guess is if we had old Earth tech we'd have had our asses handed to us. Their hands turn into pulse blasters with similar power and energy signatures to our own. Which adds credibility to the assumption that they're Kuldar." She glanced at Harris for his engineering assessment. He sat upright.

"The alloy isn't anything we know of, probably combining elements not on our periodic chart," he said. "They appeared to have been triggered by the hack from what I could tell, and acted on a pre-programmed defense mode to attack whoever was at the bunker trying to hack in. Unfortunately for Lieu- tenant Howard that was him."

Eyes glanced at Asha since he was present when Howard went down. Harris explained further.

"The weapons tech, as the commander said, is on a par with our own but they lack shielding from what I can tell. We're still in the process of taking it apart to learn more but my best guess is that they're a kind of semi-sentient artificial intelligence able to adapt to follow programming when activated."

"They were easy enough to kill," Payne offered. "But unlike biologicals, you have to destroy the brain or whatever they have to take 'em out."

"Great," Torres said. "Robotic AI space zombies killed my best navigator." He winced internally at the callousness of his statement but moved on. "What did we get from their data core?"

"Not a lot," Harris said. "If you can spare Asha, I'll need him to help with the translation."

"I must remind you, Captain Kyle Torres," Asha said, "that this is not a language I fully have the understanding of. It is like humans of your history meeting you and trying to make your computers work."

"Just do what you can," Torres reassured him. "Having you working on it sure isn't going to damage our chances of learning more."

"Anything else?"

Nobody raised any other subjects, so the captain gave his orders.

"We'll stay in orbit for twenty-four hours. Work on decrypting what we got from the surface but make sure you do it on stand-alone terminals," he said pointing a finger at Harris. "I don't want anything we don't understand connected to the *Ichi*. We're a long way from home to have our systems compromised. I don't want to limp back for repairs a second time. We'll have a ceremony for Lieutenant

Howard in the shuttle bay at eighteen hundred, mandatory attendance of not on duty or rest period. Spread the word. Dismissed."

He rose first and made his way to Asha as everyone else climbed out of their seats. Brandt hung back, joining the other two for the conversation where they could guess without spreading fear and conjecture throughout their small crew.

"What's your real take on these robots?" he asked the two of them when the room had cleared. Both humans felt a stab of unease from Asha, which told them he had a theory that he didn't like.

"My ancestors told stories about how we had developed robotics to help with labor on our home world," he said. "They did the jobs where there were hazards. They did mining and construction works, and some places used them to maintain order. They were called the Guardians, but they were not described to me like the ones that attacked us."

"Things change," Brandt said. "It's conceivable, though, that these Guardians are an evolution of what your people created?"

Asha pulled his head back slightly, an expression like Brandt furrowing her brow. She changed the wording of her question.

"It's possible these things are created by Kuldar, only newer versions?"

"Yes, this is what I fear."

"Fear?" Torres asked, furrowing his own brow.

"Learning that my ancestors became Va'alen," he said after a thoughtful pause, "has been difficult for many. Some of my people wish to go back to the planet you found us on and live simple, peaceful lives far away from war and battles with our enemy. I fear that if other Kuldar survived the purge then they have become another enemy to us and humans."

His mixture of emotions—fear, guilt, excitement—washed over Torres and Brandt.

"Agreed," the captain said. "Let's figure out what we can about them and go from there. I don't want to have to prepare for war with another alien race because we sure as hell have enough on our plates finding the Va'alen."

The ceremony for Lieutenant Howard was brief. The concept of mortality and the danger of their mission wasn't something the crew liked to consider. Having to attend a reminder of their vulnerability to the perils of being in space, of being so far from home and fighting aliens and their robots was a sobering experience.

Torres said a few words, extoling the virtues of a capable man, a good officer, finishing that he was a credit to the UN and a loss to their crew. The lieutenant's body wasn't on display, nor was the archaic necessity of having to eject his body into the void enacted. A little-known secret of all UN ships was that they all possessed an incinerator, which rendered the body of the lieutenant to fine dust in minutes. His sealed ashes would be transported back to Earth when they returned.

The analysis of the partial data recovered yielded little results. Torres wasn't sure what he was hoping for; perhaps a condensed history of the original builders of the railguns along with detailed schematics for their weapons and operating systems and a map to their new world with a friendly invitation.

As it wasn't a kid's fairytale, he had to plan for the worst while hoping for the best. He ordered simulations for Brandt's team in case they encountered these Guardians again.

Similarly, he had the *Ichi's* sensor array calibrated to check for the exact weapons signature of the orbital cannons in case they encountered them again and needed advanced warning.

The cannon's targeting software, given that the guns were no more advanced than the UN's own hardware, was the real military prize to him. It would only serve to underline that he had been the right man for the job. He wasn't so naïve as to think that there weren't dozens of other senior officers ready to take his place with more experience than he could boast.

At least that was before he'd found himself at the sharp end of the last almost year of unprecedented excitement.

When the call came over the comm requesting his attendance to the engineering department, Torres acknowledged and forced himself to walk slowly and not run. He arrived there to find Brandt had also been summoned and had arrived first.

"It is Kuldar," Asha said quickly when the captain walked in. "This is without any doubts."

"Talk to me," Torres said. He crossed to where Asha stood beside the damaged chassis of the Guardian and not a terminal like was expecting, imagining results from the data core and not the combat drone.

"Chief Engineer Ralph Harris has located a targeting subroutine in the programming of this unit," he said as his long fingers danced over a datapad. Torres smirked in mild amusement at his engineer's reaction to his name and title said out loud the way Asha did with everyone. "This routine recognizes Va'alen as enemies, just as we do, but they attacked your people because they were not classified. Before the unit was damaged by Lieutenant Nathan Rogers it had already created a targeting profile for humans wearing armor. It also explains why I was able to destroy one without it killing me. My theory is that it recognized me as one of its own creators."

"So they're wirelessly connected and think fast," Brandt said. "Great."

"Any indication of where they went?" Torres asked. "The Kuldar we're assuming left the planet?"

"Nothing yet," Harris answered, his head still bent over a terminal. "Is this something command would want to know?"

"I'd say it is," Torres answered. "Keep working on it and we'll check in with the admiral in the CS as we work along the set route."

CHAPTER 25

Gaia Neos

Eze's unit had been trained well, to a point. They were mostly new recruits bolstered with experienced NCOs and some officers taken from other units. Those who had been brought in to pass on their experience had been promoted as a reward.

These new promotions were awarded to capable troops, but ambition was something that she had to rein in from the get-go.

Her new chief, Ryers, had his hands full getting to know their new people and had to address the unit as a whole within forty-eight hours of taking charge. He informed the officers that their attendance wasn't required, which coincided with an officers briefing held by Eze.

Ryers began with a PT session that stole the air from their lungs in spite of the oxygen-rich environment on the planet. This was his way of getting their full attention before he issued the mother of all reminders—he and his NCOs were not their parents and they weren't interested in every little problem the soldiers had.

"You got a medical issue," he called out loudly after they had been beasted for almost an hour, "take it to your squad leaders and see a medic. You got an issue with your orders, *keep it to your goddamned selves!*"

After they had acknowledged his orders, Ryers put them through what he called a 'sickener' to remind them that they were UN troops and not there on vacation.

"What's a sickener, Chief?" one of the master petty officers promoted in had asked loudly for the benefit of the troops.

"Good question," Ryers answered just as loudly. "When people start chucking up their breakfast then ask me again and you'll have your answer."

He alone seemed to enjoy the mammoth PT session. At the end of it, plenty of troops wanted to see the medics but none of their complaints reached the ears of the master petty officer responsible. Lesson learned, Ryers paraded them for an hour of drill just because and dismissed them to get cleaned up.

As green as most of them were, the fact that they were being led by experienced combat troops was a reassurance.

Eze's officer briefing, in contrast, was conducted inside where the risk of being pushed to their physical limits was minimal. Her words, however, reminded them that their deployment was as much of a vacation as the troops were enjoying.

"Those kids out there," she said nodding at the window of the prefabricated building they occupied as the unit run past in formation for the third time, "are looking to you for leadership. Leadership is *not* passing up every little complaint to the top for me and the Chief to fix." She eyeballed the officers: eight ensigns, four lieutenants and two lieutenant commanders. Half of them seemed competent and the other half at least willing.

"We're deploying tomorrow night back to Gaia," she said. Issuing these orders was the main reason for the briefing. "Our task is to begin rendering the surface safe for colonization."

A hand rose at the back. Other officers leaned aside, revealing a young ensign.

"What is it, Edwards?"

"Commander, what exactly do you mean by those orders?" He seemed to know exactly what it meant but wanted it clarified before he spoke out.

"It means, Ensign," Eze said maintaining eye contact, "that there is a significant wildlife population we need to cull from our AO before the colony ship arrives in a week. That clear?"

"So we're just going to wipe out all the animals on the planet?" he shot back, bordering on insubordinate.

"Those are the orders, Ensign," Eze answered in a warning tone of her own. "But to appease your mind we are only clearing this continent. We will be issued with tranquilizer rounds to subdue the creatures and dropships will relocate them to a neighboring continent. We're not here to make anything go extinct, and that includes humans. Do you have an issue with your orders?"

Faces turned to look at the ensign who seemed to deflate under the weight of their combined scrutiny.

"Negative, Commander," he said stiffly. "Just had a moral issue with blood sports is all."

"This isn't a hunting trip," she said harshly. "And neither are our orders subjective; you get told what to do and you damn well do it. This isn't a club you can decide what to do if things aren't to your personal liking."

Edwards's jaw clenched as he bit back a smart answer. He nodded, not trusting himself to answer verbally. Eze marked him out as one to put in the thick of the action and see if he felt the same after a couple of run-ins with giant deer and carnivorous birds standing taller than he did.

"This isn't going to be easy," she warned them. "I've personally diced with a species of mammal in the mountains and it killed one trooper, in armor, while injuring another before half a squad put it down. They may not be firing weapons back at us, but you can bet your ass this won't be an easy ride." She eyeballed all of them, looking for any sign of nerves or defiance. "Get your shit together and give the orders for deployment. PT your own units tomorrow morning and rest them before we dust off at nineteen-hundred. Dismissed."

The whole unit was crammed into two dropships with a third bringing their additional kit and support group, which they needed for operating outside the wire.

The flight between the forest moon and the main planet took them almost an hour. Eze felt like a mother with kids in public—as though she was running around like a demented sheepdog making sure none of them wandered off into traffic. She gave the order as per the manual for them to close up inside their armor, but more than a few jittered in their seats as claustrophobia fought with the fear of being exposed to the freezing vacuum of open space.

Landing inside the base she had come from a week earlier gave her a strange sensation. As Ryers ordered the unit to dress off in full formation, she issued a stand down order for her troops to wait in a holding area away from the landing zone.

"You see an adjutant, Chief?" she asked Ryers. The notice-able absence of any officer from the base command had annoyed her.

"Negative," he answered. "Want me to check it out?" Eze thought for a moment before shaking her head.

"On me," she said. She called out to the lieutenant commander nearest them to keep the troops there.

"Hurry up and wait," he said happily. "Yes, ma'am."

Eze stalked toward the base headquarters with her looming command chief petty officer at her side.

"Franks," she said under her breath, as though the name was a curse word.

"Incompetence or assholery?" Ryers asked, utilizing the close bond between the two true commanders of the unit to cover the insult to a senior officer.

"Both isn't beyond the scope when it comes to him, I think," Eze answered.

The adjutant manning the desk at the headquarters was flustered but reset and coped well when Eze demanded to know why their barracks hadn't been organized and why they had to come looking for someone from HQ to tell them what the deal was.

"The commander is—" she tried placatingly.

"The commander is what?" Eze shot back, startling the lieutenant trying to mollify an armed and armored senior officer with a reputation. "Is he busy? In a meeting? Having a pedicure?"

"The commander is aware that you've landed," she said, glancing nervously behind her in the direction of Franks's office.

Eze gave a nod to Ryers. He would stay at the desk and eyeball the officer trying to cover for the asshole commanding the base.

Eze walked into his office unannounced and without knocking. Franks sat upright in his chair so fast that he dropped his datapad. It fell on the desk and showed a colorful moving display with enough exposed skin to show that he wasn't engaged in urgent matters pertaining to the effective running of the base.

"What is the meaning of—"

"Shut your mouth and sit your fat ass down," she growled, shutting the door behind her. She spoke in a low tone which promised more pain than any raised voice could suggest.

"First off," she said as she poked an armored gauntlet into his chest and making him recoil, "you withheld my orders and my promotion. Why?"

"I—I received no such ord—"

"Bullshit," she snapped, still in the low, menacing tone. She didn't want any witnesses to what she was going to do to him. "You're a liar. Secondly, get someone to billet my troops, right now, and get the resupply order for the specialist ammunition brought to our barracks in one hour." With that she smiled, her face changing from the promise of violence to calm appeasement in a flash.

"Thank you for your assistance, Commander," she said before turning on her heel and leaving his office quietly.

She kept her face an emotionless mask, as did Ryers until both had left the building. They were halfway across the parade square when they both cracked up into a fit of chuckles.

"You should've seen his face, Chief," she said.

"I think I heard his ass squeak," he replied.

Their accommodation orders were brought by a red-faced ensign less than four minutes later, along with a quartermaster's authority to draw stun munitions from the armory. Eze knew she wouldn't get the ammo brought to them—that wasn't how military stores worked. The only ammo to come to them would be a field resupply, and she hoped that wouldn't be necessary yet.

Her unit bagged their bunks, stowed their gear and filed off in squads to do what all troops landing at a new base did. They went to find food.

CHAPTER 26

Boken Sha Ichi

"Dropping out of Fold in three, two…" Rogers counted down as the *Ichi* shuddered slightly.

They had performed another twelve jumps since the planet that had once been occupied by Kuldar—or at least an unknown sub-species of Kuldar. Those lines were becoming more blurred all the time.

"Report," Torres said automatically. He didn't really need to give the order, but he'd been feeling a little redundant since they'd fallen quickly back into the monotony of jumping between empty sectors of space and unoccupied planets.

"One G-class planetoid," came the response from tactical.

"Negative for comm signatures," the communications operator announced.

"Take us into orbit and scan the surface," Torres said, idly swiping through the details on his console.

After the adrenaline rush of the orbital cannon firing on them and the brief but costly battle, the crew had fallen back into a routine that sapped the morale from them.

The only crew members not suffering from the effects of that monotony were the engineers and the two Kuldar on board. They pored over what they could recover from the damaged Guardian drone and the data from the rail gun bunker.

They'd learned precious little else since the initial discoveries but that didn't halt the efforts as the rest of the crew continued the main mission—locating the heart of their enemy and reporting back.

The sector of space they occupied was just as empty as the fifty before then. The coordinates for the next jump were calculated and engaged.

"Next stop, approaching the Crab nebula," Rogers announced before he jumped the *Ichi* into Fold space once again.

"Engage the Shroud," Torres snapped. "Tactical, tell me if they've scanned us."

"Shroud engaged," Rogers shot back. "Moving away from jump point at one-third speed."

"No indication they've seen us, sir," the tactical officer said. "Detecting active sensor pulses of our jump location."

"All stop, ready weapons. All hands, battle stations," Torres ordered.

"Captain, we've picked up a signal. It was brief but definitely originated from one of their ships."

"Probably reporting the anomaly before they went to investigate," Torres said. He was trying to sound cool but still felt his heart thumping in his chest. They'd detected two unknown signatures within thirty thousand kilometers of where they had emerged into normal space. "Keep our passive sensors up and let's see what they do."

The two ships, of no design they had ever seen, converged on their entry point in the sector only minutes after their arrival. It had woken the crew from their boredom in a rude fashion as every person onboard the *Ichi* dashed to their assigned duty station.

"Orders, sir?" Rogers asked, his voice tense but resolved and confident.

"We hold here," Torres replied. "See what they do first. Any sign that they're hostile and you jump us the hell out of here; no sense in an engagement we can avoid."

"Aye, Captain."

"Incoming signature," Sarvanto reported from the tactical station.

"Talk to me," Torres said.

"Unsure, sir," the flight officer said. "It's... it's like nothing I've ever seen before..."

"Va'alen?"

"Definitely not," Sarvanto answered with a scoff of disbelief.

"On screen," Torres instructed, leaning forward in his chair. The huge viewscreen wall came to life with what looked like a bright orange tear in space itself. He was about to ask what it was, about to ask what the hell was going on, when a ship appeared through the tear.

It was massive, bigger than their fleet carriers by half. As they stared at the image, a dozen other ships flew from the mothership and spread out in a search pattern.

"Rogers, prepare to make that jump."

Before he could respond, Sarvanto shouted up from his console.

"Five more contacts," he yelled, as they appeared on screen. "Shrouded ships, I think. Our path is blocked... they've surrounded us."

"Get us the hell out of here, Lieutenant," Torres said, before another report from the comm officer forced him to belay the order.

"Incoming transmission," she said. "Running it through translation program now... they're..."

"Spit it out, Ensign," Torres said coldly.

"Sir, they're ordering us to stand down our weapons and identify ourselves."

"Who they hell are they?" the captain asked.

"Sir, the language is the same as we found at the rail gun bunker," she told him. "They're Kuldar."

Torres stood and walked a few paces forward to stare at the massive ship coming to stop. He glanced at the tactical station to see a dozen other vessels, all a similar size to their own corvette class warships, in formation all around the *Ichi*. Realizing that their Shroud device was useless he ordered it to be dropped.

"Guns, power down but remain ready," he added before nodding at the comm officer. "Open a channel."

She tapped at her console and nodded back at him.

"Attention unidentified vessels, this is Captain Torres of the United Nations of Earth. We are not hostile. Request you stand down your own weapons systems and identify yourselves."

There was a moment of silence before eight more signatures appeared on the sensor board as additional ships unshrouded. The comm channel broke into life.

"Earth ship," came a quiet, breathy voice in uncertain English. "We are the Kuldar. We know of your people of Earth, and we know that you have sided with the hated Va'alen. Lower your shields and prepare to be boarded."

Terror rippled around the bridge as the door hissed open and Asha stumbled in looking shocked. Torres swiped the finger of his right hand across his throat to the comm officer who muted their end of the channel.

"What is it?" he asked Asha.

"The Guardian drone just came online," he said. "We had disabled the weapons, luckily, but it has injured two of our engineers."

"This ship," Torres asked, pointing at the viewscreen. "Have you seen anything like it before?"

Asha stared hard for a few seconds before shaking his head.

"Well," Torres said, "looks like we've found the rest of your people."

"Earth ship," came the same voice again, "This is Shalak Tal'ar of the Dreadnought *Koshibiyah*. You will lower your shields and comply, or we will destroy you as an enemy of the Kuldar."

"Do it," Asha said. A wave of pleading reached the captain. "They will not ask again, I do not think."

Torres fought with himself for a second, not wanting to put his ship and his crew at the mercy of anyone else. He lost that battle in his mind. He nodded to the comm officer who activated the channel again.

"Lowering shields now," he said. "We are not your enemy," he tried not to stumble over the unfamiliar sounds of the name, "Shalak Tal'ar. Do not fire on us."

There was a pause from the comm. Everyone on the bridge of the *Ichi* held their breath until the channel came alive again.

"Send your leaders to the *Koshibiyah* to discuss terms," the alien voice said.

The connection was severed. Torres let out a deep sigh of temporary relief.

"Rogers, Asha, with me," he said. "Commander Brandt, the ship is yours. If we don't return get a message back to the UN and escape at any cost." He saw Brandt's mouth open to protest, probably to insist that she came with him and that they wouldn't leave without him.

"Those are your orders, Commander," he said sternly, fixing her with a gaze that meant he wasn't asking a friend. "Get it done."

"How exactly are we going to get inside that thing, sir?" Rogers asked from the pilot's chair of the *Tanto*. Torres, sitting beside him wearing a standard flight suit, thought about it for a moment.

"I guess when we get closer, we'll figure it out."

He had ordered both Asha and Rogers to dress the same as he had, not allowing them to wear the ready suits and attend a surrender negotiation in light armor. For the same reason, he had relinquished the sidearm he usually wore, as did Rogers and Asha, the latter now routinely going armed after proving himself on the water planet.

The answer to their pilot's question became obvious as they approached the massive ship filling their viewscreen. Their controls were taken over remotely and their ship pulled toward a gaping hole in the belly of the vessel.

"Dreadnought is about right," Rogers said, craning his neck to see up. "This thing must be twice the size of the *Indomitable*."

Torres said nothing, his mind awash with too many what-ifs to relax.

"If I may, Captain Kyle Torres?" Asha asked from the nearest seat behind the cockpit.

"Shoot," Torres said, then frowned and rephrased. "Ask your question."

"If I may be permitted to speak with this Shalak Tal'ar first?" he asked.

Torres made a face again, unable to hide his stress given the gravity of the situation.

"Let's play it by ear, shall we? I don't want them to think that you're running us or we're running you, that make sense?"

"What has your ear got to do with—"

"I mean, let's just see how they are with us. If they aren't friendly toward me and the lieutenant, then you take over."

"And what's our story?" Rogers asked.

"Our story is our story," Torres said firmly. "We travelled to a new solar system, made contact with the Kuldar, got into a war defending them from the Va'alen—"

"Whose asses we kicked," Rogers interrupted.

"—whose asses we kicked, but not before they split with a dissident faction of humans who will have either given them or had taken from them the ability to jump through Fold space. Now we're looking for their base of power so we can come to some kind of peace agreement."

"Is that what we're really doing?" Rogers asked mischievously.

"In theory," Torres told him flatly. "Yes."

"And if they do not make any agreement to peace your United Nations will destroy them as they destroyed my own people?" Asha asked, bathing them in an unexpected wave of anger and hatred.

"Something like that," Torres replied. The interior of their little ship went dark inside the docking bay of the gargantuan ship. "It seems to me like they didn't exactly destroy your people as well as they thought they did."

CHAPTER 27

Va'alen Planet, Edge of the Crab Nebula

Da'kath roared in anger, dragging out the small and seemingly frail body of the Kuldar from the small, sleek fighter ship. He hurled it with an animalistic rage and leapt high in the air, stomping its skull into ragged ruin. His warriors joined in the battle cry and beat their armored chests with hardened claws to fill the air with a percussive, clattering sound.

Chakour cowered and covered his ears. He didn't want to be targeted in their wrathful frenzy. He was hauled up by his collar and felt the ground disappear from under his feet. He was lifted up until his face was only inches from the hard carapace of Da'kath's maw, which now opened to display rows of sharp teeth.

"You were allied with the Kuldar," he said in a tone that could mean a death sentence.

"No!" he cried in desperation. "Not us, not *me*! It was the UN, the other humans. They are the ones allied with the Kuldar."

Da'kath released him with a snarl, letting him drop the few feet to the dirt where he crumpled into a heap and stayed down.

Da'kath turned and gave orders to his warriors who dragged the body of the near-headless Kuldar toward one of their ships. He turned back to the leader of the warriors, pointing a sharp claw tip at him. He spoke in their language as the failed challenger bowed his head and listened. When the former supreme commander had finished, the warrior scurried away to fulfill his orders.

Chakour found himself dragged upright again by Da'kath's mate and half carried back to their ship. There he was tossed inside and instructed to strap himself in again.

As his shaking fingers fumbled at the straps, he began muttering to himself in stress and fear.

"What are you saying to me, human?" the female warrior demanded.

"Nothing," he said, keeping his head down and his voice low in what he hoped was the best way to avoid punishment.

"Speak louder when I talk to you," she snarled. "You have no courage!"

Chakour, unexpectedly annoyed at the insult, fixed her with a look of anger mixed with hate and resentment.

"I was saying that this mess is nothing to do with me. All I wanted for my people was independence from the UN who want to control all humans through power and economy." He wasn't sure how much of what he had said was understood, but she seemed to grasp his tone and defiance. She leaned back in her seat and issued a noise that he took to be a laugh.

"You think this is funny?" he asked. "You think the lives of me and my entire crew are a joke?" He didn't know where his sudden streak of rebellion came from, but he knew in that moment that being killed for angering her would be better than any alternative.

"The lives of you humans mean nothing to the Do-Ch'aal," she spat derisively.

"Is that your own opinion, or do you have to think what he thinks to stay alive? Do you even have a name? You're just as much of a prisoner as I am."

His words must have resonated with her—she shot forward to bump her hard, armored face into his and slam him back against the seat.

"My name is Cho-Da'kath," she hissed quietly as the blood ran down from his nose. Too frightened to move and wipe it away, Chakour let it drip freely onto his filthy clothing. "And I am the Cho-Do-Ch'aal. There is no higher honor for me."

"There is," Chakour whispered, shaking. "You'll never be the Do-Ch'aal, will you? You can only ever be his mate."

She drew back a claw and he closed his eyes, waiting for the end of his torment and suffering. The blow landed beside his face; the cold, smooth claw brushed his bearded cheek, and sent a soft rasping sound into his ear.

Da'kath stepped inside the ship, growling something at his mate who sat back and strapped herself in as the ship wound up for take-off. The G-forces Chakour felt during the climb out of atmosphere made his vision blur and his head swim until unconsciousness took him.

Chakour's eyes opened. One at a time, then both as he came to. He figured out from the muddled sensations feeding back to his brain that he was lying on a cold rock on his left side. Foot- steps, too heavy to be human, thumped the ground nearby as his ears began to work again with a painful pop.

He heard the unmistakable clicks and hisses and snarls of a group of Va'alen talking animatedly very close by, but his eyes focused on one smaller warrior staring straight at him. He wasn't sure if it was a female, a small male or a juvenile but the thing stared right at him and wouldn't take its gaze away.

Chakour shifted position, slowly and carefully to avoid announcing his consciousness to the congregation. He watched as the big warrior in the middle of a group of seated Va'alen thumped his chest and spoke loudly.

"I am the best leader to take our warriors into battle," Da'kath cried, all four upper limbs spread out wide as if to invite a challenge.

One of the large but dull-armored elders sitting near him spoke up.

"This may be so, Da'kath," it intoned, "but you are no longer a Do-Ch'aal. You have no army left."

"I have many warriors still with me—" Da'kath argued.

"—and only a tenth of what you left with," another elder interrupted. "You have squandered the lives of our warriors on a costly expedition. We must discuss how to defend our home worlds, not send you off into space with what army we have left for you to waste their lives again."

"I have not wasted the lives of any warrior," Da'kath spat as he turned on the elder who had spoken to him without respect. "I have brought back the best of our warriors with the greatest prize of all: the ability to move between the stars without using the Gateways."

"If what you say is true, then how quickly can we create these new devices to allow us to move unhindered?" another elder asked.

"My engineers are close to replicating the technology of the humans," he assured them. "Then we can launch an armada to find and destroy this new Kuldar threat."

Clicking and noise from the crowd swelled, growing to a level painful for Chakour. He cringed in the hope of shutting out some of the noise.

"There remains the issue of what happened to my clans- man," a booming, powerful voice rang out. One of the elders climbed to his feet. "What became of Qa'shal?"

"That traitor, that coward, that *kruh'chunn* wasted the lives of almost a thousand warriors."

Grumbling rippled through the Va'alen crowd in angry response to the insults but Da'kath carried on.

"Qa'shal disobeyed my orders. He used clan loyalty to force other warriors to obey him and abandon the expedition, and then he led an ill-fated attack on the humans which I had explicitly forbidden. He is a traitor. He died as a failed challenger."

"You are saying that you killed him, Da'kath?" another elder asked.

"Yes. He went into hiding after the humans wiped out his stolen armada. I had him brought to me to answer his challenge. He failed to kill me."

The news sent shockwaves around the aliens. A disturbance at the back of the crowd moved to the center and a large warrior stepped into the circle near where Da'kath stood. Not many warriors rivaled his height and size, but this one did. He had a shine to his armored body that spoke of a warrior fresh to the fight.

"I say to the clan elders that this traitor murdered my clan brother. I invoke the right of *Sha'rakth*."

"Are you sure you want to do this?" Da'kath offered. "I have told the truth of it as many warriors here can attest to. Do you wish to throw away your life over clan pride when the future of our entire race hangs in the balance?"

183

The warrior said nothing, merely whipped a wide short sword from behind his back and swung it in a wide arc at Da'kath's waist.

The older warrior leapt back to avoid the attack, dodging left and right to duck and avoid the wild flurry of savage blows designed to kill him. He continued to avoid the blade, dropping to the dirt to roll forward. As he stood, he brought the young warrior's right foot up with him, toppling him face first into the dirt.

"I release you from your challenge, warrior," Da'kath said. "You have brought honor to your clan by challenging me."

The warrior scrambled to his feet, no longer as confident as before. He switched the grip of his short sword, drawing another with the lower claw of his left hand to hold both like large daggers. Da'kath stared hard at him in total stillness for a few moments before rolling his neck dejectedly, as though he was being forced to put down an injured animal.

"Have it your way," he said, waiting for another flurry of wild attacks. He dodged again, faster this time with two blades to contend with. All the time he moved he seemed comfortable, while his attacker seemed desperate.

One swipe of a blade scored a line across the back of Da'kath, letting out a screech of metal on armor. Da'kath froze, turning to stare at the challenger as the atmosphere changed.

When he stepped back into the fight, he was no longer toying with the younger warrior but was pressing his own attack. Still he didn't draw his own blade but attacked with claws and feet to force the challenger to defend. When Da'kath left an opening, exposing his head and neck, the warrior roared and swung both blades in an effort to decapitate him.

Da'kath had not made a mistake in leaving his neck vulnerable. Instead his intentional goad had lured the inexperienced warrior into putting everything he had into the killing blow.

Leaning out of reach and spinning low around to his left, Da'kath rose, kicking the warrior's feet out violently from underneath him. He continued the movement upward, grabbing both claws holding the blades in his own powerful grip and slamming the warrior down to the packed dirt face first.

The tips of both blades protruded from the back of his armor directly through the chest, leaking the oily fluid onto the ground. Da'kath stood and scanned in a full circle to take in the elders and the assembled crowd.

"Do any of you challenge my ability as Do-Ch'aal?" he roared, thumping his chest again. His loyal warriors beat their own in support.

No challengers came forward, and the elders were forced to concede to his authority. The one who had demanded to know the fate of his clan warrior stood—a sign of deep disrespect. The hush that descended over the collection was deafening.

As one, every Va'alen warrior except Da'kath dropped to their knees in sudden pain, obeying an external force that they could not overcome.

A pair of Hive Lords floated noiselessly into the circle. Warriors and spectators scattered. Reaching the very center of the area they stopped, one on either side of Da'kath, and spoke in a dual voice directly into the minds of every Va'alen there.

WE DO NOT INTERFERE WITH YOUR PETTY SQUABBLES OF WHO IS THE DOMINANT CLAN, they said. IT IS BENEATH US. WE ARE FORCED TO INTER- VENE NOW, AS THE ONLY ONE OF YOU WITH THE

KNOWLEDGE AND ABILITY TO FACE THIS NEW THREAT IS THE ONE KNOWN AS DA'KATH. YOU WILL ALL OBEY HIM.

With that the Hive Lords left, floating from the area to disappear into the shadows as the aliens were released from their psychic grip.

CHAPTER 28

Dreadnought Ship Koshibiyah

The feeling of being powerless wasn't one that Rogers enjoyed. He still suffered nightmares of being tortured at the hands of an enraged alien. His prosthetic arm itched; he knew this wasn't strictly possible, but whenever the stress of a situation got to him, he always had the same sensations.

The shuttle's sensors showed a safe atmosphere outside. The Kuldar had re-pressurized the docking bay and pumped breathable air back inside. Rogers gave Torres the nod to indicate it was safe and the captain hit the ramp release button. He straightened his flight suit, as the pilot and their Kuldar ally stood beside him.

"Asha," Torres muttered quietly as the ramp lowered, "please stop that."

"I apologize, Captain Kyle Torres," he whispered. The alien got his emotions back under control so that the captain didn't feel the desperate urge to pee courtesy of Asha's nervousness.

"Here we go," Rogers murmured as the ramp revealed the heads of three Guardian drones they had recently encountered. One of them issued a robotic noise, which made Asha jump a little. He turned his head slightly to the others, but kept his eyes fixed on the robots as he spoke.

"We should step out and prove that we have no weapons," he told them.

Torres raised his hands and took a step forward, halting as one of the Guardians took a step closer and settled into what the captain hoped wasn't a firing pose. He turned a slow circle to show he wasn't hiding anything and stepped forward again. If his guess was right, they wouldn't shoot him down.

He was allowed to step clear, noticing how precise the Guardians were as they moved to maintain a perfect distance between themselves and him. One stepped forward, within arm's reach, to scan his body up close with a flat device held in one hand.

"It's okay," he told Rogers and Asha. "Do as I did, slowly. One at a time."

As the others descended the ramp to be checked, they all noticed the difference in how they treated Asha. It was almost as though they were afraid to touch him. Torres chided himself internally—a machine couldn't be frightened. The hangar doors opened after they had all been cleared and three tall Kuldar came into view.

In comparison to Asha's darker grayish green skin, theirs was a shade lighter, more of an ashen gray with an undertone of green; it seemed similar to humans who evolved in different environments on the same planet.

The one at the lead stepped directly to them, waving away the Guardians with a dismissive but elegant gesture of its left hand. It ignored Asha, much to his surprise, and addressed Torres.

"You speak for your people?" the alien asked in accented English.

Actual English, Torres noted, not a translation device changing the words.

"I am the captain of my ship and my crew all answer to me," he said, being precise with his wording as he often forgot to be with Asha. He needn't have had those concerns here; the alien leaned down to look closely into his eyes before it spoke.

"Do you speak for all humans, or are you separate from the winning faction? I know your race has splintered itself recently, and it is not inconceivable that your United Nations is fractured without us learning of it yet."

"Shalak Tal'ar," Asha said, stepping forward and bowing with both hands clutched to his chest in a gesture new to Torres. "I am Asha, mate to our Quee—"

"I know who you are," Tal'ar interrupted without any trace of kindness. "My discussion is with the humans."

Asha bowed lower and retreated a step, leaking the tiniest flash of shock and indignation before he controlled himself. Tal'ar looked at him with something resembling amusement before turning back to Torres.

"Well?" he said.

"I speak on behalf of the largest faction of humans." This was all he could genuinely claim. Tal'ar nodded slowly and turned, gesturing with another elegant gesture for them to follow as he spoke.

"Your kind has never ventured this far from the systems you inhabit," he said.

This demonstrated a knowledge that was so current and certain that Torres had to ask.

"How is you know so much about us, but we knew nothing of your people until we found Asha and the othe—"

"They are *not* our people," Tal'ar hissed, pointing a long finger at Asha. "They are the descendants of cowards who fled and left *my* people to die at the hands of the Va'alen."

Torres and Rogers stood in shock at the sudden outburst. Both had been tense. They had expected to feel emotions radiating from these new Kuldar as they were accustomed to with Asha. The new

189

alien seemed able to control it, up until when Tal'ar spoke and seemed to hit them intentionally with a burst of anger.

Asha, head still bowed in deference, said something in Kuldar. Tal'ar stood up straight and blinked in surprise at him.

"Perhaps," Tal'ar answered in English, though the two men had not understood what their companion had said.

Glancing down at his comm device, Torres read the text translation of Asha's words.

It is unjust to [punish] a child or children for misconducts pertaining to an [ancestor]

"Sins of the father?" Torres asked Rogers.

"The son shall not suffer for the iniquity of the father, nor the father for the iniquity of the son," the pilot answered. He shrugged when he saw his captain staring at him in mild confusion. "Book of Ezekiel, something or other, I forget."

Realizing that their exchange had halted the proceedings, they dropped the subject and made a mental note to revisit it in the future.

If they had a future.

"Mind if I ask how your people know so much about my people?" Torres asked.

"No," Tal'ar responded bluntly.

"Okaaay…"

"Shalak Tal'ar," Rogers said. "How do your people know so much about our people?"

"We have watched you. In your concept of time it would equate to hundreds of years," Tal'ar replied. Rogers shot a brief but smug look at his captain before wiping it off his face in a hurry.

"And in all of that time you didn't make contact with us? Never found yo—Never found Asha's people on Proxima?" Torres questioned.

"We knew the... *others* were there, but neither they nor your people were worth making contact with. It was only when you appeared in the area of the two suns you call the Centauri system that we took notice."

"What? We weren't advanced enough for you to bother with?"

"Not until you learned that space and time do not exist in one dimension," he said.

"No. You were deemed too primitive."

"Wait," Rogers said. "You were in the CS—in the Centauri system—*watching* us?"

"We took close interest in the Va'alen operations there, as we have done for many years. Our ships follow them on their expeditions and pick off groups that are small enough to guarantee success, but we have never had the opportunities we have now." He turned outside a high doorway on the long gangway they walked along, fixing Torres with a hard stare.

"When your people destroyed their way to manipulate the distances of space, we saw an opportunity to begin our offensive."

"So..." Torres said slowly, trying to wrap his brain around what they were learning. "You've just been hiding out, picking off Va'alen patrols in ones and twos until we stumbled into a war with them?"

"This is accurate," Tal'ar said. He opened the door and led them inside, gesturing at a table and chairs for them to sit.

"What about the hundreds of lives we lost fighting them? Don't you think you could've helped?" Rogers asked. The itching in his prosthetic arm bugged him almost to the point of him scratching it through his flight suit.

"This was not our concern," Tal'ar said flatly.

"The hell it wasn't," Torres responded in a quiet voice. "We could've allied ourselves and defeated the Va'alen without the losses. Without the technology falling into their hands—"

"What technology?" Tal'ar asked. "What do you speak of?"

"They've allied *them*selves with dissident factions of humans," Torres said. "That means they have the ability to travel great distances as we do."

Tal'ar's face remained a stony mask, but a bubbling sensation of fear and anger fixed both humans like a hand around the throat.

"You have given the Va'alen this gift?"

"*We* haven't," Torres corrected him. "But they have it nonetheless. What did you mean when you said you launched your offensive?"

"We have begun raiding the furthest settlements of the Va'alen's infestation in this galaxy," Tal'ar said. "We have not begun to attack their home worlds."

Torres thought of the size of the ship they were onboard and the small fleet of corvette-sized warships all no doubt capable of devastating settlements. As if reading his thoughts —which Torres genuinely hoped wasn't happening—Tal'ar looked directly at him.

"You wish to know why we do this now?" he asked. "Because the majority of their war armada cannot get back to this sector of the galaxy. We intended to allow your kind to fight with the Va'alen until they were weakened by your conflict enough for us to wipe them out. You saved us the trouble, so we have pressed our advantage towards their home worlds—*our* home worlds—instead."

Torres sat in silence for a minute just taking it in before Rogers broke the quiet.

"How is it you can speak our language?"

"We know many of your tongues," Tal'ar said. "Tell me, human, if my people were so careless as to broadcast every detail about ourselves to the galaxy, do you think we would have survived for so long? My people have watched your kind since you lived in caves, and only now it appears that you can be helpful to us."

CHAPTER 29

Gaia Neós

Eze inspected her unit, seeing up close how poorly they were equipped. She felt guilty about being in the best armor—at least the best mass-produced armor—the UN had. Most of her people had to don the armor in sections that then sealed together, in comparison to her own which opened up for her to step into.

Some of the larger or smaller of her troops were equipped with the generation of armor previous to the last one. It was the only thing available to fit them. Given the choice between old armor and no armor, they chose the old armor.

"Where are our mech-techs?" she asked Ryers during the inspection.

He didn't answer immediately, so she turned to face him. Her hard-nosed chief NCO folded as soon as she stared him down.

"Redeployed to run security for the civilian section," he said, staring directly ahead of him to attention hoping that good drill would redirect her wrath.

All of their decent gear, all of their spare parts and even their fresh rations had been diverted by orders far higher than Franks's meagre authority. It had all gone to the first colony ship to break atmosphere and land. The majority of the ship was deployed as separate pods designed to be left behind for the propulsion and crew sections returning to Earth to collect the next cargo.

They had watched that ship break atmosphere on its way out, burning a massive swathe across the evening sky. The logo of the company that built it had been visible from over a mile away.

"Hyper?" Eze asked.

"Civilian administrators," Ryers said. "Construction and mining..."

"And they need mechanized patrols *inside* a secure perimeter while we go ou—"

"*Ahem,*" Ryers cleared his throat very deliberately.

Eze took his point and stepped out of earshot of the nearest troops.

"We have to go outside the wire with green troops wearing old tech?" she demanded angrily in a low voice. "What's next? We hunt goddamned dinosaurs in grass skirts with wooden spears?"

"I hope not," Ryers answered quietly.

"Screw it," Eze said. "I'll put the requisition in again personally. Tell me we're fully loaded at least?"

"Yes, Commander. Every squad is carrying lethal and non-lethal ammo."

"Good," she said.

She tapped at her comm device, opening a channel to the suit of every member of her unit. She would address them all without having to shout like an NCO. She had NCOs for that.

"Listen in, people," she said. "Our task is simple enough, but the execution of that task will be dangerous if you do not follow my orders to the letter." She paused to let that soak in. "Squad leaders, you have the responsibility to order the deployment of lethal force if anything poses a risk to the troops under your command. Our primary goal is the subjugation of the dangerous indigenous wildlife and we will have a team of contractors flying modified transports to remove them from this continent. Should any of that indigenous wildlife pose a genuine risk to your personal safety or that of the person beside you, you *will* use lethal force. If it's an us or them scenario, it's us. Every time. Is that clear?"

She forced down the smile that threatened as her troops responded to her words. She wasn't sure she'd ever get over novelty of having her own unit, even if they were under- equipped and getting screwed over by the UN and the contractors.

She was under no illusion—they were the most expendable of all the people on the planet. Any ground-pounder can replace another but skilled engineers, pilots, construction and surveying specialist? They would require more expense and difficulty to replace in a hurry.

It was bad enough that their heavy weapons platforms, as aging as they were, had been redeployed by central command. They were deemed unnecessary to the pest control missions they were about to start running.

"On your six," came Ryers's muttered warning Eze turned to see four armored shapes approaching. "Dismiss the unit, Chief," she said.

"You *Easy*?" the one at the front asked. This was a joke Eze had heard many times, but had broken the finger, wrist, both lower arm bones and dislocated the elbow of the last person to try it. She hadn't found herself suffering the sexist jibe much after that.

"You looking to get your ass kicked?" Ryers growled as he returned from dismissing the unit.

Eze let the two men square off, like dogs circling one another, before she called a halt to it. Ryers had the guy on height, and if it wasn't for the fact that the newcomer with the smart mouth was wearing brand new prototype armor, she was sure her NCO could have taken the guy.

"Stand down, Chief," she said. "Can't you smell private corporation privilege when you step in it?"

"I can smell something, Commander," he grumbled, still eyeballing the cocky man.

He smiled, angering Ryers even more, then spoke to Eze again.

"Vickers," he said. He extended a hand to her as though Ryers leering eight inches from his face suddenly no longer existed.

"So very nice to meet you," she said. "You can call me Commander."

Vickers smiled, clearly more accustomed to dancing to this particular tune than he suspected she was.

"Pleasure is mine, Commander. I've taken the liberty of having your orders amended if you care to take a look?"

"Why don't you give me the highlights?" Eze said in a bored tone. She would not give this asshole the satisfaction of seeing her face when her orders were amended by a civilian.

"Very well," Vickers said. He seemed almost deflated that the small display of power had been denied him. "We're escorting a team of scientists who will tag and catalogue the animals for relocation. They'll also mark the ones they want stunned and the ones your..." He waved a hand uncertainly towards the troops filing away as though he didn't know what to call them. "...people can enjoy some target practice on."

Her jaw clenched a little, the muscles in her cheeks tensing and ebbing, which made his eyes light up. He seemed pleased he had got even the smallest of rises out of her.

"We'll be in the air overhead," he told her. "I'll let you know what we need, okay Commander?"

He turned away without waiting for an answer, shooting Ryers a sly wink as he went. He hoped that the chief would lose his composure and find himself put down in front of anyone still in sight.

"Leave it, Chief," she told him quietly as the four mercenaries walked away laughing.

"You know how things can go wrong in a firefight, Commander?" Ryers asked.

"Oh, I know things can get confusing," Eze admitted wryly, "and if they do, I just don't know how our corporate bullies will cope…"

"I wish," Ryers said sourly. "Knowing my luck they'd have me on camera putting two in the back of that asshole's dome."

"Then don't get caught," Eze said.

She was only half listening as she scrolled through the amendment to her orders. They put her and her unit at the disposal of a detachment of the Hyper scientific studies group.

~

It pissed her off no end that she had to take orders from privileged mercenaries. It pissed her off even more to see her own troops using out of date gear and enduring hardships when the mercenaries were riding around in dropships and sleeping in beds each night.

The mission wasn't simply a wander-around-and-see-what-pops-up deal; they were targeted toward specific areas where groups of the larger carnivorous animals congregated. The scientists called them game trails, and Eze's unit worked with another similarly underequipped unit to drive and trap the animals in large nets which were suspended underneath one of the small fleet of dropships.

If any of her people had a moral issue with what they were doing they kept it to themselves. That was lucky for them; her patience was already wearing dangerously thin with all the other problems of command. One of those major problems was their equipment, and by the end of the second day in the field she had to redeploy almost twenty of her troops from across the board due to armor failure.

Damaged charging ports here, faulty battery units there, a failed movement servo—though at least that looked hilarious when the trooper tried to report to her while dragging his right leg behind him like a zombie. By the time he arrived in front of her and saluted, she and the rest of the unit were in fits of laughter.

Eze ended up with a worryingly high attrition rate after three days. Those troops undeployable to the front line found themselves standing guard over the forward operating base.

She ordered Ryers to get the individual squad ensigns to report their figures and requirements to get their squads fully operational again. She then found herself holding a datapad with requirements for no less than twenty-three replacement armor suits and a list of spare parts that spanned four screens. Add to that the fact that they were on field rations, and the inexperienced troops who still found the tablets to be a novelty were making the rookie mistake of not taking enough water with them. That then gave her the added headache of the medics running out of laxative medication.

Without an early resupply, her unit would be at half strength at best within a week. She didn't want the professional embarrassment of having to be withdrawn from her mission due to what would no doubt be called avoidable failings.

"More goddamned lists," she complained to Ryers. "Recruiter lied to me…"

"Recruiter lied to all of us," he answered. "Told me I'd be serving somewhere with a beach and a bar."

Eze smiled at the old jokes, no funnier than they were years before. Both of them had heard the tired lines, that were now more comforting than amusing.

"What's your plan?" he asked her. "I know you're cooking something up, so spit it out, Commander."

Nobody else in the unit would have spoken to her like that. Even the two officers directly beneath her in the chain of command who permanently vied for her approval would never dare talk to her like that. The chief was different, as was their relationship. He was the true second-in-command. Her officers knew this, hence any advice he might give them was received as though their commander had given them a direct order. Eze was grateful for it; being the one in command made for a lonely existence sometimes.

"By the book first," she told him. "Urgent resupply order to base command."

"Franks?" Ryers asked incredulously. "That sack of ass wouldn't send you a re-up of water if your head was on fire!"

"I know," she said. "So I send it with an urgent marker for immediate acknowledgement with a timescale and copy fleet into it." She pointed one finger to the sky to indicate the fleet.

Ryers smiled.

"Then if said sack of ass tries to ignore your order, it gets flagged to the admiral and he gets chewed out."

"And we get our gear," Eze said.

"And if said sack of ass decides *not* to risk upsetting the admiral..."

"Then we get our gear," Eze finished.

"Sounds perfect," he admitted. "Only issue is whether they even have it in this system to give us."

"With the stores on the *Venture* and the *Anvil*?" she asked. "It's up there somewhere. We just need to find a way to get it down here."

CHAPTER 30

Dreadnought Ship Koshibiyah

It was a lot for Torres to take in. It was a lot for all of them, in truth, but Torres was fighting with his mind on fast forward trying to piece it all together.

Asha was still and quiet, with no emotions coming from him other than a small, black cloud of quiet anger. The two humans tried to ignore it, in case it opened up the floodgates of feeling blasted at them.

The dreadnought ship they were on wasn't what it had appeared to be. With something of that size, they expected a massive orbital bombardment array or dozens of smaller warships to deploy. It could have been an interstellar weapon of war.

It was all of these things, but it was much more.

The Kuldar had been open about themselves and their history. They showed their guests around the ship as though they had nothing to hide. It was a warship, a carrier, but above all it was the home of their entire race.

Vast open areas inside the ship allowed for dirt beneath their boots and trees over their heads. The foliage had dark leaves, the likes of which they hadn't seen before. As they noticed more about their surroundings, so too did the humans see differences between Asha and his people and these new Kuldar. Their eyes were smaller and the lighting on their ship much brighter than they had seen the Kuldar endure. Asha had to wear his goggles as he did in the human environment. It made him feel as much of an alien in their presence as he felt with the crew of the *Ichi*.

Children ran around in packs, hissing their laughter at the strange aliens. The rest of the Kuldar went about their business like any civilian population would.

"The outer areas of the ship are restricted to military operations," Tal'ar explained. "The protected core is where our people live. The outer layers and the docking areas are out of bounds to any Kuldar without military authority."

Rogers marveled at the sights like a child at a theme park; his mouth hung open as he spun a slow three-sixty under an open area extending maybe twenty stories. Far above him was a bright light that bathed the open area in what simulated a sun's glow. Asha stayed back to the shadows as Tal'ar spoke.

"Our smaller ships are not capable of tearing the fabric of space like your little vessel is," he said. He carried on, unaware he had slighted their ship. "Instead our ships all come home to the *Koshibi-yah* and we perform the ... what do you call it? The *jump*?"

"That's right," Rogers said. "So you're a carrier? A mothership?"

Tal'ar gave a small bow.

"That is correct, Lieutenant Nathan Rogers," Tal'ar said. "Our name, the *Koshibiyah*, means 'Life Mother' or 'Species Mother' in your tongue."

"Cool," Rogers said.

"So how can we work together?" Torres asked. "How can we form an alliance to counter the Va'alen threat?"

Tal'ar's face dropped from one of proud leader to a dark mask of controlled anger. "Not here. Our people do not know of any conflict."

Torres didn't know how he felt about that, but kept his mouth shut and his opinions to himself. They followed the tall alien off what he called the promenade and back to the darker, less comfortable outer sections of the ship. There they took a lateral lift pod to what Tal'ar called the control deck.

As the tall doorway slid open, Rogers again understated the magnificence of seeing another race's culture and technology at work.

"Huh," he said. "Like our bridge... kinda."

"Bridge?" Tal'ar asked Torres, still pointedly ignoring Asha's presence as he quietly followed the group.

"It's an old Earth term. Our ships used to sail on water and were powered by paddles. We burned fossil fuels to make steam and the steam turned the paddles. Guess we just kept the term 'bridge' because it was comfortable." He shrugged.

Rogers stared at him in mild amusement that his captain knew such archaic, though useful, facts.

"So your control deck," Tal'ar asked Rogers, "your *bridge*, it is similar to this?"

"Lemme see," Rogers said, pointing a finger at specific Kuldar at individual stations. "Helm control. Communications." He swept his finger from left to right and back again as he pointed out each station. "Sensor array. Weapons and tactical?" He looked up at Tal'ar hopefully.

"Almost correct, Lieutenant Nathan Rogers," he said. "Behind you is the weapons array. What you thought was that station is our..." He seemed to struggle for the word so spoke in his own language and gestured at their comm devices.

Torres looked down and saw the words, EXPLOSIVE DEVICE THAT TEARS SPACE AND TIME TO CREATE AN ARTIFICIAL TUNNEL FOR EXPLOITATION. He read the words twice, then shot a glance at Rogers whose raised eyebrows echoed what his captain was thinking.

"Your own ability to travel through space and time is no more safe than ours," Tal'ar said, picking up on the shock of his human guests. "Your Fold drive does the same thing to the fabric of space and time, believe me."

Torres shook off his concern. "So, what can we do to help each other out?"

Tal'ar led them to a side room, similar to their own briefing rooms, and invited them to sit. The difference between the human equivalent and this room was that there were no chairs, only a cushioned ring surrounding the table set low to the deck.

"My people have spent hundreds of your Earth years living in the void of space," Tal'ar began. "We have colonized planets and lost many of our kind to the roving patrols of the Va'alen. This is where our people developed the technology we have in common. It was based on the science used by the Gateway rings which the Va'alen took control of, but those rings existed long before our people." He waved a hand encompassing Asha, acknowledging him for the first time. "The Va'alen discovered the ability to fly in the skies, leave a planet and head for the stars. It was when we managed this that we found the rings and began to study them. But then the war broke out among us and the Va'alen took their own path."

"So you know about the Va'alen?" Torres asked. "What they are inside?"

At the mention of the autopsy, Torres felt a wave of repulsion mixed with anger wash over him from behind. From the front, he felt a sharper stab of hostility, which Tal'ar quickly brought under control.

"We know that we are all from the same beginnings, but that we took different paths. The Va'alen chose the path of war, we chose the path of science and peace, and..."

"...and *my* people had the freedom to choose removed," Asha spat.

A tense moment of silence hung heavily over them. Tal'ar broke it, speaking solemnly.

"As you know from your experience on the sector defense planet we abandoned," he said, shocking them with that reveal, "and from your lack of reaction to our Guardians, you are aware of our ground fighting capabilities. We cannot destroy them with drones and from the air alone; we need the help of humans to attack the Va'alen, destroy their ability to travel between the stars, and end this war forever."

"And what then?" Torres asked. "What happens after the Va'alen are trapped to one solar system without the ability to attack again?"

"Who said anything about trapping them?" Tal'ar asked.

CHAPTER 31

Bridge of the Indomitable

"Incoming sub space communication, Admiral," his comm officer said to Dassiova in his quarters. "Priority coding."

"Put it through," he said, getting up from the couch. He had been dozing, but he shook it off and sat at the desk in front of his terminal.

"This is Dassiova," he said, taking a sip from the coffee that had gone cold.

"Torres here, sir. Are we secure?"

"We are; how're you holding up?"

"Long story, Admiral. I need to fill you in on the details before we take this to command."

"Sounds big, Captain," Dassiova said as he sat forward. Torres seemed tired and drawn, like a man with the weight of the galaxy on his shoulders.

"It is," he replied. "Still trying to wrap my head around it.

We've located the Va'alen's home system. It's about three lightyears past the Crab Nebula."

"Well, alright then," the admiral responded. "We mobilize and take the fight to them before they can build a fleet of ships with Fold drives."

"It's more complicated than that," Torres said solemnly. "There's another player in the game now."

Torres brought Dassiova up to speed with the events of the last week—everything from the advanced tech and Guardian drones to the discovery of what he was calling the new Kuldar.

"Way above both our paygrades, I think," the admiral told him. "The distances are too far to run a conference call with Earth Command. Are you able to get back here?"

"Affirmative," Torres said. "I've bought us a week before we're due to meet them again and decide what to do."

"Okay," Dassiova told him. "How long before you can get back to the CS?"

"Two days," Torres said.

"I'll have a meeting set up for when you arrive. God speed."

By the time the *Ichi* blinked into real space a few thousand kilo- meters inside the outer reaches of the Centauri system and broadcast their identity, orders had been sent for the ship to dock with the *Indomitable*.

"Bring us in, Lieutenant," Torres said to Rogers. He tapped out a message for Brandt and Asha to meet him in the main airlock.

"Mister Sarvanto?" The tall Finn looked up. "The ship is yours."

The *Ichi* looped in, turning on the spot as she lowered to the upper hull of the massive carrier. Soon she was gently docked beside a dark-hulled corvette.

"That doesn't look military," Rogers said as the ship came into view.

"It most certainly does not," Sarvanto agreed.

Dull clanking noises reverberated around the ship as they were locked tightly to the bigger vessel and a hard seal was established. By the time the pressure had equalized, Torres,

Brandt and Asha were ready to step off their ship. They were met by two troops in dark armor with sidearms holstered against their thighs.

"CP?" Brandt said. "To what do we owe the pleasure?"

One of the special operations troops smiled at her, offering a hand for her to shake.

"Broughton," he said. "We're here with the director of the American territory UNID as our principal. We have orders to escort you to *Omaha Two*."

He led the way, a lingering gaze falling on Asha for a moment too long. Something about it made Brandt uneasy, and she knew it wasn't just Asha's emotions leaking onto her. He had been a closed book since parting ways with the new Kuldar.

The dark corvette, still smelling brand new from the ship-yards, was evidently their ride. The crew was all in darker flight suits than the usual ship's uniform.

"This a dedicated CP ship?" Torres asked.

"Yes, sir," Broughton answered. Any further details were left unsaid.

Torres guessed that he would have to ask the right, specific questions directly to get any more information. This soldier felt cagey.

Their journey to the station near to the red dwarf star was short; the captain of the ship ordered a short jump to cover the distance in a couple of minutes. They weren't given any more information until the corvette docked by the nose to the station and Broughton led them through the airlock to a well-guarded conference room.

Several people stood when they entered. Brandt recognized a few present, but what was most noticeable was the lack of any admiral ranks. Something about the atmosphere told her that the decision makers were operating behind the scenes.

At the head of the table, presiding over the meeting in spite of having no military rank, stood the UNID head man Chase Ettington.

"Come in," he said. As ever his face was an emotionless mask that never seemed to match his words. Instead of the tailored suits he usually wore, Ettington was dressed in black clothing that was seemed tactical and yet still expensive. He introduced the people sitting around the table and invited the newcomers to take the chairs at the end of the table so they could begin.

"Get the feeling we're on trial here?" Torres muttered to Brandt as they sat.

She shot him a concerned glance in answer.

"I'll get right to the point," Ettington said. "We're here to learn what you've found out about the situation in the galaxy before we decide how best to proceed."

Torres explained, starting with the discovery of the advanced tech on the abandoned planet before he was interrupted by an admiral he didn't know.

"It's *unfortunate*," he said with heavy emphasis on the word, "that you didn't recover any more of that technology. It could've been useful going forward."

"What we did recover, Admiral," Brandt said in stern challenge, "cost us the life of an officer and almost our entire crew."

"Unfortunate indeed," Ettington said flatly, conveying no emotion other than a hint of annoyance that the report had been interrupted. "Please, continue."

210

Torres explained about the Guardian drones, about what they had learned from the one they had recovered. He detailed how Asha was able to kill one of them because it didn't recognize him as a threat in its targeting matrix. He went on to say how the tear in space had opened and the dreadnought ship surrounded them with smaller warships before he was interrupted again by another officer in UNID uniform.

"We're having all of your sensor data downloaded from the..." He looked at a datapad. "*Bōken-sha Ichi*."

"We call her the *Ichi*," Brandt said. "And what do you mean you're downloading our ship's data?"

"Your ship's information on the extra-terrestrial contact will be secured by UNID to prevent any unauthorized trans- mission or security breaches," Ettington said.

Both Torres and Brandt stiffened at the implication. Ettington held up a hand to stop any protests.

"It's necessary information security, Captain," he told Torres. "No aspersions are being cast on your command or your crew, we just need to control the information. The vast majority of people on Earth are ignorant of the real situation out here; they know we've fought against a hostile alien race over territory, but the scope of that conflict is *not* public knowledge."

"So, people on Earth who are clamoring for the chance to colonize the new worlds we have don't know this place could be a war zone again?" Brandt asked.

"No, Commander," Ettington told her flatly. "They don't. And if we can resolve this issue quickly then they'll never need to know. Humanity can keep growing and colonizing Gaia without the risk of interstellar war."

"When you say *resolve* the issue," Torres asked, "you're really talking about wiping out a species of sentient aliens who have the same fundamental goals as we do, right?"

"The Va'alen are not the same as us," the angry admiral shot back. "It may not fit nicely in your little world of right and wrong, but we have to do what's right for the human race."

"And for our Kuldar allies," Ettington said with a false smile aimed at Asha.

Torres and Brandt felt a sudden stab of revulsion and worry, quickly brought under control before it spread out to the others in the room.

"So, you want to ally with the new Kuldar and wipe out the Va'alen?" Brandt asked.

"In an ideal scenario," Ettington said, "we would set territory lines in the galaxy and agree to stay out of each other's way unless through established trade routes in neutral areas. But something tells me the Va'alen wouldn't agree to peace."

"So the plan is genocide?" Torres asked.

"The plan is to defend ourselves and our interests," the admiral growled, banging a soft-handed fist onto the table. "By whatever means necessary."

"History," Ettington said in a calm voice, "has something of a habit of repeating itself, doesn't it? Look at how people spread out over Earth a thousand years ago; there were conflicts and wars but eventually we evolved into peace, on the whole, and that's what we want to achieve here."

"Might I remind you, *Captain*," the admiral said acidly, "that your duty is to follow the orders of the UN and Earth Command, not to galivant across the galaxy making friends with everyone."

Torres chewed the inside of his cheek. His jaw clenched. He let out a tense breath. He knew he wouldn't win any argument with what he was certain was a desk-admiral, and neither could his small ship and crew affect anything resembling change on a galactic scale. The wheels of human expansion couldn't be stopped, and the people in charge had decided that the small obstacle of an entire race of aliens was a small price to pay for that expansion.

"Your orders are to return to the Kuldar and invite them to meet with representatives of the combined Earth Command," Ettington told them. "Specifics will be sent to you by secure comm. I think we're done here. Unless there's anything else? Good. I know it goes without saying but I'm going to say it anyway—everything discussed inside this room is known only to those in this room. No mention of this meeting, the points discussed or any part of the *Ichi's* mission is to leave the minds or mouth of anyone. I trust you'll make that abundantly clear to your crew, Captain Torres?"

Torres nodded.

"There is something more," Asha said quietly. He gained the full attention of everyone in the room. His crewmates beside him felt nothing—no leaking of emotions they could use to gauge what he would say. His focus was absolute.

"Please," Ettington said, "enlighten us."

"Have you considered the next logical step after all-out war against the Va'alen is complete?"

"The next logical step is to form a peaceful alliance with your people and agree territory, like we sai—"

"They are not *my* people," Asha told the admiral who had spoken. "My question was what you would call rhetorical." He stumbled over the word and glanced at his comm device to be sure he had spoken correctly. "*My* people were left behind like your cavemen while these new Kuldar became more like the Va'alen than they understand. They want war. They want to do what the Va'alen did to all of us—to all Kuldar and Va'alen. They want to rule as the supreme race. So, I ask you, what will stop them turning on your people and my people when you have killed every last Va'alen with them?"

The room was silent as faces turned to look at one another. "That question," Asha said, "was not a rhetorical one."

CHAPTER 32

Gaia Neós

"You're sure about this, Commander?" Ryers asked for the tenth time.

"Yes," Eze told him. "We'll be at sixty percent combat effective if we don't get a full resupply and new gear soon. There's no other way."

"You could report up the chain of command," Ryers said in gentle admonishment, "instead of circumventing it entirely."

Eze shot him a look, feeling slightly guilty that he was right. He was only trying to help her out. But crying to the admiral and withdrawing her unit from the field wasn't the greatest start to her first real command.

"I'm hardly circumventing anything, Chief," she lied. "I'm just omitting certain facts from the orders."

"Which is a court-martial offence," Ryers said. Eze threw her armored hands up in mock surrender.

"Fine, Chief," she said. "Have it your way, but we're going out with five squads. Five. And those five aren't even fully equipped as it is. I've got willing troops without combat armor, and I'm leaving behind three squads because they lack the right gear. That puts the remaining five at heightened risk, which I won't allow."

"Then we should report that we're unable to deploy and ask for an urgent resupply or reinforcements."

215

Eze sighed. She knew her chief was right, but her pride and ambition were getting in her way. With an angry stab of her finger, she deleted the orders she had written and started again.

She wrote about their failure of equipment, their lack of appropriate gear and support lines. She also requested that the resupply contain the list on the attached file, which included everything they needed to be fully combat effective again.

Hitting send, she satisfied herself that she had done all she could, including laying the blame on a few key people who wouldn't want their names attached to loss of life reports.

Ryers took the datapad from her and checked it, issuing a small huff at what he saw. The subject heading seemed a little melodramatic and the admiral was personally copied into the comm sent to base command, fleet deployment control and the quartermaster general's office.

"Happy?" she asked him.

"Commander," he said wryly, "when have you *ever* seen me happy?"

~

Deploying to the least dangerous areas with her diminished force was a constant source of conflict between Eze and the Hyper mercenaries running the science team. Their apparent leader, Vickers, was too blasé about the risks to unarmored troops—as any asshole riding above the battlefield in a dropship would be. As far as he saw it, the risks were negligible. The problem was that he was only considering the risks to himself and the scientists.

Twice already her urgent requests for resupply had been declined; the last comm advising her to 'use her initiative' and 'make do'. She half expected someone to tell her that there was a war on, didn't she know?

Eze took half of her unit, leaving the mostly unequipped half behind at their forward operating base. With forty of her troops, along with their NCOs and officers, left defending the hilltop against what they were referring to as 'critters', she led the mission. They were to clear a particularly dense stretch of jungle where creatures that resembled large crabs lived in the shady leaf mulch beneath the canopy. They were believed to be similar to the scorpion crabs Brandt and her team had found on the nearby forest moon where they'd trained before deploying.

The description of the animals—or whatever they were designated as—made her certain that she didn't want to be stepping through the dark without armor. Her brief to the troops was flat and bordered on ruthless.

"These things are pests here," she told them. "This isn't a capture mission, luckily."

Chuckles ran through the assembled ranks as she addressed them. She had been unable to stifle a shudder down her spine when describing their targets.

"They're mainly nocturnal, so expect to find them sleeping off whatever they did last night. Live rounds only, squad leaders will inspect you all before we move out."

The plan was archaically simple; start at one stretch of the patch of jungle and proceed with one squad through the dense undergrowth to the far end, shooting everything they encountered. Any of the critters who made it out of cover on either flank would be picked off by the units there. The last unit comprised mostly of her heavies—the support squad with their 12mm squad support weapons—would be at the far end of the trees ready to dispatch their quarry.

"I'll lead the squad inside the trees," she said. "The Chief will command the stopper squad. Questions?"

"What do we do with the ones we kill, Commander?" asked a petty officer.

"Leave them," she told him. "It's all part of the great circle of life or something like that. Move out."

When they were set up, she linked the squad leaders to her net on a closed loop and connected to the squad net that she moved with. After a comm check with Ryers and the other squad leaders on either flank, she called the advance.

It didn't take long for the plan to fall apart. She had to call a halt after a hundred paces; her line was so strung out across the difficult terrain that the plan was no longer effective.

"Eze to overwatch," she called on a separate channel. "Vickers, go."

She stifled a curse at having to speak to the man.

"The plan's ineffective," she reported. "We can't get

through this terrain on foot. Recommend withdrawing and using the gunships, over."

The gunships were a resource that she couldn't authorize because they were a Hyper asset and not under UN control. Having to report to a civilian and ask to use their toys was degrading and insulting.

"Negative on gunships," Vickers told her. "But there's an alternative..."

"Which is?"

"Scanners up here have detected a central warren of some kind. Looks like it's their nest or whatever. Recommend deploying heavy ordnance directly."

"Define *heavy ordnance*, over."

"We've got something for it," Vickers told her. "My team will deploy it if you can spare a few competent people as a protection detail?"

Eze muted her mic and swore using language that would make her chief blush. Once she had centered herself she re-opened the comm link.

"My squad converge on my position," she ordered. "All other squads to remain in place and standby to engage anything coming out of the trees that isn't us."

She waited for her acknowledgements before advancing her squad to the marker Vickers sent to her HUD. As they approached, the trees above began to shake violently under the onslaught of a hovering dropship. Thick cords snaked down through the canopy. The sound of heavy zipping filled the air and Vickers's team of four mercs descended, followed by a heavy case strapped to two lines. They touched down deftly, stepping away from the lines as the crate thumped down. Two of them to step forward to pick it up.

"All-round defense on my team," Vickers ordered Eze over the open channel for all of her troops to hear.

She bit back the first thirty things she wanted to say to him and gave her own orders, ignoring him. It was the only professional way to make her point in front of the troops.

The advance took close to fifteen minutes. Finally they arrived at the HUD coordinates and Vickers began giving orders on his own channel without even bothering to include Eze. His team assembled the device from the crate and started to move back before one of the armored goons literally dropped through the dirt in front of them.

Eze tried to break into their channel via her suit's software but couldn't. She hailed Vickers with no response. He spun in circles with his rifle aimed at the ground. She stepped toward him quickly and hit him hard on the shoulder. He spun, bringing up his rifle and squeezing off a burst of automatic fire, which luckily missed everyone since Eze had grabbed the barrel of his gun and kept it pointed at the deck. She released him and tapped a finger to the side of her helmet. After a pause her comm filled with panicked breathing.

"Where's Navidi?" he yelled, on the edge of losing control. "Where the hell is Navidi?"

"Get your people back," Eze yelled at him. She suddenly saw the measure of the man and didn't want the panic to spread among her untested troops.

Shouts sounded all around her as the ground below them began to churn. Massive claws poked through the dirt to grab at the ankles of the troops.

"Light 'em up," she bawled, though her troops didn't need the order to open fire when they were being ambushed in close quarters. The air filled with the percussive cracks of burst fire as her squad began to withdraw.

"Stay together," she ordered. "Break cover. Go go go!" She turned back to Vickers who had his reflective visor fixed on hers. "Is the device armed?"

"Navidi's dow—"

"Is the goddamned device armed?" she snapped, slapping her gauntlet against his helmet for his undivided attention.

"Yes."

"How long?"

"Three minutes," Vickers told her weakly. She took a breath to master herself. Now was not the time to kick his ass for not sharing relevant intelligence. She spun him toward the gaping hole in the wet dirt where his Hyper underling had disappeared.

"We can't go d—"

"Navidi?" she yelled.

She dropped into the hole and her HUD swam with red outlines. She spun to find a massive armored creature reaching out a fat claw the size of her head. She opened up with her rifle and smashed a ragged hole into its hard shell. It dropped, blocking the path of one behind it, trying to climb over the body. She drilled it through what she hoped was its head, then reached down to her feet where her gauntlet met the resistance of more alloy. Grabbing it, she hauled up while still firing her rifle one-handed. The resistance fell away as Navidi came with her. She climbed out of the hole, spinning Vickers again and forcing him ahead of her as they crashed recklessly through the dense undergrowth to escape the imminent blast.

The rumbling ground announced the detonation before the blast shockwave rushed past them. It then sucked them back to the source of the implosion hard enough to bend trees. They burst out into the open ground from the tree line, running away from the cover that could still contain massive animals capable of damaging them even in armor. Once clear, they turned to assess their casualties.

The troops from the cut-off groups had converged on her. They all seemed to be staring or turning away to remove their helmets and double over.

From Navidi's upper body, entrails had uncoiled during their rapid retreat and streaked away from his severed waist. She dropped the dead hand she held and turned to fix Vickers with a hard stare.

221

Before she could say anything, her helmet speaker burst to life hailing her unit's callsign from what sounded like a flying dropship.

"Send it," she said, after acknowledging the hail and identifying herself.

"Orders from fleet," the voice said. "Current tasking is rescinded. Report to base for immediate redeployment."

"Be advised, my unit is down to half strength due to lack of refit and resupply, we're unable to re-deplo—"

"Refit and re-arm scheduled in orbit, Commander," the voice said before signing off.

Eze turned away, not even bothering to acknowledge Vickers's presence again.

CHAPTER 33

Bridge of the Ichi

"Everything?" Torres asked.

"Everything," Harris confirmed. "They damn near purged the entire ship's operating system while they were at it. Ended up with a gun in my face when I tried to stop them messing with the new shield harmonics subroutines."

Torres blinked in surprise, turning to look at Specter who nodded slowly.

"A UN trooper pulled a live firearm on you for protecting your ship from having its coding purged?"

"Not for long," Harris said with a smirk, also glancing at Specter.

"Something I need to know?"

Specter smiled crookedly, his scarred face contorting the lines of his cheeks. "I took it away from him," he said simply with a shrug. "I gave it back, eventually…"

Harris chuckled before he got a hold of himself. "In two pieces."

Torres glanced at Specter again, trying to look stern but he was losing the internal battle not to smile. He turned on his heel and went for the console beside the command chair.

"Other than the removal of the hardware—the drone and the terminal," Sarvanto said, "they have purged every trace of the sensor data from our servers. She literally has no memory of what we've done for the last weeks."

223

Torres bit back his thoughts about the shady dealings of the UN, since he had returned to find their ship had been effectively quarantined. He made a move to protect his crew. Hitting the icons on the console he opened a ship-wide channel.

"All hands, this is the captain. You're aware by now that all data we recovered from our mission has been seized and is treated as highly classified." He paused, taking a deep breath. "Now, while I trust each and every one of you implicitly, the UN Intelligence Directorate is less than happy about classified information getting out, so I'll remind you: no details of our mission or our findings are to be discussed outside of the confines of this ship and crew... Now, take twenty-four hours to refit before we head back out there. Torres out."

Before they left the system again, Torres accepted an invitation for coffee from Dassiova. Ten minutes before the appointment, he left the airlock of the *Ichi* intent on making his way to the carrier's bridge when a low whistle sounded from the dim corridor. He turned toward the sound, ready to admonish whoever it was for whistling at a senior officer, when the whistler stepped forward into the glow of a deck light. The fleet admiral stood before him.

"Sir, what are y—"

Dassiova held a finger to his lips to silence Torres before jerking his head to indicate he should follow. A hundred yards down the gangway, the older man dropped back to fall in step with the younger.

"UNID corvette turns up and quarantines your ship, you get whisked away to *Omaha* while troops have your docking level locked down, then you come back and say nothing?" Dassiova summarized. "Doesn't take a genius to figure out that some shit's going down.

Also strange that I get two new members of bridge crew rotated in who happened to hitch a ride on the very same UNID corvette."

"Not even subtle," Torres said with amusement.

"Not in the slightest," the admiral agreed. "Anyway, thought you'd appreciate the chance to stretch your legs."

Torres followed the lead toward the aft section of the carrier. He was enjoying the chance to move unrestrained and not on a treadmill as he'd been forced to for weeks of being confined to the *Ichi*. Even being onboard a UN recon ship as luxuriously appointed as the theirs was gave a sense of claustrophobia after a while.

Climbing down three decks of ladders, they arrived at the cargo and docking areas, near the large storage bays designed for storing parts and gear that kept the fleet of dropships and the eight gun barges all running smoothly.

Given that they had a permanent station in the sector and the massive forge ship in the *Anvil* to fill those requirements, the bays had been mostly empty.

Until now.

Two armored troops, minus their helmets, stood guard with rifles locked to their backs. Both snapped to attention when the admiral and the captain approached, but neither threw up a salute—no doubt adhering to Dassiova's standing orders for anyone on his ship. The door was activated and they stepped inside.

It was like an open-air UN field camp inside the hangar. Areas were separated off and duffle bags piled in neat sections. Everything looked efficient. Urgent activity indicated the threat of someone coming to kick their asses for slacking off.

Elsewhere they saw knots of troops sleeping, resting and otherwise conserving energy.

"Hurry up and wait," Torres murmured with a smile of appreciation.

"I've heard their CO is a real ball-breaker," Dassiova said as he took long strides toward the central hub of activity.

Torres already knew who it would be before he arrived at the desk littered with datapads and with a gaggle of junior officers hovering nervously nearby. They made their way to the woman sitting behind the pile of urgent work. She had the sleeves of her fatigue shirt rolled up and was sweating in the artificially warmed metal cavern.

"Yes?" Eze asked, not looking up. She was skim reading a report, but sensed the presence of someone standing in front of her.

"Ahem…" Ryers said deliberately.

Eze looked up, her face splitting into a broad smile. "Kyle!" She stood and rounded the desk, hesitating a moment before throwing her arms around his neck. "When did you get back?"

"Late yesterday," he told her. "Got caught up in… stuff." If she was annoyed, it didn't show at all.

"I trust you found your resupply, Commander?" Dassiova asked. She released Torres, lowering her height as she rested her boot soles back on the deck.

"I certainly did, Admiral," she said enthusiastically. "And if you're responsible I'd like to thank you on behalf of my unit. I had guys with old rifles and no armor throwing insults at bugs the size of dogs down there."

Dassiova reflected her serious words with a feigned ignorance.

"I'm sure I have no idea what you're talking about, Commander. It's not my personal responsibility if a resupply vessel is found to have faulty repulsers in need of an overhaul, resulting in the need to ship their cargo off-deck for repairs."

226

In that one sentence he explained exactly how he circum- vented the bureaucracy of fleet logistics after the official request had been denied. Eze's troops had armor, whether it worked or not. Since they weren't on the priority list, the resupply query was dismissed as an attempt to get an upgrade in the confusion of deployment.

"And if I *was* responsible," Dassiova went on, "then I wouldn't have necessarily done you a favor. You're being re-deployed."

Eze's face fell; luckily for Torres she didn't turn her disappointment in his direction. He would've done anything to see her happy. He needn't have worried, though, as Dassiova filled her in quickly.

"I now have eight units at my disposal assigned to the *Indomitable*. Yours is one of them. Can't say much for the accommodation but I'm assured these areas were actually designed for troop transport, among other things."

"Fine by me, Admiral," she replied. "Where are we going?"

"Can't say yet," he shot back a little too quickly. "But they're shipping out more troops and contractors from Earth over the next few days. Planet side operations will be left to the civilians."

Eze looked at Torres, putting two and two together. They must have found the Va'alen home world and the UN were gearing up for an invasion.

She turned and barked. "Dismissed."

The officers loitering around her open-air headquarters all scattered.

"Commander," Ryers said as he watched the others go and moved to take a pace backward.

"You stay, Chief," she said. "Chief Ryers, meet Fleet Admiral Dassiova. Captain Torres you already know."

"Honor to meet you, sir," Ryers snapped as he stood straight.

"Good to have you here, Chief," Dassiova said. He knew the man by reputation via his own former chief.

"So we're invading?" Eze asked in a lower voice. The three men leaned in to hear her.

"Not quite as simple as that," Dassiova said. "You leave that part to others for now. Not sure if you've noticed, but I have four units and eight dropships. That leaves me no drop- ships and to spare if I assign each unit even half of their allotted two each. That means I need at least half of your unit qualified on combat drops. How many you got so far?"

Eze and Ryers looked at one another, exchanging a knowing look.

"Two," they said in unison.

"We'll get it done, sir," Eze assured the admiral.

"Sir," Torres interjected. "Might I borrow the commander for a debrief on the most recent combat drop training before they start?"

Dassiova smiled in mock disappointment.

"Start tomorrow, Commander," he said. He gave them a nod and stepped away.

Torres said a brief goodbye to Eze and caught up with the admiral. The two walked in silence for a while after Torres thanked him. Dassiova ignored the thanks but spoke eventually.

"I wouldn't ask you to breach protocol and discuss anything you're not allowed to discuss," he said carefully. "And I certainly don't want UNID breathing down my neck any more than they already are. But I'm going to go ahead and take a guess at something to see what you think..."

Torres counted the steps in his head, reaching six before Dassiova spoke again.

"You found the roaches' planet and we're going there," he said.

"Admiral, I'm unfortunately unable to discuss classified intelligence without direct authority from Director Ettington," he responded woodenly.

Dassiova took that as a yes and carried on.

"But you found something else there," the admiral guessed. "Something that left you and the cloak and dagger brigade with your panties all twisted."

"Again, Admiral," Torres replied quietly, "I'm afraid I can't discuss any matters relating to the Va'alen threat or the proposed alliance with the new breed of Kuldar we discovered unless Director Ettington authorizes me to do so."

"Understood, son," Dassiova said. "Understood."

CHAPTER 34

Crab Nebula

The *Ichi* jumped out of the CS, making the series of long jumps back to their objective. Before they left, before Eze's unit began dropping from the hull of a familiar frigate onto the planet's surface, no fewer than nine ships had arrived near to their orbit of Gaia Néos to transport people and equipment down to the surface.

Of those nine ships, five belonged to Hyper while another two were from other large private corporations. Two were UN, both troop carriers built on the same scale as Dassiova's first flagship, the *Venture*. They were retrofitted with a double-skinned array of shield emitters and new pulse cannons acting as what they were now calling PDTs—point defense turrets. They were really not more than glorified buses with the sole purpose of jumping into a sector and deploying the twenty-eight large dropships. This would then get the fourteen units of ground-pounders onto the deck of an enemy planet to do what they did best.

Arriving in empty space at the agreed coordinates, Torres called for an all-stop. He set his bridge crew to using the sensors to locate the shrouded ships he was certain were out there. The sensor data from their first meeting with the new breed of Kuldar had been wiped, leaving only their personal memories of the brief encounter to develop a way to detect the ships.

They waited for over six hours, constantly on high alert. Finally, an alert from the tactical station sounded and made the ensign in front of the console jump.

"Sub space tear detected," he called out.

Torres stood, requesting the signature to be put up on the viewscreen. The rip in space showed a planet on the far side that was quickly obscured by the dreadnought ship and at least a dozen smaller vessels.

"Incoming hail, Captain," reported the comm officer.

"Put it through." The face of Tal'ar replaced the image of the tear in space.

The tear closed up and the Kuldar got straight to business. "Have your leaders agreed to our proposal?"

"They have," Torres responded. "They want a representative from your people to accompany us and discuss the finer details."

Tal'ar turned to one side and spoke in his own language before looking back at the human captain.

"I will send an envoy to you," he told Torres. "They have my full authority to negotiate on behalf of my people. Also," he leaned forward, "if you fail to return we will eradicate your presence in the system before returning to destroy the Va'alen."

"I assure you," Torres responded stiffly, "that won't happen. We are offering you an alliance, not looking for war."

The Kuldar made a noise which Torres took as a scoff.

"Humans only know war," he said. "Your history speaks of nothing more."

The comm went dead, cut off abruptly.

"Friendly bunch, aren't they, sir?" Rogers said from the helm.

Torres was saved any response by the report from tactical. A Kuldar shuttle was inbound requesting docking clearance. Torres gave orders for the shuttle bay to accommodate their visitors, then turned to Brandt to ask if she would show them to the guest quarters held in reserve.

Brandt went to the shuttle bay to meet their wary and seemingly unfriendly new allies, picking up Specter on the way. He fell in step beside her. Without his armor, he walked soundlessly like a predator.

They waited as the shuttle bay re-pressurized. When the lights went green and the door slid open, the two soldiers walked forward to meet the envoy, standing at the rear of the smooth-lined ship waiting for the ramp to lower.

They waited over a minute until Brandt's boredom and annoyance overcame her manners. She stepped forward and banged her boot against the fuselage.

"Bridge to Commander Brandt," her comm sounded. She acknowledged the hail, hearing the voice of the comm officer on the bridge.

"Message from the Kuldar, Commander. They said they'll stay inside their ship until we arrive at the meeting."

"They know it's going to be a couple days?" Brandt asked. She couldn't understand why anyone would want to stay holed up inside a shuttle when they didn't have to.

"I've informed them," came the terse reply. "They're adamant."

"Fine by me," Brandt said, considering another futile jab of her boot at the shuttle. She left the shuttle bay, ordering it locked down. She detailed Beale to organize a two-troop guard on the doors at all times.

"They want to play not-friendly," she muttered to Specter. "I'll respond in kind."

"Commander Brandt to the bridge," her comm said.

Specter said he'd stay on the outer doors until the troops arrived. Brandt acknowledged the order and made her way back up to see the captain.

"That's wise," Torres told her as she followed him into the briefing room.

She grunted her acceptance of the compliment, still seething at the lack of cooperation from their envoy.

"I think it's a case of us being the middle-men," Torres went on. "They don't see us as the decision makers, so they aren't wasting their time building any kind of relationship. Don't take it personally."

"Fine," she said. "But put me on record saying that I don't trust them."

Torres stiffened, becoming formal to match her tone.

"Noted, Commander," he said. "But try to remember that we follow orders. Perhaps running around the galaxy with too much autonomy has made you forget that point?"

"Not at all, Captain," Brandt told him. "I'll follow my orders, wipe out our enemy. I'm just saying that we need to consider the risks of getting in bed with another alien race that might turn out to be just as bad."

Torres stared hard at her for a while before standing. "Dismissed." He left the briefing room and marching onto the bridge to order their jumps calculated back to the Centauri system.

He was angry.

He was angry with the Kuldar, angry with the UNID for pulling their strings, putting victory and wealth over the moral obligations that should rule them. He was a soldier with a diplomat's heart. He wanted to seek a peaceful resolution to the boiling pot that threatened to throw them in to all-out war, but he was also prepared to put himself, his ship and his crew on the line to get the job done.

He sat in the command chair in a pensive silence. The *Ichi* moved between the points in space and time back to their objective, and he couldn't shake the feeling of dread that Brandt was right.

That was why he was angry with her.

Arriving back in the CS, he hailed the *Indomitable* from his quarters to inform the admiral that they had their principals onboard—away from prying ears on Dassiova's own bridge. It was a small victory over their political handlers. He then ordered another jump back to the space station where Ettington would no doubt shut him out of the negotiations.

"Sir," the comm officer said, "*Omaha Two* is requesting we hold our position."

"They give a reason why?"

"Negative, Captain," she told him. "They're requesting acknowledgment."

"Hold position, signal the station we're complying."

The wait was close to thirty minutes. Torres's mind ran riot with the possible reasons their precious cargo would be delayed.

Their answer came when a trio of smaller ships dropped from Fold space less than ten thousand kilometers off their stern. Not one of the ships hailed them. Instead they moved straight in for one of them to dock with the station before the *Ichi* was cleared to dock, though they had been waiting almost an hour.

CHAPTER 35

Omaha Two

With no shuttle bay large enough to accommodate the *Ichi*, Torres had to personally go to the shuttle bay after asking his comm officer to alert the Kuldar that they had arrived and would have to walk through the ship to the negotiations. They sent a curt acknowledgment and only made the slightest concession.

The other ships held all of the negotiators from Earth Command, a large contingent of which met them by the airlock. The visiting Kuldar, just three of them wearing simple robes, said nothing to the crew of the *Ichi* as they were led through. This behavior further solidified Torres's mistrust of them, and when they were escorted away on the locked-down station the captain and his entourage were left standing by the airlock at a loss.

"Come on," Brandt said. "Let's see what this place calls coffee." She tried to walk to the crew quarters of the station but found her way barred by an armored trooper bearing the logo of the CP team on his shoulder.

"Stand aside," she said, mustering the power of her rank and moving to bypass the guard.

He moved to block her again, his reflective visor giving nothing away and only showing her own angry expression back to her.

"I said move, soldier."

"The station is on lockdown," he said, his voice slightly distorted through his suit's speakers.

No 'ma'am. No 'commander'. Just a flat tone leaving no room for argument. Brandt began to draw herself up, a vein in her neck pulsating as though her angry indignation was looking for a way out. Before it could find its way to her mouth, Torres stepped in.

"Let's go," he said.

He pulled her arm gently and felt her tense against him like she was going to throw down with the guy, armor or not. He pulled her arm a little more forcefully, leading her away back to the airlock. She stayed silent and bottled up her anger.

As they reached the heavy doors to the airlock the *Ichi* was docked to, another small group walked out of the nearest airlock. Admiral Dassiova stepped out along with three other senior officers. He locked eyes with Torres for a brief moment before being escorted away in the same direction as the Kuldar had been taken.

Brandt held her tongue until their airlock opened. Once on the other side of the door, she let fly a string of curses dripping with angry indignation before Torres silenced her with a hand on her shoulder. She deflated, shrugging his hand off her and speaking quietly.

"I know, but you'd think after everything we've done, we'd at least get a seat at the table."

"I think our last meeting had a bearing on that decision, don't you?"

Back on the bridge Torres gave a nod to Sarvanto who vacated the command chair and reported the latest news.

"The Tenth Fleet are dropping in," he said.

Dassiova took a seat at the table, three places own from where Director Ettington sat presiding over the meeting. He began by welcoming the Kuldar representatives. He spent some time assuring them that the United Earth Command was serious about forming an alliance with them and that the purpose of the meeting was to agree a plan to remove the Va'alen threat from the galaxy.

The way he so casually spoke of genocide made Dassiova shift uncomfortably in his seat. The admiral was fine with a war. He'd suffered enough and lost enough of the men and women under his command to feel justified in killing the warriors who threatened the survival of humanity and hindered their efforts to expand. Ettington's implication of wiping out every one of the aliens left on their home worlds to gift the planets back to the nomadic Kuldar just felt wrong.

The aliens responded with their own pleasantries, speaking accented English and surprising most the assembled UN uniforms seated around them.

"We agree to form an alliance with your people," the one who was speaking on behalf of his race said. "The details of which are what we have come to arrange here, in this place." He gestured around him at the bulkheads of the conference room.

"And after which," the Kuldar to his left said in a softer voice as she leaned forward, "we will agree territory that will not be breached by your kind."

"All in good time," Ettington said with the falsest smile as Dassiova had ever seen. "First we need to deal with the threat to both of our people. Now, as you know the Va'alen have captured technology from a dissident faction of humans. That faction that is no longer a problem to us, bu—"

"It is our understanding that this faction chose to ally themselves with our enemy, which makes them our enemy also," one of the aliens interrupted.

"I assure you," Ettington said firmly, although still wearing his politician's smile, "the humans calling themselves the Middle Eastern Alliance are finished. They hold no military or political power and the territories they claimed to back them are back under United Nations control. You have my word."

"We are…" The lead Kuldar hesitated as he thought of the right word to use. "…*unaccustomed*, to taking anything on the word of anyone—human or Kuldar. We believe in actions, not promises."

"Well, *we* operate on good faith," Dassiova cut in. Every head in the room turn toward him. "That's what we're offering."

The room was silent as the alien regarded the admiral for a time. Ettington cleared his throat to speak but the slender fingers of the Kuldar's hand raised to silence him.

"You are a warrior of your people, are you not?" the alien asked.

"I am," Dassiova said. "All my life. I've fought against humans and Va'alen, and *both* have been treated as enemies so long as they put the lives of my people in jeopardy." He held the gaze of the Kuldar just as intently as it was mirrored. The intimation that he would defend the interests of humanity was so strong that Ettington cut in to steer the conversation back to where he wanted it.

"And with our alliance, that staunch defense extends to your people also," he said smoothly. "Your message said that you wished to join our forces together to fight our common enemy, which is what we're here to discuss. That's a given. Perhaps it would be better if we discussed what happens after that?"

The subtle tactic of showing the negotiators the final prize was a good one. Ettington had used this maneuver during many conversations when he was tasked to convince someone to do something. The lead Kuldar looked to his right and his companion produced a disc-shaped device, which it slid onto the expansive table. This prompted a small gasp from one of the younger officers, which caused a moment of embarrassment.

The device sparked to life, flickering a bright green and red display over the table. The lead Kuldar manipulated it with slender fingers to expand the display and fill the open space between the assembly.

"The Va'alen occupy *our* true home worlds here," he said. He magnified a system with four highlighted planets orbiting a large star. "Everything on this side of the nebula will remain Kuldar territory after they have been removed. No human will pass the nebular without an invitation, and any incursion will be seen as an act of war."

"You have my assurance that we will respect your boundaries," Ettington said confidently. "We will draw up a line through the galaxy to mark your claimed territory. Might I suggest we make arrangements for a buffering zone or at least a system classed as neutral where our two races can mix freely and trade?"

The three aliens glanced at one another before the leader moved the holo-display to a system without any habitable planets.

"We would suggest this area for our people to establish permanent stations," he said. "It must remain free of military presence, however."

"We can make that happen," Ettington said. It was simple to make promises that he didn't have to keep just yet. "In the meantime, shall we discuss how best to defeat the Va'alen?"

CHAPTER 36

Va'alen Home Worlds

The appointment of Da'kath as the supreme commander of all Va'alen sent strong ripples through the clans that threatened to spark a civil war.

Only the interdiction of the Hive Lords stopped tribal bloodshed from erupting. They visited each clan to enforce their subservience. The message to their entire race was clear: eradicate the new threat to their galactic dominance or face annihilation.

In a brutal mirroring of the negotiations taking place lightyears away, Va'alen clan leaders were demanding greater territories. Their claims depended on the number of warriors they could put into the war and clan allegiances, though these were mixed so fluidly that they seemed destined to tear them- selves apart before any invading force could attack.

Da'kath stayed out of the squabbling, trusting the senior clan leadership to absorb the lesser houses into their own when the time came. The clan leadership would force all of them to swear their allegiance to him as their supreme commander. His only direction was to remind clan leaders that the lives of their warriors were required in sacrifice for the good of all Va'alen and not to be wasted in petty clan warfare.

He wasn't so naïve as to think that he could hold his warmongering race together without the support of the Hive Lords. However, as most were more concerned with what their own clan could gain from winning the war, he focused on waging that war against an enemy they knew almost nothing about.

His engineers, brought in from all over their empire, picked apart the downed Kuldar ship to its individual components. At the same time, others were busy stripping the interior from the captured human ship and forcing the remaining aliens to explain how the schematics for their Fold drive were to be interpreted.

The engineers Da'kath had working on the remnants of technology left behind when their gateway was destroyed had a head start. Soon the construction of other carrier ships was underway.

They lacked the time and the materials to equip each of the smaller vessels with the technology. Instead they focused on the quickest and easiest way to transport their warriors over vast distances—just as the humans did with the ship they had captured. That vessel was stripped of all human comforts, allowing it to hold hundreds of Va'alen ships, just as the bridge was retrofitted with controls suited to their anatomy.

It took them only two weeks to build reconnaissance ships from their existing fleet by merging the new technology with their own. Of those ships only four were lost to catastrophic malfunctions, losses the supreme commander dismissed as an acceptably small number.

"Bring me the human," he ordered his honor guard. It was comprised of the best warriors each clan had to offer.

Chakour was dragged to him whimpering and cast down at the foot of his throne in the clan citadel. He stayed in the dirt. He had learned from experience not to move unless he was told to.

241

Da'kath ordered him to stand.

He did, struggling to his feet awkwardly. His emaciated frame barely held the weight of his body upright.

"Tell me," Da'kath said, "what use do I have for you now that we have your technology?"

Chakour was exhausted, but he retained enough self-preservation to come up with an answer—any answer—to prolong his life.

"You think my species isn't still out there, looking for you?" he asked, careful not to look directly in the face of his tormentor. "They are, believe me. Do you know enough about how they think? About their tactics? You need me to advise you."

"Why you?" Da'kath asked. "Why not any of your people that still live?"

"Because I am the most senior among us," he said. His lip twitched as his words consigned the other captives to death. "I know people on Earth, influential people, people with power and money. People who could help in the future."

"I have no interest in speaking with your people," Da'kath said with a dismissive wave of his claw, "only eradicating them like vermin. You may still serve a purpose. That is the only reason you yet live."

He stood and swept a claw through Chakour sending him sprawling to the ground. A warrior snatched him up by his ragged collar and dragged him back to the cage they kept him in.

The speed at which the Va'alen engineers and warriors worked to build and repurpose almost everything they could use to create an armada-carrying fleet was astonishing.

The small group of three ships, including what had once been the *Weapon of God*, seemed paltry in comparison with the massive numbers of vessels the humans had fielded. Each of those three ships, however, was quite literally crammed with many of the smaller fighting vessels the Va'alen preferred.

Every possible weapon not assigned to orbital or planetary defense systems was taken under the authority of the supreme commander and transported to the stations orbiting their world. There they were rigged to the hulls of the ships.

There were only three. The creation of working replicas of the Fold drive on Chakour's ship had been the slowest part. Creating the massive superstructures of the new ships had been easy, but it took twice that time to fit the drive cores, shield emitters and Fold drive technology. Under the guidance of one of the surviving humans, they had connected the drive to a separate power source linked to the forward shield array. This would prevent any mishaps that might lead to their ship dropping out of Fold space in parts spread halfway across the galaxy.

He alone seemed unfazed by their status as hostages, living only for his work and deciding that this new occupation was what kept him alive. He threw himself into it.

Senior engineer rating Al-Hashim had formed an interesting working relationship with the Va'alen engineers. He had been given to them like someone might hand over an operating manual. Once he saw their potentially catastrophic efforts to recreate the technology, he jumped up to wave his arms at them. Anything to stop them. Even the threat of a claw grip- ping his face and squeezing with just enough pressure to distort his moustache—an oddity the Va'alen found distracting—wasn't enough to dissuade him from protesting. When it became clear that he was trying to help them build it properly, he quickly became a key member of the team. Al-Hashim was so useful, in fact, that the Fold drive he helped construct was completed a full three days ahead of the other. He was trans- ported to oversee the final stages of that, and it felt curious to be escorted by his three large Va'alen comrades. They in turn felt a pet-like fondness for the short man with stick-thin legs and a barrel of a torso underneath his fearsome moustache.

Al-Hashim's efforts and cooperation earned him preferential treatment, which did not go unnoticed by the other captives. They began to offer their own help and expertise to their captors with renewed fervor, giving a small boost to the speed of the fleet's readiness. He and two others—a navigator and a shield technician—were aboard the first of the new ships when it was ready to conduct test flights.

With no ceremony at all, no deep breath of anticipation and hope, the Va'alen pilot keyed in the coordinates and jump pattern. The chief engineer assigned as the test run captain called out the order without hesitation. Al-Hashim drifted away from his position as the ship vibrated violently. He dragged himself upright to look at the nearest console, fighting the sickening sensations of the zero-G—the Va'alen didn't use grav emitters as humans did. The icons on the screen meant nothing to him, but they weren't flashing in warning colors. That gave him a small hope of surviving.

The Va'alen at the helm turned to click and rattle some guttural noise at the captain who responded similarly. Al-Hashim felt the ship come about—something he would barely be able to detect in a new Earth vessel with gravity-creating emitters at strategic points throughout the ship. He guessed that the jump was successful. They repeated the sequence of uncomfortable events to return to their start point.

A clicking noise, sounding both dull and shrill at the same time, reverberated throughout the bridge. The Va'alen seemed to be congratulating themselves on a successful mission.

The wide hangar doors slid open to accommodate the intended cargo to continue testing. The ship had been constructed simply, resembling a long tube with wider, flatter outer edges. Al-Hashim founding himself wishing there was a viewing window he could watch from, marveling in the purity of engineering being to solve any problem. If he could have witnessed the inaugural carrier flight of the Va'alen, he would have seen ten of their fighter ships spin on their horizontal axis and back into the exposed sections of the hold, which all ran toward the central spine of the simple vessel. They took one section each, their ships clamping to the flat deck purposefully built to be large enough to fit the ships in columns before the doors sealed them inside their ships like coffins.

He imagined for a moment what it would look like for one of these ships to arrive in battle, without warning, and disgorge the hundreds of ships it could hold into a battle like the emptying of a wasp's nest.

He imagined what two of those ships would look like, expelling fighter ships in unison. He settled on a single word that didn't quite do it justice.

Terrifying.

He couldn't shake the imagery of the swarming wasps pouring angrily from nests, even as he was led away to help fix some new problem.

Until that point, he hadn't considered the consequences of his work, only the work itself. Imagining those wasp's nests pouring out their incensed occupants in Earth orbit sobered him in a heartbeat.

CHAPTER 37

Station Omaha Two

"The full fighting force of the Ninth Fleet remains under my command," Dassiova responded flatly. He stared Ettington in the face until the man had the good sense to look away at some unnecessary piece of information on a datapad.

"Admiral," Ettington said, "I assure you that all military decisions in combat will be left to you and your officers. However, I will place an advi—"

"Don't you say it," Dassiova interrupted in a warning tone. "Don't you dare say that you're putting an advisor on my goddamned bridge. You can appoint an observer, nothing more. Because *advisors* only give the advice that serves their primary purpose. *My* primary purpose is to keep our people alive and make the enemy the opposite of that."

Ettington regarded him for a few moments before speaking with exquisite control, as though the man hadn't just erupted at him.

"You know, Earth Command wanted to put Admiral Vernay's Tenth Fleet into the fight and leave your people here in the CS."

The threat, so deftly implied, was clear as spring water. "Vernay would be a fine choice," Dassiova said. "She's a highly capable leader with more than enough experience in command. What she isn't, however," he said as he leaned back to show his own cards, "is experienced in fighting large-scale pitched battles with Va'alen fleets. She also, and correct me if I'm wrong, isn't and has never been a ground-pounder."

He leaned forward to force his intense gaze on the real string-puller.

"I know the battle up in the black, as do my people. They're running the best weapons of war our species has ever created. I also know the battle down on the deck where politics don't stand for a goddamn. Down there," he pointed at the deck, "low on ammo with no comms and visibility shittier than a Lunar mining tunnel, you need people like me to get it done."

He stabbed his finger into the tabletop with a hard tap. His point had been made.

"It's my recommendation," Ettington said carefully, "that the Tenth assume protective duties in the CS and keep the supply lines open to Earth while the colonization and other operations continue unimpeded by the war. Private contractors are already taking over those few military duties on the surface of the planets to free up the troops you'll need."

"I have the troops," Dassiova said. "What I don't have are the supplies."

"They're coming," Ettington said.

"On which convoy?" the admiral shot back. "All I see coming in is mining operators and colony-builders. If we don't win this fight then whatever lucrative deal the UN has with the big companies won't be worth a single credit come the Va'alen invasion."

"I'll advise you once to be careful, *Admiral*," Ettington said. Placing emphasis on Dassiova's rank made it clear that he could be replaced at any time.

The politicians couldn't understand the crucial nature of experience and local intelligence; they thought all admirals were the same and all enemies just needed killing. They didn't realize that in war the Va'alen showed the deadliest behavior the human race could sum up in its entirety. They were kamikaze suicide bombers, each and every one of them willing and unwavering when it came to laying down their lives to kill the enemy. In personal combat they were like the berserkers of legend, fighting with all the intensity and fanaticism of zealots. The Va'alen were, Dassiova had to admit, goddamned hard to kill.

But *he* had fought them. He had killed them. The memory of his last encounter sent a sudden stabbing pain through his gut, which must have registered on his face in spite of every effort to hide it. Ettington saw it, understood it, but to Dassiova's surprise he didn't use it. Not yet anyway.

"I am aware of the importance of winning the conflict, however our best analysts have assimilated the data from the Kuldar and in all of our simulations victory is assured."

Dassiova scoffed.

"Your simulations factor in Mrs. Murphy's boy?" he asked bitterly.

Ettington ignored the question. Murphy's Law, a way to justify unquantifiable fear of defeat in his opinion, was a statistical nonsense. He'd heard all the sayings about the likelihood of plans surviving contact with the enemy, but those sayings came from a time when they didn't have computers capable of analyzing every scrap of recorded data. He was certain they had correctly calculated the odds of success down to the third decimal point.

"The facts remain the same, Admiral," Ettington said, eager to return to the point of the meeting. He turned to include the six other people around the table waiting nervously for the peacocking to abate. "A full resupply is inbound. Now, to the point?"

The lights were dimmed, and a holo-display flickered to life in the center of the table. It showed the system on the far side of the Crab Nebula. The four planets were highlighted as targets and the 3D image moved with the briefing as the officer spoke.

"Our Kuldar allies will lead the fight, moving in ahead of our fleet to secure the airspace in the system."

Symbols and icons showed the predictive model of their ships and the alien ships spreading out to secure the darkness at strategic points.

"Their ships will engage any Va'alen resistance. Our predictions show that will be centered around the four main planets with little or no resistance in deeper space. We don't anticipate that they'll have any real defenses outside of orbit."

"What about the gateway device they have?" a gruff frigate captain asked, catching Dassiova's eye and smirking in amusement at the video game they were being shown.

"It's set in a region fairly central to the four planets," the briefing officer said. He manipulated the display to show it.

"And these system schematics have been supplied by our new friends?" the captain asked.

"They have," the officer answered.

"So, you're basing guesswork on unconfirmed intelligence. We're supposed to commit not only half of Earth's armada but a vast number of troops on information that could be at best outdated, or at worse the complete opposite of what we'll find?"

"Captain Hayes," another admiral called out from across the table. "If *I* were your commanding officer, I'd have grave concerns about how you view the amount of water in your glass."

Hayes leaned forward to look at Dassiova, unsure if the admiral from the intelligence corps was right.

"Actually," Dassiova said, "the captain raises valid points regarding the quality of the intel. You do still grade intelligence reports, right?" He turned his gaze onto the intelligence officer again.

The younger man looked around as though seeking support. He found none. Left on the spot, he swallowed and tried to wriggle out of giving a straight answer.

"The time stamps translated show these system scans to be—"

"Not what I asked, son," Dassiova said, sounding more patient than he was. "Do you, as an intelligence officer, use a system to grade the intelligence you receive?"

"Yes, sir."

"And how do you grade this?"

The intelligence officer was defeated. "It's uncorroborated, known personally to the source of the information and not to ourselves. The information can't be judged—we haven't acted on previous intelligence from the same source to assess the strength of it yet."

"So, it's trust work?" Dassiova asked.

"Yes, Admiral." Ettington's voice came from the shadowy corner behind him and made his skin crawl. "It is trust, and we're going to trust the Kuldar and form a battle plan based on their report."

Dassiova opened his mouth to speak, to make his objections clear for the record if it was even being kept of the briefing. But Ettington spoke again.

"That said," the UNID director went on, "I would expect that such experienced captains and officers as this fleet possesses to be ready for any and all conceivable contingencies."

"You're telling us to plan for a betrayal?" a female captain asked.

"I'm not telling you anything," Ettington lied smoothly. "I'm just mentioning in passing what my expectations would be. Please," he added to the intelligence officer, "continue."

The known details of the gateway device were provided, explaining through the movement of the holo-images that a detachment of Kuldar strikers—their equivalent of the UN corvette class ships—would be sent through a tear. Once through, they would secure the immediate area of the device and remove any resistance.

"That's not our fight," the admiral who had spoken earlier interjected. "We will concentrate on landing our troops on the four planets to secure the bases of power located as per the briefing package. Each troop-carrying ship will have set coordinates to hit and deploy their troops, then remain in orbit to provide fire support if required."

Hayes caught the eye of his counterpart, Captain Nicola Halstead, and the two exchanged a knowing look. They were going on trust to escort troop ships and be on station to glass a planet full of roaches. They were fine with killing the enemy; that was what they did. What neither of them enjoyed was the risk of wiping out thousands of civilians. Before either of them made an objection Dassiova spoke again.

"I have to raise a moral objection to what I think you're saying here," he started. He held up a hand to stop the desk-pilot from interrupting him. "I think we're a little further evolved from the days of crying 'no prisoners' from horseback carrying spears and swords, don't you?"

"Our intelligence, in fact every experience we have regarding the Va'alen, is that there are no civilians. Each and every one of them is a combatant," the intel admiral insisted.

"That may be true," Dassiova said evenly, "but my standing orders are that any Va'alen offering surrender will be given the opportunity to comply with instructions."

"Prisoners are allowed for, although unexpected. The Kuldar will take charge of any captured Va'alen at the conclusion of the campaign and we will withdraw to our side of the open corridor."

The open corridor, as the politicians were calling it, was a demilitarized zone between UN and Kuldar agreed territories.

There was a proposed neutral area with no habitable planets in the system where trade stations would be established, assuming everything else went to plan. The buffer zone allowed for either race to miscalculate jump coordinates and stray into the neutral area without making a risky incursion into claimed space without an invitation. That was the theory, anyway.

"Very well," Dassiova said.

He settled in to hear the more precise rundown on each of the planets and the assigned vessels carrying troops to each one. The briefing only came to a close when the door opened to interrupt with the news that the Tenth Fleet had arrived bringing the resupply and relief.

CHAPTER 38

Cargo Bay 12, The Indomitable

Eze chose to refit her unit to full strength and test their gear in the final drop to the surface. They were delayed from completing the last qualification jump because of a lack of the rocket pods. Plus, there was an unexpected shortage of the stimulant medication required to stop the jumpers passing out through the excessive Gs of the descent. They had to wait.

When the resupply was announced inbound, she deployed her troops operating without armor to do the grunt work—two squads' worth. They didn't complain about the detail; they'd be getting new upgraded armor out of it. Eze sent one of the master petty officers with them in charge, although the detachment was nominally under the command of the two ensigns. She was pleasantly surprised when she was brought a large weapons crate on their return. She scanned the shipping tag to see where it was intended. It had been marked for the private security contractors on Gaia Néos; Eze only just managed to hide her grin.

"For me?" she said sarcastically. "You shouldn't have…"

"These weren't exactly on our docket, if you catch my drift, Commander…" the petty officer said.

Eze straightened and eyed him seriously, making everyone around them in the HQ area go silent.

"Master Petty Officer Travers," she said sternly after opening up the crate bearing the Hyper logo. "Did you unlawfully acquire a crate of sniper railguns that wasn't issued to you?"

"No, ma'am," Travers said stiffly. "I also got a crate of new pulse rifles and two bricks of charge packs for them." He kept his expression perfectly straight as he gave the admission.

"Nice," she said. "I'll take one, as will the Chief. Other than that, I want them distributed among the squads to the best shots. Redistribute the explosive ordnance ammunition so everyone is carrying as much as possible."

"Yes, ma'am," Travers said as he tried to hide his relief at not getting chewed out. Coming away from stores as a UN trooper with anything even remotely resembling what you needed was unheard of. Distracting the quartermaster's underlings while loading a few crates of bonus content was the stuff of legend.

Once, as a petty officer class one, he had been sent to the stores by his chief to replace some gear his squad had lost. At the time, he'd carried with him a data slate from the chief. He left feeling confused when the stores guys laughed at him. He was red-faced as he walked out, without having fulfilled his requisition order for the kit he needed, let alone the chief's requisition for one box of unicorn shit. He ground his jaw as he heard the last words echoing behind him.

"It's called *stores* asshole," someone shouted after him. "If we were going to issue it, the place would be called *issues*."

"And Boss Travers?" Eze called out after he'd made it ten paces. He turned and stood waiting for the dressing down. "Next time, get enough for everybody."

"Yes, ma'am."

They didn't lose anyone in training which, given the risks of an orbital jump, was a success worth celebrating. As they waited for their turn to be recovered from the surface and head back to the *Indomitable*, Eze ran through squad and full unit exercises. They were to expend all of the ammunition they'd carried down, safe in the knowledge that they had double that amount back in their unit stores.

She assessed and even took her turn to lead the full culminating exercise, still fighting the urge to lead every squad personally. She had to trust her troops. Trust her NCOs and her officers even down to the argumentative young ensign called Edwards. She knew that they in turn trusted her not to lead them blindly into a battle they had no hope of winning.

Those fears were separate from her concerns about everything else. Only her chief was aware of the trepidation she felt. She knew from experience, being of the minority who had fought and won a battle against a Va'alen army, that the enemy could be beaten. She knew that it was mostly that human instinct, that fear of monsters, which could be debilitating to anyone facing the roaches in open combat.

Checking where their ride was in the queue, Eze assembled her unit. Every one of them was dusty and tired from the final build-up exercise, but every one of them gleaming to her eyes. She opened her suit's comm to all of them.

"Listen up," she began. "I'll go over this again when we hit the AO but these are our orders. We will be transported on the *Indomitable* to the planet in the Va'alen system with the largest concentration of warriors." She paused, letting it sink in. They weren't on another bug hunt and there would be no 'hurry up and wait' until the job was done. "But that only means that you'll all have to work as hard as I know you can. Listen to your squad leaders, follow your orders, and fight like the salty sons of bitches I know you are."

She paused again, walking along the front rank as she eyeballed as many troops as she could wearing her best—though blood-thirsty—smile.

"We're part of the largest human offensive maneuver in living history," she told them. "Never before has there been this kind of fight. Believe me when I tell you that if we don't destroy our enemy, they *will* find a way back to Earth and they *will* bring with them every goddamned roach they can to make sure we don't get back up."

She stopped, scanning her gaze up and down the line of soldiers. She saw a few concerned faces trying to remain resolute. She considered whether to release the final piece of intelligence or whether to save it for just before their deployment. Something in her wanted to be as up-front as possible to gain their willing support.

"The Va'alen are in possession of Fold drive tech, courtesy of the former Middle Eastern Alliance" she said flatly. There was a collective gasp. "And we need to ensure that doesn't end up being used against us. We're heading into the fight, and we're going to fight hard. We *will* be going home as heroes."

A cheer broke out, nervously at first. All fresh troops were inclined to be hesitant when standing on the precipice of war. But the cheer grew, swelling in intensity, and ended as a deafening roar of promise.

CHAPTER 39

Bridge of the Indomitable

"All ships signal ready for departure, Admiral," the young ensign said from the fleet comm terminal.

Dassiova nodded gravely from his command chair, tapping out an encoded text message to Admiral Vernay, addressed to *Neptune* actual.

"Look after the CS until we get back. ED." To his surprise he received an answer almost immediately, also a single line: "*Dieu vous garde et bonne chance.*" He smiled again, translating it as wishing him god speed and good luck. He looked up and asked for a fleet-wide channel.

"Standby for comm from Fleet Admiral Dassiova," the comm officer announced, turning back to give the admiral the nod.

He stood, straightening his uniform and clearing his throat.

"*'hemm.* All ships of the Ninth Fleet," he said. "This is the Admiral. You have your jump coordinates, you have your orders, and you have my full, unwavering faith that all of you will do your jobs to the best of your abilities." He paused, wishing he'd tried to write something down or even practice his speech, instead of winging it.

"Take a look at the people beside you," he said. "Take a look at your crewmembers, your brothers and sisters, your *family*, because each and every one of you in this fleet is vital to what we're trying to achieve. We might not all make it back, but by god we're going to

257

leave a crater in the genetic memory of the Va'alen so wide and so deep that they'll never even dream of seeking us out again. Dassiova out."

He sat, swiped two fingers across his throat for the ensign to cut the comm, and checked the console beside him to see another text comm addressed directly to him. It was from Captain Hayes onboard the *Hammer*, and it read, 'get some.'

He smiled. The screen flashed again with another message from the same officer, showing a single word as an afterthought: 'Sir'

"Lieutenant Commander Moon," he said loudly with, "Take us out."

CHAPTER 40

Approaching the Crab Nebula

The telemetry data of the *Ichi's* previous forays had allowed the fleet to cover the distance in nine long jumps. Each time they dropped from Fold space they went into full defensive array centered around the troop-carrying ships. Those were the most vulnerable and not built for battle in the void of space.

Riding on the back of the carrier flagship, the *Ichi* remained apart from the fleet maneuvers until they were needed. Torres insisted that he was going to the surface with the team, though not to take over command from Brandt. He spent the time obsessively checking his new gear—he had swung an upgrade to the prototype armor courtesy of Doctor Paterson who remained safely on the *Anvil* back in the Centauri system.

Once the captain had left the ready room to eat, Kekoa glanced after him then back to Payne and Zero.

"How come we have to babysit the captain?" he asked.

Payne glanced at Zero who only betrayed that he had heard by the slight raising of both eyebrows. The responsibility of putting their baby straight fell on Payne's shoulders.

"I wouldn't let anyone else hear you say that shit, man," she told Kekoa. "The captain was CP and UNID through and through. He had a confirmed terrorist kill when you were in diapers."

"I thought he was a flight jock…" Kekoa began, his words trailing off as the unsettlingly quiet sniper raised his gaze to him.

"He's no flight jock," Payne corrected him. "He's a ground-pounder like us. You may be big and all, but he's the real deal. You haven't heard the story about the little ensign in charge of Specter's patrol when he got…?" She waved her hands vaguely over her body in a way that tried to convey being blown up.

"Oh," Kekoa said. "I'll shut up now."

"You do that, honey," Zero said quietly, "and while you're at it just make sure you don't vent too much steam from your mouth that you could use elsewhere."

Kekoa looked at Payne for a translation. She shrugged. "Worry about yourself, not anyone else, okay?" Kekoa nodded and put his head back down to his comm device.

Torres, eating alone, chewed fast in time with the involuntary jigging of his right leg. His thoughts were gathering more momentum with each jump toward their objective. He didn't even realize he was shaking the whole table until Brandt dropped heavily into the seat beside him.

"New thermos-dynamic energy source you're working on there, Cap?" she asked with a smile. She was as nervous as he was, but she kept it deep inside so nobody else saw. If she had concerns, she'd let the team know; otherwise her stress stayed bottled up tight.

Torres followed her gaze, stopped jigging his leg and smiled back at her.

"Just going over things again," he told her quietly. He glanced around to see that nobody else was in easy eavesdrop- ping range.

"The board's set," she told him. "All we can affect now is our own performance; leave out the rest until it happens."

Torres nodded—she had it right. They could plan all they liked but if their enemy did something outside of their expectations then they had to adapt.

Adaptation required trust—trust in their training and trust in the abilities of the team and trust in their leader. Not wanting to explain all of his fears to Brandt, he fell back on discussing the obvious concerns.

"Amare's unit is dropping on the same planet as us," he explained.

"And they'll be fine," she reassured him. "She's a good commander and from what I can tell her people will follow her anywhere."

Torres nodded as though accepting her reassuring words, when in fact he was still worrying about all the things he couldn't control.

What if there's more resistance at their objective site? What if there was a new tech level they didn't already know about? What would the Hive Lords do when they were threatened?

That last question could at least be answered with some previous intelligence and educated guesswork; Brandt and Specter had seen a Hive Lord personally control a Va'alen warrior when Rogers had lost his arm. They had to expect that every single one they'd encounter would be in a berserker rage. They were equipped for that, trained for it, and if they expected it and planned for it anything different would be easy.

Unless it was worse. That was what kept running through his mind as he conjured more and more outrageous scenarios where he'd get people killed. Torres tried to push it all away, managing only to put it back to the fringes of his immediate thoughts so he could be present for this conversation.

He looked down at the sub sandwich he was eating—he hadn't even been enjoying the fresh ingredients that had been a welcome addition to their most recent resupply. He swallowed before taking another bite; the crewman working in the galley had put more mustard on the slices of protein just as he liked it. "Heard anything about the other CP teams?" she asked.

Changing the subject allowed him to forget his worries for a moment.

"Nothing," he responded truthfully. "I know where their target locations are but nothing about who is on them."

"Standard," Brandt replied with disinterest. "They probably know nothing about us either."

Torres knew that was true, having spoken with Dassiova during the last jump to go over the last-minute details again. Each of the four ships carrying troops also contained a drop- ship that would launch during the massive offensive. It would then head to the targets and hit the identified sites where the telepathic aliens were believed to be.

What had come out of the briefing with the Kuldar was that there were believed to be *four* pairs of these controlling aliens. As one pair had been with the Va'alen expedition to the Centauri system, it had left their race under the control of the three remaining pairs. Torres had no idea if that was relevant, but he liked the symmetrical appeal of having four planets, four locations for the strike teams to hit, and four chances to capture one of the pairs.

He hadn't given much thought to the purpose of their orders until the long wait of being in Fold space began. They moved ever closer toward the inevitable battles. As much as it nagged at him, he didn't want to think too hard about what the UNID or Global Command or the United Earth Command or whatever they wanted to call themselves that week wanted with the creatures.

He had to fall back on the comfort of being a soldier and the security of having orders to carry out.

"We're all set?" he asked.

"As set as we're going to be," she told him.

"Good," he said. He pushed away the rest of the sandwich he couldn't stomach. "Last jump and we're in the fight."

Before she could respond, the ambient lighting in the galley turned a muted red and a double-ping sounded through the ship to signal battle stations. Both officers stood, expecting that something had gone wrong and their timeline accelerated, but the voice of Rogers over the comm settled them back down.

"Contact made with Kuldar fleet," he said. "Prepare for final orders before jump."

The battle started sooner than the plans dictated, which was as unsurprising. As was the fact that a ship identified as Va'alen, although of no composition they'd seen yet, disappeared from sensors. The fact that the enemy had already managed to manufacture Fold drive technology was concerning.

Torres left the galley at a run and turned automatically for the bridge. He tutted loudly at himself in annoyance and doubled back to the armory where he stepped into his armor. He felt the familiar sense of claustrophobia envelop him, until three deep breaths steadied his nerves. By the time he had mastered himself, the armor had already synced to his body and moved so effortlessly that he felt a sense of resting power course through him. He walked into the ready room and deactivated his helmet to consult a display showing the whole system.

The large icon of the Kuldar dreadnought in the central position caught his attention. He imagined smaller ships streaming from it to head off in five different locations, a sub-fleet to each planet and one to the gateway device. He tapped a command on the display and watched as the screen showed five projectiles sear from the dreadnought for the individual ships to fly through and arrive ahead of the human vessels.

The first wave—the aerial battle in orbit of the four planets—began in devastating earnest as the numbers scrolling on the display counted the enemy and allied icons blinking out of existence.

"*Ichi* from *Indomitable* Actual," came the comm from the carrier. "Prepare to disengage."

Torres fought the urge to respond personally. He had left the bridge operations under the command of his flight officer. He imagined more than felt their ship detach from the spine of the bigger vessel, imagined how Rogers expertly maneuvered them through the pattern of the eight gun barges deploying to fly a steel ring of protection around the *Indomitable*. He thought he felt the slight hitch of the grav emitter not catching up with how fast their pilot threw them into a rolling dive toward the surface.

Torres felt the vibrations of their guns firing, sending heavy concentrations of energy bolts to the surface and saturating the defensive cannons of their enemy. Unsure if it would work, he had agreed that the Shroud device would be active from the moment they entered the battle. They needed a pilot of exceptional skill to avoid hitting the other ships who would be partially blind to them with their transponder shut down and their comms dark.

"Team to the shuttle bay," Brandt's voice announced.

She snapped his attention away from the bigger picture and put him back in the comfortable setting of fighting only the battle he could directly influence. Torres could focus on his own actions, and not have to worry about so many people.

That trust, that relief of giving up the wider concerns, put him in a mindset of total control and focus.

Picking up the pulse rifle from the rack on the wall, he stepped into the tube and dropped into the shuttle bay without a shred of indecision.

It was time to fight.

Eze was in the first rank where a leader should be. She knew a lot of her troops were already nervous about an orbital drop. A drop into combat under direct fire from the ground and through a global dogfight between the ships of two alien races was another thing entirely.

She had no words to say, no final speech of encouragement to give. She was busy mastering her own thoughts and feelings. All she had to do was get her people on the ground and light up anything with more than two arms.

"First wave," announced the deck boss on the carrier, "*drop!*"

Eze went with it; the artificial gravity fell away so forcefully that it momentarily disorientated her. She hurtled towards the dust-colored gray orb beneath her, and felt the armor constrict her legs to keep the blood in her vital organs where it was needed.

"Second wave," the voice in her comm called out, "*drop!*"

Rogers handled the control like the skilled pilot he was. If he allowed himself a hint of pride—which always came across as arrogance to the unfamiliar—he was more than a skilled pilot. He was god behind the controls. This was what he was born to do.

He jinked the *Ichi* this way and that, never maintaining a steady descent, never allowing any rail gun on the surface to take its time, draw a bead on them and end their part in the war. Ever since coming face to face with the Va'alen, he had been desperate to get back to the fight. He knew it made him seem reckless, so he'd kept those thoughts and feelings out of every psych report they'd put him through.

Rogers was no warrior, no ground-pounder, but his own war was fought by being the best stick in the fleet and delivering his payload of ass-kicking friends to the surface where they could do what *they* did best.

The annoying ensign at the tactical station over his right shoulder kept making noises like he was playing a video game and giving himself small sounds of congratulations every time he fired a successful shot. Rogers ignored him at first, but with each hiss of satisfaction he grew braver and more convinced that they'd make it.

"Standby for atmosphere in three, two..." he shouted as the ship began to shudder violently.

The angle wasn't perfect, but then again, he wasn't going for smooth; he was going for tactical. That term had been used by pilots for hundreds of years to justify a rough landing. Rogers didn't care one bit for comfort or what anyone else thought of his piloting right then. The ship's shields could take the punishment of a thin ozone layer. The shuddering stopped but a light buffeting of wind resistance replaced it. Flying a ship even as small as the *Ichi* in atmosphere required a whole new set of skills he had developed on his own.

Flying in the void of space was child's play in comparison to what he fought inside the bubble of the planet.

"Adjust course to two-oh-eight," Sarvanto called out to him.

Rogers flashed his eyes at the display to his left. He saw no need to adjust but trusted the man left in command to know the bigger picture. He corrected course, slowing before adding a crushing burst of full burn to throw off anything pointing a building-sized barrel at them.

"Combat drop troops," Sarvanto told him, explaining the course change.

Rogers was too professional to have argued with those orders, and as he imagined wiping out his captain's girlfriend by failing to follow the order, he was glad he hadn't hesitated.

"Drop coordinates in twenty seconds," he reported. Sarvanto addressed the team over the comm.

"Standby to drop on my mark," he ordered in his stoic, unflappable voice.

"...*mark*!"

"Request from drop-troops for fire support, sir," said the comm officer on the bridge. "*Indomitable* is responding unable to comply."

"Ensign?" Sarvanto asked calmly, as though someone had enquired after their dinner plans.

"Firing," he said, sending a juddering report through their hull. "Effect on target. Window is now closed."

"Carry on, Lieutenant Rogers," Sarvanto said.

CHAPTER 41

2,500 Feet Above Planet Designated 'Cathedral'

Eze plummeted to the deck with one eye on her HUD, checking the progress of her team, with the other eye fixed on the ground below to stop her feeling disorientated.

She was impressed that her team kept disciplined comms as they dropped, but that happiness was destroyed as a fat bolt of orange energy seared past her so close she could've touched it. She didn't—she likely would have found her entire arm burned off. That would've made the start of her fight uncomfortable.

"Ground units engaging," she reported, switching comm channels with a blink of her eyes. She hailed the *Indomitable*. "Requesting insertion saturation for five seconds."

She received a curt, "standby," in response before the answer. "Be advised, negative firing solution at this time."

"Shit," she cursed to herself, then switched back to the unit comms. "First wave, incoming fire from enemies on the ground. Engage on landing."

There was little else she could do, but even stating the obvious showed her troops that she was aware of the threat and had a plan for it, no matter how simple that plan was.

Her suit began to fire thrusters to begin arresting her fall, but she rapidly scrolled to the safety override on her HUD. A few of the first wave did the same and effectively eyeballed the landing. Behind and above her, signified by a green arrow pointing backward on her visor's display, one of her team was hit and let out the smallest strangled cry before their comm went dead. She pushed the concern aside as two more went down in the hail of intensified fire. As she was preparing to fire her suit's retro-thrusters hard, a series of pluming dust clouds appeared beneath her at angle to her left. She had no idea who had given the order to fire the half-second burst of pulse cannons or what ship they originated from, but she was grateful as the shapes on the ground were thrown about by the destructive force of the weapons.

Eze flared hard and hit the ground hard to roll. She came up drawing the rifle in one fluid movement and sent a stream of automatic fire into the broad torso of the nearest Va'alen twenty feet away. It seemed to convulse like it was electrocuted. Black scorch marks covered its upper body before it dropped backward like a felled tree. She fired on two more who still hadn't reacted to her landing, as her own shots were joined by the rattling sound of a rifle firing traditional ammunition joined in. Her shots blew the arms off one side of her target before the additional bullets exploded and cracked open the shell. The alien dropped to the deck in a fountain of black gore. All around her the rest of the first wave of troops was landing; heavy thuds signaled their arrival. Three heavier sounds indicated the bodies of the troops hit by the ground fire, but she forced that out of her mind.

A shot to her back pitched her over. Her HUD flashed and blinked in and out as she rolled again. As she came back up, she held her fire, smiling as the Va'alen took aim at her again before being crushed to the dirt by the leader of the second wave. He had timed the stomp of his landing perfectly to drive the alien attacker down with a resounding crack of destroyed armor.

"Nice of you to drop by, Chief," she said in a voice cooler than she thought possible.

"Commander," Ryers said in a tone just as calm. He pointed his own pulse rifle at the dying alien and fired twice into the crack in the hard shell of its back.

"Rally on me," Eze called out over the team channel as the third wave was coming in to land.

A quick check of her HUD showed a loss of eight troops in the drop which, given the circumstances, wasn't as bad as she was expecting.

The unit formed on her as the last of the Va'alen retreated back up a small rise. Ryers was busy with the two lieutenant commanders organizing the unit into their squads. Eze established comms with the carrier in orbit to prepare for the fire mission she anticipated.

"They're runnin'!" one of the soldiers called out. He emerged from the cover of the shallow crater their fire support had created.

"Get your ass back down," a petty officer snarled at him, reaching up to drag the idiot out of sight.

Eze didn't think she needed to explain what a tactical withdrawal to high ground looked like but, evidently, she did. As though the Va'alen were had heard the scolding, a flurry of shots rattled over the trooper's head and forced him to dive for the dust.

"Our objective is that high ground," she said over unit comm. "Advance by squad after fire mission. Head's down until I give the order to move."

Eze switched channel again to link with the orbital fire support onboard the carrier. She looked up to the carrier and saw bright flashes in the dusky sky where the carrier was engaging the enemy both in the void and on the ground.

"High ground six hundred meters," she said. "Flashing coordinates now."

Her HUD responded to her commands and outlined the distant ridge. A few seconds passed before the acknowledgement came; she held her breath as the bright blue streaks radiated out from the ship high above and seemed to head directly for her. She covered up. The impossibly strong concussive reports of rail gun fire impacted the ground a half mile in the distance, and she counted to ten before she gave the order to move out.

She went with the third squad, following protocol now—her troops were in the fight and didn't need to follow her like she was their flag. Eze gave the order for them to move, in the hope that they would have covered at least half of the distance before the dust had settled and exposed them.

The clouds of dust didn't seem to stifle their enemy's aim. Shots cut through the debris thrown up by the bombardment after they'd covered only a few hundred meters. Throwing herself into cover, Eze called for a second orbital strike in spite of being dangerously close to the target. It wasn't as though she hadn't survived a similar situation before.

"Cover," she ordered.

Her unit collectively hit the deck. The supercharged projectiles hit the planet with more kinetic energy than anything should've been able to survive. She had them up, on their feet and moving again before the rumbling echo of the last shot dissipated.

She used the power of her armor to push herself up the incline that was much steeper than it looked. From there, she held her position just below the ridgeline until the rest of her unit had caught up. As one, they crested the rise with their guns up, expecting to find the broken remains of an enemy company. Instead, they found only the empty, churned-up ground and a small fleet of incoming Va'alen ships.

"Take cover!" Eze bawled, dragging out the last words.

She expected to feel the incoming thuds of heavy pulse cannons tearing up their cover and them in in turn. Instead she heard the screaming *whoosh* of an unfamiliar sound. Risking a glance upward, she saw a string of shiny, flat ships no bigger than a ground transport. They flew in tight formations, like migrating geese, and their guns spat fury.

The Va'alen ships switched their aim from defenseless ground troops to the more menacing threat of the Kuldar fighter wing. Their three lead ships exploded in mid-flight. The rest peeled off, either hugging the deck or fighting to gain altitude as their guns returned fire.

The Kuldar were outmatched in both shielding and the weight of their guns, but they had the numbers. Eze was locked in awe as she became a spectator to the aerial battle. After a moment, she shook herself out of her stupor and advanced her unit while the distraction played out.

A few opportunistic shots from the Va'alen ships landed among her troops, but she had no time to dwell on the potential losses; there was only time to dominate the high ground and dig in to repel any attempts to dislodge them. Her troops were spread out. Those with the heavier guns could deploy them at regularly spaced intervals, with the option of inter- locking arcs of fire should they face a concerted attack by ground forces.

She detailed the squad ensigns—only one had perished in the drop—to pre-set orbital strike coordinates on the unit's data channel. They needed to be ready for rapid deployment of fire support in case their screen of Kuldar ships were destroyed or moved on.

Every tenth troop along the ridge line was equipped with a brand new sniper rail gun, courtesy of the empty-handed assholes back on Gaia. To those marksmen only Eze gave the order to fire at will.

The metallic, electric *twang* of those weapons firing filled the air at irregular intervals. The Va'alen warriors were showing themselves.

Eze stood, walking along her line and shouting encourage- ment to her troops. She kept her own fears locked up tight, hoping that they could hold the high ground and not die.

CHAPTER 42

Hive Lord Cathedral

Brandt's team had nicknamed their objective the cathedral. It had a complex spire that put them all in mind of a religious building, which had, in turn, led to the planetary designation. The size was intimidating, but their intelligence reported it was mostly a cavernous interior without the need to conduct protracted room clearances.

As they stood on the deck of the shuttle bay waiting for the order to jump, it struck Torres that he didn't know how the Kuldar could have got that kind of depth to their intel without having boots on the ground. He was saved any further introspection by Brandt slapping an armored hand on the back of his shoulder and yelling, "Shields on... *jump!*"

He activated his shield by tensing his body and tricking the armor into thinking he had a fright reflex. Torres smiled to himself as he took two long paces to the open ramp and hurled himself out into the slipstream behind the *Ichi*.

Something about stepping off the edge, about literally throwing himself into battle, shocked him out of every ounce of doubt he carried. The time for worrying was over. The time for action had begun.

That jump into the air, that release, that letting go, centered him in a way that nothing else could.

He settled out into a standard freefall pattern, not being strapped to a rocket as the others from the *Indomitable* had been. Instead he saw the green arrows on his HUD sweep around as the rest of the team settled in for the short drop to their target site.

"Eight hundred meters," Zero called out over their channel.

This was information they all had available to them, but relaying it was his way of staying calm during a drop. Anyone who didn't know him would just see the implacable, stone-cold exterior but the signs to his inner fears were there if one looked closely enough.

"Four hundred meters," he said after a short silence. "Bart out."

Torres kept his eyes on the horizon as he fell. He had been spared the need to jump out of a perfectly serviceable vessel for quite some time. He experienced the god's eye view provided by their marksman's little buddy for the first time, smiling at the sight. His smile quickly faded away as the drone accelerated toward their target and began to mark numerous red outlines of Va'alen warriors ahead of them.

"Count six," Brandt said. "Flaring."

"Flaring," the rest of the team echoed. They slowed under the force of their retro-thrusters and went vertical to come in to land. Torres, like a rookie, involuntarily closed his eyes before he touched down—the ground rushed up at him faster than he liked. That left him as the only one of the team not to stick their landing with just a crouch to soften the impact. Instead, he pitched forward, rolling and then scrambling to his feet to get his gun up.

"Sound off," Brandt said.

"Torres."

"Beale."

"Specter."

"Zero."

"Payne."

"Turner."

"Kekoa."

"Fangs."

"Drop."

"We've got company," Specter said. Brandt turned to look at him—the rifle came off his back in such a fast and fluid motion that it was almost mesmerizing. The barrel flashed, sending bolts of energy at a target she hadn't seen yet. She turned her head toward the red icon that appeared on her HUD and raised her own weapon. The red arrow flashed into an outline of a Va'alen for a brief moment before it flickered out, hit by both Specter and a rail gun shot from Zero.

"Zero, Beale, Fangs and Drop—high ground," she said, pointing to where the dead Va'alen had been. "Everyone else on me. Specter on point."

They moved. They had dropped within a hundred meters of the tall building and not given themselves much space to maneuver. The troops then found themselves engaging four Va'alen warriors behind cover near the entrance. It took ten seconds exchanging fire between their respective covers for Zero to get in position on the high ground. The detachment then poured fire into the exposed flank of the enemy. Brandt moved with Specter under the distraction of that fire and closed the ground, putting down the surviving pair before the last Va'alen could become enraged and be harder to kill.

"Counted six," Payne said. She spun to cover their six and point the heavy gun attached to the cradle of her armor. "That's five."

"Where's the last one?" Brandt snapped. "Anyone have eyes on it?"

"Bart's got nothing," Zero said.

"It must've gone inside," Specter said.

He peered off into the gloom; his eyes saw better than the optics on most suits of armor. Brandt and Torres peered with him, squinting into the dark chasm and using their suits' soft- ware to enhance the imagery as much as possible.

The darkness ahead erupted into light—orange flashes of the pulse rifles the Va'alen fired at them. The watching humans scattered.

CHAPTER 43

The Indomitable

A sickening, shuddering vibration rocked the bridge so violently that it interfered with the artificial gravity. Dassiova floated up awkwardly out of his seat a few inches before his ass dropped back down. He straightened himself and cleared his throat, as though reassuring himself.

"Ensign," he said calmly, "what was that?"

Ensign Romano was always suffering under some reprimand from Dassiova just because he looked about twelve years old and had an annoying habit of speaking too loud and high-pitched around the admiral. He swallowed hard, wanting to be sure of himself before responding.

"Gun barge four, sir," he said.

"What about it?"

"It... uh..." Romano stuttered.

"Take your time, son," Dassiova said with heavy sarcasm.

"Nobody's in a rush for anything here."

"It crashed," Romano blurted out. "Crashed into us. Into our outer shields, I mean."

"Status?" Dassiova asked. Romano groaned inwardly. If he provided a status update about their shields, then Dassiova would say he meant the gun barge. If he told him about the gun barge, then he'd be yelled at for not giving the status of their outer shields.

"Gone, sir," he said. "Third layer shields are holding at ninety-eigh—" Another series of thudding vibrations rumbled under their feet. "Ninety-four percent."

"Barge four?" Dassiova asked.

"Also gone, sir," Romano reported. "Their shields went down at the same time as their guide thrusters from what I could see. They lost control and wiped out into the barrier."

Dassiova balled a fist with his left hand and thumped it into the arm of his chair.

"Dammit," he snarled. "Push the barges out another five kilometers."

One of the comm officers acknowledged the order and began speaking rapidly into his headset without offering an opinion. Romano would have asked about the gap it would leave in their defenses instead of just following order. Demonstrating that he was learning to shut up and follow orders, he kept his eyes on the console and his fingers dancing over the icons as his mind raced. If their shields had been intact still, no matter how weak, they would have passed through the protective energy barriers of the *Indomitable* as they ran the exact same harmonic resonance. He weighed the pros and cons of their shields failing first—there was no way that the crew of the barge could have survived.

"Ventral and port defense cannons on stack four are down," snapped the lieutenant at one of the weapons stations. She was managing the firing solutions and protocols of the defensive guns, her fingers working over an interactive schematic of the carrier.

"Cause?" Dassiova asked.

"Power failure," she shot back. Her hands moved quickly. "Attempting remote reroute... *got it*. Guns coming back online now."

279

Dassiova said nothing. There was no need to waste the oxygen acknowledging the report. She was just doing her job.

There were no participation medals on his bridge.

"Give me the bigger picture, tactical," Dassiova said loudly. Romano, as prepared for the question as he ever could be, stammered through an answer.

"All dropships away," he started. "We lost two to enemy fire. Some losses with the drop troops but not known at this time."

Dassiova bit down his anger at the losses. As admiral, he felt personally responsible for each one. But he wasn't so naïve as to think those losses would not increase when the troops on the surface took it to the Va'alen.

"Further afield?" the admiral asked, nudging the ensign towards the greater concerns of the conflict.

He swept the view out wider and checked other numbers scrolling down one side of the wide display. "Kuldar ships are engaging on the surface of all four planets... Ground teams are away..."

"All going to plan then," Dassiova said sarcastically.

"Sir, I'm showing debris where two of our ships' transponders were," Romano said heavily. Dassiova sat back, his expression unreadable.

"Acknowledged," he said simply.

⸺

Flying a fast, low orbit, the twin frigates under the direct command of the *Indomitable* skimmed the upper edge of the atmosphere. Their cannons and rail guns pounded everything on the surface designated as a target. The crews on board trusted in the strength of their shields and their breakneck velocity to keep them safe from all but the luck-iest of orbital defense gunners.

They suffered some hits, although all deflected by the outer shielding. Any stray energy weapons that found their mark only served to restore minute amounts of power to the shields.

Captain Hayes, strapped in to the command chair on the bridge of the *Hammer*, smiled at the display showing their shield integrity. The outer layer dropped a little under twenty percent from a rico-cheting rail gun projectile and then climbed up three percent from a flurry of energy cannon shots finding them.

His gunners and tactical officers worked silently as they rapidly selected targets and gauged the firing solution, sending munitions of varying types hurtling down.

This wasn't what they were designed for, but the frigates were unleashing death like wrathful gods from the heavens.

"Incoming hail from the *Vengeance*," his comm officer called out. He put Captain Halstead on the screen without being prompted.

"Count thirty Va'alen fighters inbound," she said immediately. "Peel off?"

"Break orbit," Hayes ordered.

The grav emitters fought against the pull of the planet as the ships angled off into the void. The two frigates employed a maneuver they'd practiced and perfected ever since their first harrying action on the massive Va'alen armada they faced on their last deployment. The attack pattern was shared with the rest of the UN fleet, but as Hayes and Halstead were the two captains who had invented it, their crews performed their roles sublimely.

Halstead slowed her ship, the pilot spinning the vessel on the horizontal axis to present its broadside to the oncoming enemy. The Va'alen weren't suicidal, at least not when their mates still lived, so they slowed their approaches and spread out. They didn't present easy targets to the humans and their singularity warheads.

The *Vengeance* let rip with a full salvo of energy cannons, orange bolts of light rippling out to saturate the enemy. The Va'alen ships opened up with their own guns a moment later. Their projectiles raced toward each other like tidal waves of destruction. As they fired, the *Hammer*, which had veered off below, executed a micro-jump. This put the ship just ahead and to one flank of the main body of assaulting ships, immediately firing off a spread of singularity nukes. The nukes detonated among the enemy ships, and blinked out almost a third of their number in the first attack.

As the attack faltered, with half of the remaining alien ships changing course to attack the new threat, the *Hammer* blinked out of existence. A confused mass of ships was left behind, unsure where to go. Turning their attention back to the *Vengeance*, the aliens found that ship no longer there. Instead it reappeared beneath them and launched its own warheads, before joining up with the *Hammer* at their rear.

"Eight incoming," Hayes's tactical officer reported. "Eight still heading for the planet."

"Ignore the ones heading for us," the captain ordered. "It's a feint to keep us from the planet. Helm, jump us ahead of them."

Both frigates reappeared between the last four pairs of attacking ships to block their route to the *Indomitable*. Both captains held the guns of their crews ready until the Va'alen were inside of effective weapons range when Hayes's tactical officer called out again.

"New signatures," he snapped. "Count sixty."

"Theirs?" Hayes asked.

"Negative, sir. Kuldar fighters on direct intercept course." Hayes tapped an icon on his console to open up a direct comm to the bridge of the other frigate.

"Stay and play or back to the planet?" he asked.

"You go," Halstead responded. "We'll stay and make sure they don't break though." Hayes gave his orders to return them to their orbital strike pattern when an emergency hail sounded from the *Indomitable*.

General Chakour watched from the corner of the room. He saw the interactive holo-displays flashing brightly with colors and icons he could decipher as the battle raged outside in the void and far away from where he cowered. He held still, not wanting to move in case he got kicked or stomped again by the warrior assigned to watch him.

He shifted position, wincing but not crying out. He had learned the hard way about attracting attention to himself in the company of the Va'alen. Chakour was certain that the bones of his right forearm were broken. More specifically, he suspected he had spiral fractures to the radius given how the warrior had gripped his limb and twisted it violently to throw him down. The swelling was making his skin tighten and the throbbing pain grew in intensity with each pulse of his heart. The rising agony was a locomotive gathering speed every second.

From his new position, he could see Da'kath manipulating the main display with all four of his arms. He shot them out to zoom in on one icon that grew into a shape Chakour recognized instantly.

He felt a wave of hatred and revulsion to contend with the pain, as he recognized the outline of what had once been his own ship. It was no longer his, however. It was now cannibalized and bastardized to be the host for the malevolent infection of these big bugs.

They had ruined his ship, his *flagship*, the pride of his fleet and his command. By changing the vessel, they had stolen his pride, what little he had left, along with it. Swallowing hard to fight down a strangled cry, Chakour watched as his ship spewed out wave after wave of alien ships.

It was as though someone had kicked a hornet's nest or burst a venomous spider's egg sack. Ship after ship exited his former command, his weapon of god. As those enemy ships flew into the raging battle, the general's gaze lingered on the husk that had once been his greatest achievement.

The pain pulsed in his arm once more. He closed his eyes. He tried to find a peaceful place in his mind to retreat to.

Specter emptied the entire battery pack of his pulse rifle into the dark maw of the cathedral's entrance before diving for cover. A pack of warriors, crushed together in the confines of the tunnel, burst into the open as the enfilading fire of Zero and the others on the high ground tore into their exposed flank.

Some dropped only to get back up again, firing and rushing the human invaders with a fury that they recognized all too well. The berserker rage of the now mate-less warriors sped them toward the team, pinned down in cover under threat of being overwhelmed. The rhythmic *twang* of Zero's rail gun sounded as he crushed them to the ground at diagonal angles from his elevated position.

As devastating as their sniper's fire was, he couldn't fire fast enough to stop the charge.

Specter, with his HUD showing multiple red outlines and red arrow target indicators approaching quickly, didn't reload the spent rifle. Instead, he rose up with both heavy blaster pistols to break for cover to their left flank and draw some of the enemy away. Brandt and Payne popped up from cover to add their fire, as Specter took a flurry of shots to his torso and rolled hard into the dust.

His green indicator flashed. Brandt pulled her eyes away from the enemy for a half second to check his neural readings spiking on her display.

"Jake!" she called out. She dropped back into cover to slap a fresh energy pack into the gun and resume firing. "Jake!"

He didn't answer. Brandt called for suppressing fire automatically, as though her people weren't giving it everything they had already.

"Shit," Zero cursed over the comm.

Before Brandt could react, before she could ask him what it was or make a move to drag Specter into cover, a screaming, whooshing sound filled the air, amidst the electric thumps of a ship's cannons firing in atmosphere. She glanced up, seeing the high ground disappear in a massive plume of dirt and rock. A second screaming sound caught her senses, making her turn to see a second Va'alen fighter bearing down on their position.

"Cover!" she yelled.

Another huge explosion sounded above them. The ship smashed brutally into the open ground between her position and the entrance to the cathedral. Her HUD flashed the location of the *Ichi's* transponder as it shot overhead. She looked up, seeing their ship bank hard to go after the first alien ship and hunt it down before it crashed into them.

Kekoa rolled from cover to riddle the only Va'alen warrior still standing, scorching the alien with shot after shot. It tried in vain to raise its weapon, as Payne added her heavy blaster fire and dropped it in ruin to the dirt.

"Zero," Payne called over the comm. "Come in, Zero!"

"I'm here," he replied, sounding almost hungover. "The LT and his boys are gone."

Brandt hadn't realized that, hadn't seen the four flatline readings on her team display. She was running hard on the heels of Turner, who was heading for Specter.

CHAPTER 44

The Indomitable

Five successive orbital rail gun strikes pounded the outer shields of the carrier, collapsing them and lowering the third layer close to failure. Sparks showered over a console at the back of the bridge, earning a cry of fright from the unlucky crewmember there.

"We've got a feedback loop in the third layer," shouted the petty officer specializing in the defensive barriers.

"Recommendations?" Dassiova barked.

"Shut it down," she said. "Kill all power feeds to it. It's the only way to avoid a cascade effect."

"Do it."

She turned back to the console, finger dancing over the controls before she reported that she'd done it. "Down to fifty percent shields."

That wasn't as accurate as it sounded, even though they'd lost two out their four shield emitters. The smaller barriers closer to the hull used less energy and provided less protection.

"Sir, we need to break orbit," Moon shouted from the pilot's chair. "We can't outrun their orbital cannons."

"Noted," Dassiova answered. He kept his face stoic but allowed himself a gentle stroke on the arm of his command chair, as though to reassure his ship that if she just looked after them a little longer then he'd look after her right back. "Comm, update on the ground troops?"

"They're still heavily engaged, sir. If we break off, they'll be sitting ducks on their advance."

"Hold orbit and keep pounding the enemy," the admiral ordered. "We're not leaving them exposed."

"Incoming wave of Va'alen fighters," Romano shouted from tactical. "Count forty. No idea where they came from, Admiral."

"Doesn't matter where they came from, son," Dassiova said. "Matters that we take 'em out."

He looked at the display beside him, multiple icons smothering the board. He focused on the tightly packed attack wing heading straight for them. If the admiral had to guess, he'd say they took off from the far side of the planet like a reserve force. Further out, the board showed a few more incoming enemy ships with a Kuldar flight in between his ship and them. He also spotted a familiar frigate transponder in that area.

"Get the *Vengeance* to intercept," he said before changing his mind. "Correction. Hail the Kuldar and ask that attack wing of fighters to lend a hand."

"Aye, sir," one of the comm officers said. She began working her station to raise their allies.

"No response, Admiral," she said.

"Try their dreadnought ship. Highest priority. Tell them we'll lose our orbital foothold if those fighters get too close."

He waited as patiently as he could for the request to be relayed, getting a thumbs-up from the comm officer as she spoke into her headset.

"ETA four minutes," she told him.

"Sir," Romano squeaked. "Time to enemy contact is two minutes."

Dassiova sat back and drummed his fingers on the arm of his chair for a second before sitting forward.

"Resupply drop requested," said the comm officer. "Dropping two pods... now."

"Recall the frigates," Dassiova ordered. He sensed a moment of hesitation before his orders were affirmed. "If we go down, so do our troops on the ground."

Eze waited for reports from her squad leaders as she mentally totaled up the losses. With so many troops under her command, she couldn't realistically keep tabs on them all through her command software in her HUD. Instead, she relied on the individual squads reporting back to her.

She ran the count again, willing it to be wrong. It wasn't. She had started the drop with ninety-two troops including her. Now that her entire unit was down to sixty-three, she worried that she was to blame for those losses.

Get a grip.

She heard barking from the back of her mind echoing Brandt. She was in command, but she wasn't their babysitter. Those troops—all twenty-nine of them—were dead from the drop or the savage, gutter-fight of trench warfare under the heavy soundtrack of orbital bombardment. They had given their lives doing their jobs, just as she fully expected to lose her own life before the day ended.

Something in that thought calmed her nerves. It freed her, un-locked her bravery and stopped her from worrying about all the things she couldn't control. When she accepted her imminent death, or the very realistic prospect of it, she freed up the space in her brain to do *her* job: closing the gap between her troops and the enemy.

She was never one for rousing speeches, always among the first to roll her eyes when subjected to narcissistic senior officers who loved the sound of their own voices. In spite of this, she found that those same principles drove her onward.

Taking a few precious seconds to run through the squad lists, she found that the squad leader tags had moved from those officers and NCOs who had gone down. The baton of leadership had been passed on; others were stepping up to perform the roles needed to get her people to their objective.

That objective, only a few hundred meters away but as inaccessible as walking the Centauri system, was filled with craters and trenches containing both dead and living Va'alen. The closer they got to their goal, the more savage, more brutal the fighting became. It was as though the aliens that still lived and offered them fierce resistance simply refused to die.

Every so often, usually when one of her remaining snipers spotted a brave or foolish enemy popping their insectoid heads out of cover, an animalistic scream of rage would pierce the gaps in the sounds of bombardment. Such a wretched cry would fill her mind with terror that another enraged berserker was heading over the open ground for them.

Eze hated how they moved when they went berserk. The sounds were terrifying enough, but the sight of them frantically tearing over the battlefield toward her lines signaled a profound and dangerous rage. Seeing the deep score marks crisscrossing their torsos usually meant the death of one or two more of her soldiers, unless the enemy could be taken down with concentrated gunfire before it reached them.

She had expended all of the battery packs for her pulse rifle and left it locked to her back as she apologized to a dead trooper at her feet for taking his rifle and spare ammunition. Grateful the bullet counter still showed a nearly full magazine, she brought it to her shoulder in response to yet another bellow of rage. She gave the target a good lead to account for its speed and her eyes widened before she could squeeze the trigger. It had turned directly to face her, coming head on for her position. She pulled the rifle in tight and began firing off controlled bursts, resetting her aim after every pull. Despite her armor, the gun recoiled more than the pulse rifle had. It took a few more seconds of firing to fully adapt. Eze's first shots punctured the outer layer of thick, shell-like armor and began to detonate.

Chunks of the enraged thing blew away, but still it came. It ran toward her, ignoring the dark gore dripping from multiple holes in its body. The Va'alen seemed to be protected by some deity or luck; no matter how many bullets she put into it the damned thing just wouldn't go down.

A whirring noise from her right sounded as heavier caliber bullets ripped into it. She had to drop the magazine out to replenish it. Their one remaining support gun, resting on an unsecured tripod, sent bullets flying wildly at the charging beast. Each impact sounded much harder than those her own gun had made. They must be twice as hard, she realized, given that the 12mm bullets packed double the punch. As the larger explosions started to tear more chunks away from the charging alien, she thought for a brief moment that it would finally be stopped, that it would go down and stay there. Despite the huge injuries and one missing claw, however, it jumped impossibly high through the air and landed behind her position.

As the alien sailed overhead, maw open exposing sharp teeth as it roared, Eze thought just how terrifying even one of those would be if it got loose on Earth. If it could endure the sustained fire of her remaining troops and still be mobile, then this one Va'alen alone could kill hundreds of unarmed civilians before enough guns could be brought to bear on it.

She shook the thought out of her head and squeezed the trigger of her rifle again, firing from the hip and mashing the explosive rounds into its back from only a few paces away.

The creature went stiff, arching its back. Its fight evaporated just as her second magazine ran dry. Dropping it out and slapping in the last one, Eze called out for her chief.

"He's over on the left flank," said a lieutenant to her left. "I think."

Eze realized it didn't matter who called in the request, and gave the order to the lieutenant.

"Re-up," she said as she pointed to a large crater that would give protection to even the tallest trooper. "Right there."

The lieutenant nodded, turning away to make contact with their orbital benefactor. He nodded to the reply only he could hear. "Ninety seconds."

He yelled at the nearest troops to get their heads up and clear the area. Eze heard them before she saw them—a screaming whistle that signaled a metal dart plummeting from space.

She covered up; she wouldn't see the tactical resupply drones until they impacted and she didn't want to get knocked off her feet by their arrival. The double thump of the ammo canisters hit the dirt, embedding twelve feet into the ground until it hit bedrock.

"Ammo up," she called over the unit comm channel.

Her troops dropped back from the line in ones and twos, they were dry on bullets. She helped herself to six more magazines from the open pods, taking a seventh for good luck and mag-locking it to a spare patch of armor on her left thigh.

When the pods had been emptied, she rallied her troops and, without any pomp or circumstance, led them out of cover and to the enemy.

"Jake," Turner said as he rolled him over onto his back. "Say something, buddy."

"Aaaasssshole," he groaned. "Did... did you get it?"

"That Va'alen took a roach ship to the face," Turner told him. He synced with the prototype armor to assess the damage. "It ain't getting up."

"Good," Specter said, as he twitched in a way that was distinctly non-human.

"Dammit, Commander," Turner said. "I can't even tell what's wrong... he needs a mechanic, not a medic. No offence."

"None... taken..." Specter gasped in pain or malfunction. "I... aw, *shit*."

"Shit what?" Brandt demanded. "What's shit?"

"It damaged... my... power core..." Specter said.

"Okay, we can fix that, right?" she said as she looked at Turner. "We can fix that?" Turner gave a slight shrug as he searched for the words to explain that he didn't have the first clue.

"Afraid... not..." Specter said as he began to recover slightly. "Not here. I'm okay, I just need to take it slow." He stood, in spite of Brandt protesting, and teetered slightly before reiterating he was okay.

"Come on," he said. "We need to get to these floating suckers. Maybe we can use them as leverage and force a surrender."

"On me," Brandt ordered the remnants of her team.

Kekoa stepped up to take point. They pushed into the darkness, going through the long tunnel. The intel was correct. After the tunnel, the interior of the cathedral opened up into the largest artificially created cavern any of them had ever seen. Directly at the center of the massive space was eight floating figures in long robes.

"Crap," Brandt cursed. "Payne, call it in; all of the Hive Lords are here."

She ran forward. The losses on the other planets would all be for nothing if they couldn't finish the job right there and then.

Before they reached the circle of levitating aliens, a solid, insistent humming noise pierced their suit sensors.

Sssstop! announced a voice, that seemed to be many voices all speaking in unison.

Brandt whipped around to look at the others. They'd all stopped, hands to their helmets. They had heard it too, only not with their ears. The Hive Lords were projecting it to their minds.

Your crude, filthy race will pay for your invasion, the voice said. *When the rite is complete all Va'alen will experience the path of ending and destroy your fleets, and kill your warriors. Any that survive will seek out you home world, your Earth, and end it.*

"Oh *hell* no," Turner said.

He raised his rifle and fired at the nearest alien. He faltered, seeming to choke and go rigid before a strangled cry tore from his mouth over the comm.

"Turne—" Brandt called out

She stopped as she saw the inside of his visor splashed with blood. His body froze for a heartbeat, then fell to the ground as his flatline appeared on Brandt's HUD.

"No!" Payne yelled. She swung her heavy gun up before Brandt held out a hand to stop her.

An eerie, mocking, hissing noise filled their minds as though the Hive Lords laughed collectively at them. At Turner's death.

The rite is almost complete, the voice said scathingly.

"We need to shut this down," Kekoa said uneasily. "Like, *now*."

"Anyone got comm links topside?" Brandt called out. Her own comms were dark, as were those of her troops.

The humming noise intensified, rising in pitch and urgency until it created a painful pressure in their heads.

Awaken, warriors, chanted the collective voices. *AWAKEN!*

"We need to shut this down," Brandt said, echoing Kekoa's words. "We can't risk all the remaining roaches turning berserk. Withdraw and light 'em up."

"No," Specter said. He bent to Turner's body and picked it up haltingly, as though he was in pain and struggling with the burden. "There's no time and they'll kill you. Go. I've got this."

"What? Jake, no!" Brandt said.

He handed Turner's body to Kekoa and deactivated his own helmet to show his scarred face and the lopsided smile he wore despite the pain he felt.

"I'll follow you out," he lied. "Just get out of here. Now."

CHAPTER 45

Va'alen Planet

Eze's unit took the high ground with heavy losses. In the space of only a few minutes she had lost another dozen of her troops but that was the price of achieving their objective. The squads, hammered with losses and, in some cases, down to only a handful of soldiers in dusty, scorched armor, formed around her. They drew up in rally square to defend the single position against the new waves of Va'alen warriors advancing on them.

"Lieutenant," she said, "get us another resupply ready."

"The, err…" a trooper beside her said. "Commander, the LT bought it on the hill."

She cursed silently but tried not to show any reaction that could erode the confidence of her remaining people.

"Get on the comm, Seaman," she instructed. "Order us a re-up."

He nodded as she looked back down the length of her rifle at the advancing enemy. She still had one of her lieutenant commanders calling orbital strikes. Eze watched as the ordnance and cannon fire thumped into the ground ahead of her, churning up building-sized plumes of rock and dirt, with the occasional spinning and broken form of an alien.

"Hold your fire until effective range," she said over the unit channel. "How many support guns still operational?"

"Two, Commander," Ryers said, as he stepped into position beside her.

"Get them up front and ready to fire; interlocking arcs."

Her chief took personal responsibility for placing the guns, noting with apprehension that they had started the action with eight of the Gatling-style weapons.

The orbital bombardment ceased. Looking back to her front and the oncoming wave of enemy, Eze's mouth dropped open and her heart sank, leaving a cold, empty feeling in her chest. She couldn't see anything in the skies through the thick dust blown up into the air.

"*Indomitable* has gone dark, Commander," the officer liaising with the orbiting ship told her.

She bit her lip, so as not to curse him out for giving that piece of information over the open channel. At his rank he should have known better than to spread panic among the others.

Then she realized that he was panicking himself. He was as terrified as the others were. Looking back for any visible sign that their ship was still above them, Eze saw the awful signs of something terribly wrong. Scores of tiny meteors showered overhead as innumerable things burned up in the atmosphere.

She looked back to their front. The advancing Va'alen had stopped running toward them and were all also looking at the sky. She glanced back up involuntarily—maybe they had seen something that she hadn't—and when she returned her eyes to the enemy, she saw something that churned her up and threatened to explode in a scream.

As one, all of the aliens were dragging their claws across their chests to score deep X marks, then resuming their charge at close to twice their original speed, each one with its mouth open wide in a roar of pure and utterly horrifying rage.

CHAPTER 46

The Indomitable

Forty Va'alen ships were as much as Dassiova had faced before. Then, however, his shields had been running a little higher and his gun barges numbered eight and not the five he had remaining now.

As they prepared for the incoming attack, an orbital gun battery comprising of two quad-barreled rail guns had been unveiled on the surface. It hammered them with a devastating amount of fire, requiring the admiral to divert the frigate on their way to reinforce the carrier to deal with it.

Captain Halstead grudgingly gave the orders to break away from their intercept course and begin pounding the site with everything they had left. They could try and break down the energy shields and destroy the guns.

"You'll be on your own, sir," she told Dassiova.

"I think we can handle these roach sons of bitches for a few minutes until our new friends arrive," he told her. "But not if those guns are hitting us."

At one of the weapons stations, an officer recoiled, a hand shooting up to his mouth in shock.

"Two gun barges..." he croaked. "...gone..."

"Give the order for the remaining five to push out on an intercept course at full burn," the admiral ordered.

He would kill two birds with one stone and sacrifice the remaining barges to slow or halt the Va'alen ships if necessary. It also put them out of harm's way from the orbital defense guns that would destroy them much easier than the Va'alen could.

"Keep that bombardment up," he told his weapons opera- tors, "and if you can spare any warheads send them down the throats of those damned guns."

He waited tense seconds as his five barges closed on the enemy. Listened as his bridge officers reported their engagement. Leapt from his seat to take rapid steps to the large console to see for himself what was happening.

"The barges are gone. They were rammed and... and they're gone. They've all gone kamikaze," Romano said, sounding like he'd cry. "They shouldn't do that, right, sir? They shouldn't turn suicide bomber unless their partner ships get taken out?"

"Son," Dassiova said gravely, "I've seen up close what these sick cockroaches are capable of."

He turned to the weapons stations and gave new orders.

"All defense turrets to target that incoming wave and fire like you mean it. Comm, get a hold of the Kuldar again and ask them to do whatever they can to take out those ships. Tell them it is mission critical if they want this planet taken."

"Incoming missiles!" Romano cried out before hitting the ship-wide comm. "All hands—*brace, brace, brace!*"

Dassiova didn't have time to return to his chair and strap in. He held on tightly to the side of the tactical station and tensed, ready for the thumping booms of explosions tearing through their shields and into the hull. The explosions were worse than he feared, rocking the ship so violently that he was thrown back in spite of his iron grip. He landed hard on his back, seeing blood on his hands—he'd held on so hard that he'd snapped off a corner of the toughened glass display when he fell.

"Shields to nineteen percent."

Dassiova's ears were ringing as he struggled to roll and get to his feet. He wiped the blood coming from his cut hand onto the leg of his pants as he got back into the chair.

"Sir, we need to divert guns," Romano shouted to him. "Sir! I said we need to divert guns; the enemy are on a direct run at us."

"Guns," Dassiova growled. "Fire everything on those bastards."

Thirty-five Va'alen ships burned hard, heading right for the carrier. There was no thought spared for the five warriors who had already slammed into the gun barges that tried to block their path. No remorse or seconds wasted mourning loss of life; there was only the rage. The rage had consumed them so unexpectedly that all of them had their final cognitive thought that their mates must have been killed and that they were experiencing the Path of Ending. None of them looked at their displays to see that almost all of their ships remained intact, but that was what the rage did to them.

Ignoring the incoming fire that killed another twelve Va'alen, they all aimed their ships at the human vessel and kept the power at full.

The shields of the *Indomitable* absorbed nine of the twenty-three impacts before their last layer of protective barrier failed. The last fourteen smashed headfirst into the hull. Explosions rippled throughout the ship, shutting down the engines and the grav emitters and the life support. The ship was left rolling slowly, inexorably toward the planet below.

Dassiova, slamming a bloody hand onto the console in the desperate hope that violence could restore power, knew in his gut that his carrier was dead in the water.

"We…" He shook his head to clear his hearing. "We have power left anywhere?"

"Nothing, sir," the young ensign answered. His face was streaked with blood streaming from the cut high up in his hair line.

"Auxiliary power? Can we get the engines running again at least?"

Romano's console flickered back to life, the display showing bright colors intermittently that the young officer could still decipher. The grav emitters, or at least the one to the bridge, came back online, dumping them all back to the deck. This small improvement gave the admiral hope that his ship could yet be saved.

"I can access it, but it won't be enough," Romano said. "I'm reading critical damage to three singularity reactors."

That sealed it for Dassiova, crushing any remaining hope he had for saving the flagship. "Divert any and all remaining power to shipwide comm."

"You're on, Admiral," Romano told him after a few seconds.

"All hands of the *Indomitable*," he said loudly. He swallowed before he uttered the next words that he had never wanted to hear said even in jest. "Abandon ship. Repeat, abandon ship."

He sat back in his chair, straightening his torso and tugging down his disheveled uniform.

"You too, sir," Romano said to him.

The admiral regarded the young ensign with a smile, possibly the first one he'd rewarded the annoying young officer with.

"My ship, Ensign," he said flatly. "My responsibility. Go on now, son, that's an order."

"With all due resp—"

"Don't you dare *all due respect me*," the admiral snapped. "I gave you an order and I expect that order to be followed. Now go, get out of here."

"Fine," Romano said, throwing himself down into the chair beside the admiral and turning a sullen look on him.

"Fine *what*, Ensign?"

"That's fine, Admiral," the boy said calmly. "But it's also my bridge and that makes it my responsibility also."

Dassiova sighed heavily. "You're not going to get in an escape pod unless I make you, are you?"

"Correction, sir," Romano said with a smile. "I'm not getting in an escape pod unless you're in there first."

Dassiova sucked in a loud breath and leaned back to let it out slowly. Rumbling explosions vibrated through their seats as the catastrophic damage spread across the dying ship.

"Ah, screw you, you little shit," Dassiova said. He stood up abruptly and grabbed the ensign by his uniform. "If that's what it takes to save your scrawny ass so you can grow up to be an admiral then I guess that's what it takes."

CHAPTER 47

Hive Lord Cathedral

Jake Santana tapped at the device on his right forearm to make his armor pop open. Stepping out, he walked to the ring of floating aliens, slowly, as though each pace took great effort.

You, the multiple voices said in perfect unison. *You are not like the others of your kind. I know you.*

"We've met before," Jake said as he approached. He held his arms out to the side, showing them he was unarmed. "I captured one of you."

The loud humming took on a threatening edge as the memory of that time rippled through their collective consciousness.

"Can I come closer?" he asked.

The angry sense of the humming subsided, not calmed but more in amusement or curiosity.

Jake took a tentative pace toward them, concern etched on his scarred face. He was risking being killed like Turner had been.

"How was it you could control my friend?"

Our power combines together, the echoing, haunting voice explained, *and only together can we connect with your primitive kind in the way that we can control the warrior caste.*

"The warrior caste?" Jake asked, taking another tentative step closer. "You mean the Va'alen?"

The voice ululated in derisive laughter that seemed to come from all directions.

Kuldar, Va'alen, these are all castes of the same beings.

"And us humans are too primitive for you?" Jake asked, now inside their circle as he turned to speak to all of them. "We're not evolved enough or strong enough or fanatic enough for you like your pet Va'alen?"

The warrior caste is a tool, they said. *We have bent them all to our will for millennia and will continue to do so, to grow from the ashes after we have eradicated your kind from the galaxy.*

"Huh," Jake scoffed. He closed his eyes and made a face of pained concentration. "What if *I'm* a tool for my masters? What if I'm a—" He looked down at his hands, opening and closing them stiffly. "A *weapon?*"

The humming took on an angry tone like a wasp's nest that had been disturbed. Jake bunched his prosthetic hands into tight fists. He tensed his arms and torso like a bodybuilder showing off their physique.

Only he wasn't showing off. He wasn't tensing his artificial muscles as a display. He was trying to force as much power as he could through the power regulator attached to his micro singularity source hidden inside his abdomen. He hadn't lied about how bad the damage was; it was serious but survivable, as long as he kept his power output low.

That was the opposite of what he was doing now.

The Hive Lords were unaware of exactly what was about to befall them but they sensed they had been lulled into a vulnerable situation. As one, they reached for him with their mind, seizing him and dragging him up from the ground.

Jake Santana threw back his arms and roared in defiance.

Brandt broke cover from the darkness of the tunnel just as her HUD showed external comms once again. Before she could call out for Zero, the sniper's voice rang loudly inside her helmet.

"Enemy left flank!" he yelled.

He was twenty paces ahead under the flimsy cover of a chunk of rock dislodged from high ground. He didn't look back to indicate he'd seen their approach; Bart was still in the air acting as his eyes.

"Two pairs in the defilade," Zero said. "They were in crazy-ass mode but just stopped and dropped literally just before you came out. Wait... is that—"

"Turner's down," Brandt told him abruptly, quick like she was tearing off a band-aid. "The brain bastards got him."

"How did th—" Zero began.

"Where's Specter?" Torres interrupted. "Shouldn't he have made it out—"

The ground shook, like they were standing too close to massive machinery. Before any of them could guess at an explanation, an eruption of dust burst from the tunnel behind them, riding on an angry rush of air.

"Jake," Brandt croaked, taking an involuntary step toward the tunnel entrance.

"It's coming down," Kekoa roared.

He noticed the upper layers of the tall spire begin to crumple in. He reached out for his commander to drag her away but she was already moving.

A singularity collapse wasn't much of a spectacle in space, but on the surface of a planet was another story. It brought all the noises and sensations that the dark void took away, leaving only the visual elements.

It began with what seemed to be a regular explosion radiating from Jake's chest, with a shockwave which had a blue tinge to the leading edge. It cut out in all directions like a ripple in still water, quickly followed by the booming, cracking sound of the detonation.

That leading edge, cutting like a spectral blade, pulsed out and passed through the hovering aliens before they understood what was happening. There was no opportunity to understand it, no time to wonder how it had happened when they had sensed no weapons on the human at all. There was only time for the Hive Lords to feel the concussive wave that followed the now bright blue pulse of the explosion.

The concussive shockwave blew them back, out of forma- tion and severed their bond. Their single consciousness suddenly and violently fractured into eight.

Those eight, only now beginning to understand that they were in great peril, were flung back through the air by the force of the shockwave. Their movement from the source of the flash was arrested with such intensity, such violence, that most of them cried out in pain.

Pain wasn't something they were accustomed to. Most of them hadn't felt the sensation for hundreds of years or more. Still, they didn't understand the severity of their situation.

The Hive Lords hung in the air for a brief moment but the sensation lasted much longer in their minds. That outward movement had been aggressively halted and turned inward. They experienced a split second of unnerving sensation as one direction replaced another.

It was a split-second of weightlessness, like when the floor of an elevator dropped away slightly too fast, or when reaching the apex of a jump before heading back to the deck.

Before any of them could understand what the unexpected change in direction meant, the strength of the pull forced their frail bodies back to the source of their death. The sound of the rushing wind of the shockwave raced past them as though eager to return to the center.

The Hive Lords were unable to see the human any longer; his body had been absorbed by the growing ball of dark light that rippled angrily with tiny strikes of blue and purple lightning. They accelerated toward that ball, driven at a growing velocity by an unseen force until all eight were slammed into it. They were crushed into nothingness in an instant.

Brandt stood staring as the massive structure fell in on itself. Anything near the center was swallowed up into the dying singularity she could see through the dust in the air.

She knew what that singularity was—or rather *who* it had been. She replayed everything that happened inside and realized that as certain as she was that Jake was gone, she had been sure that he would be following them to safety.

Her helmet speakers buzzed in vibration, but in her ears and brain didn't register any words. Slowly, as though she had fallen asleep underwater and was lifting her head out of the liquid, Brandt heard her name being screamed. It felt like a time lapse recording. Nothing moved or sounded or even *looked* right.

"Commander!" Kekoa yelled.

She turned to see him lower Turner's body to the dust as carefully as he could, before leaping into close quarter battle mode and extending the spikes on his gauntlets.

"Get down!" Payne yelled from her left.

This call forced Brandt's head to swing back that way. She was made dizzy with the speed of the movement. She saw Payne, support gun resting on her hip, brace as she leaned her armored body back and shot a stream of fire ahead of her.

Brandt looked back to the front, her mind catching up with real time suddenly, as she found herself staring down the barrel of a Va'alen pulse rifle. The alien staggered slightly, as unsteady on its feet as if newborn and confused, but it steadied itself quickly and leaned into the gun.

Brandt was fast. She ignored the rifle mag-locked over her right shoulder—it would take too long to draw. Instead, she crouched slightly before launching herself into the air and activating the melee weapon built into her right forearm bracer. The powerful servos in the suit gave her all the extra help she needed to clear the distance otherwise impossible for any human to achieve unaided. She trusted gravity to provide more power to the killing blow. But her face dropped in fear and disappointment when she realized her poor calculation.

The Va'alen warrior, chest scored deeply with the self-inflicted marks, fell back as it tracked her unexpected movement through the air. In the second before the blade punctured the outer layer of armor and lodged firmly inside the brain of the smaller, weaker being inside, the creature depressed its trigger and hit her at near point-blank range.

Da'kath, Supreme Commander of all Va'alen and the greatest warrior of his kind in living memory, staggered back as his mind returned to him.

He was confused, disorientated. It took him a while to comprehend what had happened. He looked down at one of his right claws—there was a bloody chunk of flesh still gripped in the pincer. Looking around to understand where it came from, his eyes rested on the ruined, torn and bloody pile of biological detritus that sat twisted and broken against the far wall. He looked at the body then back at the chunk of flesh still held in his grip as though the explanation would present itself to his muddled brain. The scrap of material attached to the lump of flesh bore a partial emblem that he recognized. He must have destroyed the human he had been keeping alive for amusement and information. He dropped the chunk, hearing it land wetly against the dust-covered ground. As his eyes followed the path of the meat, he saw the deep score marks running crossways over his torso.

He couldn't comprehend it at first, but when he understood that he had entered the Path of Ending he searched the room frantically for his mate. He had expected to find her body, so his mind was thrown into even more turmoil when she emerged from a dark corner, touching the deep gashes in her own carapace and looking up at him. He felt a sense of great unease, of confusion and even fear emanating from her as only their unbreakable mental link would allow. Both should have been dead, based on the reaction of the other. But they both stood there, still alive. Neither could comprehend what had happened, or how they had come to be in this situation.

An alarm sounded on the main console under the holo-display. It now showed almost zero Va'alen ships still flying. The low klaxon, insistent and repeating fast, was linked to a warning icon on the display. Da'kath reached for it, almost robotically, to silence the noise.

The icon burst wide to fill the display. It showed a human ship building the charge on an orbital bombardment weapon targeting their position. Da'kath turned to look at his mate one last time before the explosions of the incoming ordnance buried them both under tons of rock and metal forever.

"*Hammer,* this is *Ichi* actual," Torres said. "Requesting permission to dock."

"Permission granted, *Ichi.*"

They had called their ship in for immediate casualty evacuation right on top of where the Hive Lord's cathedral had been. Brandt, unconscious and unable to be ejected from her armor without medical presence, had been picked up by Torres. He carried her like a baby, and ran up the ramp, straight to their small medical wing. The gun pods chattered five separate times as the rest of the team recovered the bodies of their fallen—all except Specter.

All over the planet, all over the entire system, the Va'alen warriors who had so suddenly gone mentally blind with rage slowly regained their senses. The process of having that controlling link to the Hive Lords severed so abruptly had left them confused and subdued.

It was more of a depression they felt, not exhaustion. Many of them lacked the will to fight their victorious enemy any longer and simply lay down dazed on the ground.

With almost all of their personnel recovered, the *Ichi* took off, burning hard for the atmosphere at escape velocity. Punching through with a slight orange glow, their pilot turned the nose of the craft and plotted a short jump that would allow them to join the rescue mission.

All of the other ships in the system that weren't heavily damaged, destroyed or otherwise employed were converging on the cloud of debris that used to be the *Indomitable* to recover the multitude of escape pods.

Torres, looking at his display with numerous tiny blinks of emergency pod beacons, felt hope swell that they would find the admiral among those beacons. They soon learned via the fleet comm that the *Hammer* had jumped in first and recovered Dassiova. Torres breathed a sigh of relief before ordering his bridge crew to pick up as many pods as they could carry.

"No sense in going in empty handed," he mused out loud. He rubbed a hand on his chin and glanced down at the dried blood ingrained in his skin.

He didn't know if the blood was Turner's from when they'd opened his visor, his own from some as yet undiscovered injury, or Brandt's as he laid her on a med station.

Torres had left Brandt under the care of Doctor Curtis, who searched for any exposed patch of skin to inject Nanomites. He was unsure if she would make it. Torres headed for the bridge, stopping off only long enough to step out of his armor on one of the storage platforms in the troop ready room.

Lowering his hand and hoping that nobody had witnessed him halting at the sight of blood, the captain held his compo- sure. His ship spun to dock to the frigate where the fleet admiral was currently in overall command.

Torres felt that same peculiar pull as he moved from a small ship to a larger one via an airlock hatch. His body was caught in a brief tug of war over whose grav emitter had a hold of him. Steadying himself for a second, he stood tall and made his way to the bridge. There a harassed-looking Captain Hayes gave him a solid nod of greeting.

It was the kind of nod that came from a man unaccustomed to gestures and the sharing of feelings. It said simply, "Glad you didn't die. You're not bad at your job."

Torres returned the nod, a little more warmly than Hayes's had been but still fleeting and distracted. Torres glanced left and right, then saw Hayes point toward the frigate's bridge briefing room.

He walked through the door and found Dassiova sitting amongst a throng of officers and ratings, all trying to shove datapads under his nose and get his attention. Dassiova seemed to ignore them, taping away awkwardly with just his left index finger on the pad while his right hand was being treated for a deep cut by an exasperated medic.

"Everybody quiet," the admiral said loudly enough to cut over everyone. He looked up, fixing Torres with a glassy-eyed, emotionless stare and raised his eyebrows in question.

"You want to know why all the Va'alen went into berserk and then shutdown modes?" the captain clarified.

"It would be great if you could explain it," Dassiova said.

Torres cleared his throat and described finding all of the Hive Lords together performing some kind of power-up ritual meant to send all Va'alen into suicidal killer mode.

Dassiova responded with how that part had coincided with him having all of his gun barges and his carrier taken out.

"Continue," he told Torres. "This is the part when you explain why they all went into limp-home-mode like the first ground transport I bought always did."

Others chuckled at the joke, but Torres's face remained like a statue.

"Sir," he said formally. "It is our understanding at this time that specialist Jake Santana detonated his own power source in order to prevent the Hive Lords from completing the ritual. He..." Torres bowed his head and swallowed as he tensed, trying to exert control over his facial features. "He recognized the threat not only to our people here, but to Earth and every- where else humanity could settle..." Torres seemed like he was going to say more but his voice abandoned him.

"Any other losses?" Dassiova asked quietly.

"Half my team, sir," he said. "More than half, actually. Commander Brandt is still a maybe."

That news gave Dassiova pause. His own face flickered in betrayal of his emotions before he mastered himself.

"I'm sure she's in good hands, Captain," Dassiova reassured him. "Right now our priority is to recover and treat the rest of our wounded on the surfaces of these god damned dust balls and get them fixed up. After that we can recover our dead and give them the honors they deserve." He nodded as though thanking Torres and dismissing him, but the younger man wasn't finished.

"If I might know, sir," he asked, "what are the casualties on the surface?"

Dassiova flashed him a brief, grave, tight-lipped smile.

"She made it, son," he said. "Now go get your ship picking up our people. The sooner we collect up everyone the sooner we can get the hell out of this system and never come back."

EPILOGUE

Torres groaned as he leaned back into the bubbling water of the large hot tub. He stretched out, draping an arm over the Eze's rich, brown skin. She smiled and leaned into him, the champagne flute moving back up to her lips as an errant bubble shot up to splash her mouth.

Brandt laughed from her position sitting opposite them, the light pink skin of the burn repair showing on her left shoulder and up her neck. She leaned back, taking in the massive, expansive view through the clear dome of the grand panorama of Earth.

Their reward of an all-credits paid week in one of the vacation domes on the Moon was much appreciated after everything they'd endured. It had been months since the peace they had known before stepping outside their solar system for the first time. As much as they complained about the UN, they had to admit that they chose the best location for their enforced decompression leave. It certainly beat a Mars base rec room.

"Move over, beefsteak," Rogers said to Kekoa.

He dropped the towel from his waist to expose a set of trunks that had to be two sizes too small. The people in the hot tub recoiled as multiple shouts of alarm and disgust greeted the reveal.

"What?" the pilot asked, arms out wide as he paraded himself without shame.

"They hatin' on the smugglers?" Zero asked. He approached from behind the exhibition, dropping his own towel to expose a similar pair only with a more garish color scheme.

"What the hell?" Payne complained.

She moved away from the steps awkwardly, trying to escape the bulges and she shielded her eyes with a hand in case the imagery was burned onto her retinas.

"Smugglers?" Torres asked, confused.

"Budgie smugglers," Eze educated him. The two stared at one another for a long moment until Torres's face cracked into a smile. He glanced automatically at the offending articles and instantly regretted it.

"You okay bringing that thing in the water?" Kekoa asked, nodding at Rogers's prosthetic arm. "Not going to electrocute us or anything, right?"

"What's the worst that could happen?" Rogers asked with a shrug and an air of recklessness.

"Err, we could all be electrocuted?" the Hawaiian repeated, glancing around for support.

"Relax," Brandt told him. "You're too big to get killed by mere electricity."

Kekoa nodded, accepting the reassurance as gospel because it came from the mouth of his commander.

The champagne was poured, and they sat around, crowded together and cozy in the hot tub. The conversation quickly ebbed away as they lapsed into thoughtful silence about the people missing from their group.

"It was here I first met Jake," Torres said. "The Lunar base, I mean."

"You weren't on our dropship on the way up?" Brandt asked him.

316

"I was," he said. "Just didn't know anyone's names until we got there. I was only posted to Dassiova's unit about four hours before we lifted."

"Man," Brandt laughed, "you were so small back then!"

"Little Kyle the Wheel," Eze teased.

"Ha," Kekoa snorted loudly. "Fifth wheel."

"Yeah," Zero said sarcastically. "We get it."

Kekoa looked a little embarrassed for half a second before he forgot about it.

They lapsed back into silence again as their thoughts returned to the absentees.

"You reckon we're all done now?" Zero asked in a rare moment of loquaciousness. "You think they'll just scatter us to finish out our service like normal people?"

"We're not normal?" Payne asked.

"Not even close," Brandt said smoothly, taking a long, awkward sip of champagne. "I'm going to miss them."

She had flipped the subject back so suddenly that they all dropped their heads.

"Me too," said Zero.

"Yeah," agreed Kekoa. Torres raised a glass, his face no longer the mask a senior officer would wear to get the job done. Instead, it was the face of a man among friends, toasting the lives of the good people no longer with them.

"They paid the ultimate price," he said. He feared that he sounded a little melodramatic, that both of them would mock him if they were able. "I know Jake would've been sick in his mouth if he'd heard me say that…"

"If he ate, that was," Rogers quipped.

"He ate," Zero said. "Just not much. Isn't your calorie intake lower with only three quarters of the limbs you were born with?"

Rogers accepted his point with a pensive face and gave a nod.

"None of us would be here without them," Brandt said, sipping her own champagne with her stare fixed on a point a thousand yards away. "And believe me, back when he was your age, he'd rival you for food intake. He always joked that the only reason he joined up was for food."

"So, what do we do?" Payne asked.

She was trying to make the question sound off the cuff and rhetorical, but Brandt knew she desperately wanted to have the way to cope shown to her.

"We get a grip," Brandt said. "We carry on."

"Warriors in peacetime?" Payne asked.

"Plenty of call for people like us, even without any roaches left to kill," Zero told them, sipping his champagne with the pinky finger ironically extended. When Brandt noticed, she coughed bubbles out of her nose. "Bug hunts, terrorists, separatists... there'll still be work to do."

They drank, they joked, and they told stories about all the people who should've been there and weren't.

Brandt leaned back, resting her head on the edge of the luxury spa pool. Her head began to swim with the bubbly alcohol. She tried to recall the last time she'd drank, that it must've been on the last night of freedom she'd enjoyed, right before she'd been attacked by some Middle Eastern Alliance opera- tors. That felt like a hundred years ago.

The line of thought led her back to Morello. She'd finally managed to track him down after a long time spent making calls from their enforced vacation.

She sat back, finally relaxing and dropping her hyper-vigilance after months on edge. She stared up at the starry black-ness of space with a wide arc of blue at the top of her vision as she tried to figure out which continent she was looking at.

As she stared, Brandt imagined a fiery yellow rift exploding in the darkness as space tore wide open before her eyes. She daren't breathe in case letting out her breath made it real. She didn't speak, in case she broke the spell and what was in her mind became a reality.

She blinked involuntarily, and realized that the tear in space was no longer there. She breathed out a long sigh of relief.

Her mind wouldn't let the image go, however. She conjured the imagery of the tear growing, as small, smooth wedges zipped through it ahead of the gargantuan nose of the Kuldar dreadnought ship.

Were they fools to think that they could stay at peace? Fools to believe the tenuous alliance would hold and the territories would be respected?

Humanity, she feared, wasn't the only force in the galaxy intent on destruction.

THE END OF THE EXPANSION SERIES

Remember to sign up for my emailing list at **www. devoncford.com**
Follow me on social media for cover reveals, release information and general shenanigans:
Facebook: @devoncfordofficial
Instagram: @dcf_actual

Also by Devon C Ford
The *After It Happened* series:
(Also on Audible)
1 – Survival (Performed by R.C Bray)
2 – Humanity (Performed by R.C Bray)
3 – Society (Performed by R.C Bray)
4 – Hope (Performed by R.C Bray)
5 – Sanctuary (Performed by R.C Bray)
6 – Rebellion (Performed by R.C Bray)
7 – Andorra (The Leah Chronicles, performed by Kate Reading)
8 – Piracy (The Leah Chronicles, performed by Kate Reading)
9 – Home (Performed by R.C Bray)

The *New Earth* series:
(Also on Audible Performed by Marc Vietor)
1 – ARC
2 -SWARM (with Chris Harris)

The *Burning Skies* Multi-Author series:
(Also on Audible read by Neil Hellegers)
1 – The Fall
2 – Fallout (by Jacqueline Druga)
3 – Uprising (by Chris Harris)